SCHOLAR'S MATE

*To Jean
with best wishes
John Foster*

JOHN FOSTER

jsf
Lucerne Villa
58B Norfolk Road
Sheffield
S2 2SY
Email: johnfosterstories@gmail.com
Web: www.johnfosterstories.com
ISBN 978-0-9929459-0-9
British Library Cataloguing in Publication Data
A catalogue record for this book is available from the British Library
Printed in UK by TJ International

for the 11,200

ACKNOWLEDGMENTS

I am indebted to Bill Murray, leading expert on the Devonshire dialect, without whose generous help Chapter XI could not have been written, and to Tom Foster for his professional advice on mental health matters.

Warm thanks go to Sarah Burgoyne, Mike Daly, Roger Holden, Aimée Taylor and Ken Woodhouse, who kindly read drafts of all or part of this novel and responded with the enthusiastic encouragement and constructive criticism that I needed. Above all, I thank Margaret Daly, who followed this project from the first draft of the first chapter and provided the critical sounding board that every writer needs.

Finally, I am grateful to Sue Beaver, who proof-read the final draft, and to Samantha Watt, who skilfully orchestrated my ideas for the book cover.

CONTENTS

Prologue

This account is based on a journal which I began on my 70th birthday, rather late in life to begin writing a diary, perhaps. I had a good reason for writing it. I had begun to see sense in the universally accepted theory that, with advancing age, our short-term memory, our memory for recent events, experiences, emotions and insights, begins increasingly and incrementally to fail us, whereas memories from previous decades remain clear, some of them as clear as if they had happened yesterday.

Although not the most self-aware of men, a man who had on no previous occasion recognised a significant moment in his life until well after the event, I did have the presence of mind to realise that I had on that day sailed into uncharted waters, that I was about to meet a new kind of challenge, one perhaps greater than I had ever faced.

I wrote the journal so that I would not forget.

It is prefaced by a quotation from Alfred Lord Tennyson's *Ulysses*:

> *Old age hath yet his honour and his toil.*
> *Death closes all; but something ere the end,*
> *Some work of noble note, may yet be done,*
> *Not unbecoming men that strove with Gods.*

I must have been feeling particularly maudlin on that day. It *was* my 70th birthday. Perhaps I had the right.

Over a life-long career in secondary education, a teacher meets thousands of pupils and students, leaving on each one, willy-nilly, his or her mark, for good or ill. This morning, in an idle moment, I made a back-of-an-envelope calculation of the number of young people who had crossed my own path over my 42 years in secondary schools. Taking into account the seven different schools, attributing an average figure of 900 pupils or students to each, an average annual intake of 140, with my average stay of six years, I calculated that I met, either in the classroom, in the corridors, on the playing fields, at after-school clubs and on excursions locally and abroad, in a pedagogical, pastoral or social role, in the first year at each school 900 new pupils and subsequently in the rest of my stay 700 more. I multiplied the sum of 1600 per school by the number of schools and came to a staggering career total of 11,200 pupils who had crossed my path.

I hope they will forgive me if I do not remember them all as well as they remember me.

This is the story of just one of those 11,200 pupils, the story of how his life and mine became inextricably entangled, of how the relationship between us became as close as, if not closer than any I have experienced, although he only ever spoke two words to me.

David York, Sheffield, 31 October 2013.

I

IRREGULAR OPENING

(A chess opening with an unusual first move from White, categorized under the ECO code as A00.)

2011

I am on my way to number 5 Love Lane. In Wakefield. Not for the first time, but this time is different. This will be the last time, and this time I shall not go through that demoralising entrance.

It is Monday January 31, 2011. My birthday. I am 70 years old. As yet I have received no birthday cards, as the postman does not arrive until 10.30 or later, and my wife has not remembered my birthday. She remembers very little these days. I have left her in the safe hands of Suzi, our Croatian charlady, who comes every Monday, cleans the bathroom and kitchen a little and talks a great deal, which Marilyn seems to like. I usually invent an excuse to be out of the house. Today I do not need to. I have a genuine reason.

If I'm honest, as media people, especially football pundits, are disposed to say constantly, if I'm honest I am here to assuage my guilty conscience. Even after all these years, I still think it's my fault. I should have stood up to them, taken the flak, but I didn't. As the poet said: I have something to expiate: a pettiness. I want to atone for this pettiness; this time I want to give him the best chance I can.

I arrive early. I don't want to miss him, and I'm not certain he knows that I'm coming. I drive the accustomed route: A638, says my satnav bully, continue forward onto the A642, turn left into Parliament Street, right onto Back Lane then left into a narrow side-street, some quarter of a mile long. You have reached your destination: 5 Love Lane, WF2 9AG. My tyres crunch on the vestiges of the recent snow, frozen into dirty brown ice in the gutters. I pull up on the double yellow lines partly concealed by the frozen slush and switch off the engine of the Jaguar. I can't remember ever parking on double yellow lines before. I am one of life's conformists. Let's live a little, break a law or two. No car park for me today. I want to make sure he sees me.

No, Love Lane is not as romantic as it sounds. In fact there is nothing remotely romantic about it. It is probably the least romantic part of Wakefield, and Wakefield is, well, Wakefield. Love Lane is neither the venue for a lovers' tryst nor the picnic spot that its name might suggest. For one thing, the view is not good. All I see from my driver's window is a long, blank, high wall, whose length and blankness is relieved only by the small, black door from which, I am informed, he will emerge. Wakefield Prison, the 'Monster Mansion', has none of the grandeur of Armley Gaol, with its pseudo-mediaeval turrets, towers and ramparts and its daunting main gate of stout English oak. As one of my inside contacts once put it so appositely, 'Armley scares the bejazus out of you, but Wakefield just depresses you to hell'.

To give it its due, like Dr Who's Tardis, Wakefield Prison is a good deal more exciting inside than it is outside. A 'Category A' high security unit, it has housed and still houses many very colourful prisoners. No, colourful is too kind. Perhaps I should say famous, or legendary, or celebrated. Let's settle for infamous. The atomic physicist and spy, Klaus Fuchs, served his sentence here in the fifties. Dr Harold Shipman, who murdered at least fifteen of his patients, hanged himself here in 2004. Radislav Krstić, the Serbian war criminal convicted of genocide, has been here since Christmas 2004. Colin Ireland, the so-called Gay Slayer, took such a pathological exception to homosexual men, especially those with a sadomasochistic tendency, that he lured them back to his pad with the promise of action, before torturing and then killing them. He has been here since 1993 and will remain here until he dies. He is 56. Ian Huntley, the school caretaker whose murder of two little girls appalled the nation, was sentenced to serve at least forty years and incarcerated here until 2008. He is not quite 37. David Bieber, the American son of a headteacher, shot three traffic policemen in Leeds on Boxing Day, 2003, among them PC Ian Broadhurst, whom he first shot in the back, and then in the head, as he lay helpless on the pavement. Bieber will be here until at least 2041, when he may become eligible for parole. He is 44. Robert Maudsley, the British version of Hannibal the Cannibal, alleged to have eaten the brain of one of his victims, is kept here in solitary confinement in a perspex cell with cardboard furniture, watched over at all times by five guards. He is 57. Charles Bronson, who has with full justification earned the title of 'the most dangerous prisoner in Britain', has served several terms here and spent almost all of his adult life in solitary confinement in prisons and psychiatric units. Inexplicably released in 1992 from HMP Parkhurst, Isle of Wight, Bronson returned immediately to a life of violent crime and was subsequently locked up here in the 'Hannibal Cage'. Bronson is a self-proclaimed poet, artist and fitness fanatic. A year older than Maudsley, at 58, he can manage 172 press-ups in 60 seconds. I have never set eyes on him, but the very thought of his presence behind these high walls sends a shiver down my spine.

It is after ten. He is late. Ah! The small black door moves, then opens inwards. A uniformed officer emerges, followed by a morbidly pale man, in his forties, below average in stature, his mid-brown hair cut severely short and greying at the temples, carrying a green sports bag. The officer speaks to the man, who appears not to hear him, then walks away from the door towards the main road and me. I get out of the car and walk round to open the passenger door. I am sure he sees me, but his face is expressionless, as always, the gaze blank, eyes red-rimmed behind the round spectacle lenses. He does not acknowledge my presence. He never did. I step into his path and halt him on the narrow pavement. I do not speak. Nor does he. Of course not. I motion him to get in. He looks around, as if checking for a better alternative, then complies. George Campbell, released on licence from Wakefield prison after serving twelve years for the brutally violent murder of his own father, gets into my car, clutching his green sports bag as though it contains his life savings, and fastens his seatbelt. A nursery rhyme runs through my head, insistent:

Here we go round the mulberry bush,
The mulberry bush, the mulberry bush.
Here we go round the mulberry bush,
On a cold and frosty morning.

I remember. They say it is what female inmates used to sing as they exercised around the mulberry tree in this prison yard. They say that this is where the rhyme originated. It is a good story, but almost certainly not true. The mulberry tree is still there, flourishing, but the women are not. Now there are only monsters.

My passenger and I do not speak. We do not even look at each other. I drive back to Sheffield in our silence. All the way down the M1 the mulberry bush goes round in my head. It seems fitting, and it reminds me of childhood; it reminds me of the first time I met George Campbell.

●

1978

A small boy sits opposite me, looking down at his feet, his satchel still swinging from his shoulder. His blazer is buttoned up wrongly, which gives him a lopsided look. His national health spectacles are bent, so that one lens sits higher than the other. He is scruffy, with greasy, unruly hair, but I am used to this; many of our pupils come from a deprived area of the city. He is twelve years old and I note that he is tiny for his age.

'Good morning, George,' I say.

George does not acknowledge my greeting. He does not look up. I turn to the third point of our triangle, Angela Davis, the First Year Tutor.

'I'm sure you'll have lots to do, Miss Davis. George and I are just going to have a little chat. Aren't we, George?'

She shakes her head vigorously. I nod firmly, walk over to the door and hold it open for her. She leaves, but not without giving me a look that speaks volumes: 'On your own head be it; I wash my hands'.

I study the back of the boy's head and his grimy shirt-collar, contemplating my next move.

'Let me take your satchel, George.'

Not a flicker from the boy. I take the satchel and place it by the side of his armchair. He picks it up and puts it back on his shoulder. I am back in my seat now. He is looking out of the window onto the staff car park. I turn my head to see what he is looking at. Nothing.

George is here because I am following up, as I promised, a concern raised in 'any other business' at last night's staff meeting by Gordon Peck, master in charge of woodwork and an old stalwart with thirty years' service at the school. Colleagues listen to him, because he makes a lot of noise.

'Something has to be done about George Campbell. It's got past a joke now. Colleagues are spending more time on him than the rest of the class put together.'

And so on. I won't bore you with the rest. His tirade was greeted with a mixture of nods and murmurs of approval from one half of the staff and eye-rolling from the other half. Angela Davis raised her hand:

'He's one of mine, in 1R. I am forever . . .'

I looked at my watch. It was 5.40. I cut her short.

'Let me intervene, Miss Davis. It's been a long day, and a long meeting. You and I will talk about this first thing in the morning.' I shuffled my papers and put on my best reassuring smile for the assembled staff. 'We'll deal with it, I promise.'

Undaunted by the minor slights over the satchel and the good morning, I try again: 'Just you and me now,

7

George. Nothing to worry about. You're not here to be punished or told off. I just want to chat.'

Again nothing. The boy's expression remains blank. He adjusts his satchel, continues to look out of the window, eyes clouded and unfocused. I try asking him how he's finding it at the school, whether he has made any new friends, which lessons he likes best, how many brothers and sisters he has, what he likes doing in his spare time, all to no avail. I am uncertain whether George is very shy or just downright rude. My pride is hurt: I'm supposed to be good at this; at least that's what it says in all my references: highly experienced and skilled in dealing with difficult children, forms positive and trusting relationships, demonstrates empathy and communicates well with children of all ages and backgrounds.

Res non verba, I resolve, remembering my old school motto: 'Let me see your specs, George. They've gone a bit wonky. Mine are always doing it – I'll fix them for you.'

No movement from George, no change of expression. I reach over and remove his glasses. He flinches a little, and the red-rimmed grey eyes blink furiously for two or three seconds, but he does not resist. I rummage amongst the jumble of paperwork on my desk to find the little screwdriver I keep handy for such occasions. I bend the frame back into shape as best I can, use the tool to tighten the arms and then polish the grubby lenses. I hand the glasses to him. He does not take them from me. I rest them gently back on his nose and curl the earpieces round his ears. I am unable to resist re-buttoning his blazer. He says nothing.

'Thank you, George. I've enjoyed our little chat,' I say, realising just how ridiculous that sounds to me and probably to him. 'We'll talk again soon, and you can tell me how it's going.'

I walk over to the door and hold it open for him. As he walks out, he catches his satchel strap on the door handle. I unhook it for him. He continues with neither a word nor a glance.

•

I pull into my driveway and switch off the engine. I turn to my passenger:

'George, you're going to stay with my wife and me for a while, until we find you a place of your own. Is that okay?'

There is no reply, no gesture of acquiescence or refusal. Not that I expected any. I get out of the car and walk round to open the passenger door. George fumbles with his seatbelt, and I resist the temptation to help him. Finally he releases the buckle and gets out of the car. He follows me into the house.

Tuppence, lying in ambush behind the glass recycling bin, examines George for signs of clear and present danger to his regime, concludes there are none and returns to his hobby of stalking small birds.

Marilyn, surprisingly, is not disconcerted by our arrival together. Has she remembered that I have warned her about the guest? No. She thinks it is my old friend, Jürgen, and speaks to him in broken German. She goes off to put the kettle on. Suzi breaks the ice in her inimitable manner, haranguing George with a multitude of questions to which she fortunately does not appear to require any answer. Marilyn returns from the kitchen having forgotten what she went in for. I leave the three of them together. Good luck to them all. I suddenly feel very tired. I retreat to the kitchen and open the birthday cards from my son and my sister. His is the typical ageist 'humorous' card, but with thankfully no mention of a milestone 70th birthday. Perhaps he is being tactful, perhaps he does not know my age. Hers is a picture of a dog, with warm wishes for a speedy recovery. She must be psychic. I make a pot of tea.

II

ISOLATED PAWN

(A pawn with no pawn of the same colour on an adjacent file.)

1978

To the annoyance of his Year Tutor and the Head of Pastoral Care, I took a special interest in George Campbell from that morning when I had my first brush with him. He was a challenge I could not ignore. I made enquiries at his primary school and discovered that he had appeared perfectly normal until the age of nine, when suddenly he had refused to either speak or write in class. Prior to that, he had made above average progress in school.

I called in the local authority child psychologist, a freckled, sandy-haired young man overburdened with a huge caseload, who was already aware of George. He had diagnosed the boy's problem as 'elective mutism' and bombarded me with catchphrases such as 'inherited predisposition to anxiety', 'sensory integration dysfunction' and 'hypersensitivity of the amygdala'. He told me that sufferers typically had difficulty in maintaining eye contact, especially with adults, were reluctant to smile, worried a lot, were often depressed, and had difficulty in

10

expressing their feelings. As to a cure, or even to effective treatment, he was less forthcoming. It seemed that the boy would just have to grow out of it. It was his choice not to speak, after all. I placated Gordon Peck by assuring him he was not expected to teach the boy anything, but merely to accept him in the room and keep him safe. I explained, lying through my teeth, that he was under the supervision of the school psychologist.

Peck was unimpressed: 'These psychos and therapists are all the same, if you ask me – it's the emperor's new clothes!'

I decided to visit the boy's home. Diplomatically, I invited Angela Davis to go with me. We walked to the house, only 400 yards from the school. On the way, Angela explained to me that George was the eldest of five children, that his mother was known to the police as a shoplifter and his father was long-term unemployed, a drinker, and from time to time missing from the family home for weeks. The family was well known for the frequency with which police were called out to 'domestic incidents' and late night disturbances. There was also an Uncle Cameron, who Angela thought was Mr Campbell's brother.

The front door of number 27 Khartoum Street led directly into the kitchen. Mrs Campbell stood in the doorway, arms folded, waiting for us. She had a broad stain on her cheek, either a bruise or a faded birthmark. Two mugs of instant coffee stood cooling by the sink. I asked her whether we were expecting her husband to be present, and she gave me a meaningful look, as if to say it was a stupid question. Our discussion was short. She was not surprised that George was silent at school; he had stopped speaking to her ages ago. If the boy did not do what he was told in class, then we should 'give him a good hiding and be done with it'. I asked whether she or George's father ever punished the boy. She said she would if she could catch him, and that her husband did give the kids a thick ear when he was that way out. 'When he gets in before they're in bed,' she added.

She showed us into the living room, where there were three dogs. We picked our way through a minefield of toys, empty crisp packets and drinks cans to a window at the rear of the house. A rusting car engine lay in one corner of

11

the murky, walled back yard, next to some rotting kitchen units and a cracked lavatory bowl. The five children were engaged in a highly organised game, with George very much in charge. He was using a pile of three tyres, in front of the outside toilet, as a platform from which to issue instructions for what appeared to be a dramatic production. He spoke loud and clear. His mother wrenched open the metal-framed window, which screeched in protest at being disturbed, and called him over. He hopped down from his precarious podium, came halfway towards the house and stopped when he saw us. I tried to engage him in conversation, skilfully and sensitively, I thought. He did not respond in any way. No, that is not strictly accurate. He did respond, by looking down at his feet. Elective mutism it was, then. He just didn't want to talk to us. This was the second time that this 12-year-old boy had left me feeling totally inadequate. We said our goodbyes and thanked Mrs Campbell for the coffee.

'It's a big family. I wonder where they all sleep,' I remarked to my colleague.

'The three girls share the back bedroom and the two lads sleep in the attic.'

'What about the uncle?'

She shook her head and put on a pained expression:

'One of the little girls told her teacher that Uncle Cameron sometimes sleeps in the attic with the boys, sometimes on the settee and sometimes with Mummy and Daddy.'

'How the other half live', was all the wisdom I could sum up.

Our problems with George Campbell did not diminish. Rather they worsened. To his refusal to speak or write George added ever increasing truancy. In his second year at the school, being almost totally dysfunctional, he was relegated to the slow learners' set in every subject. I resisted pressure to remove him from French classes – his French teacher declared him impossible to teach and a drain on her energy:

'Not only does he never speak, he never writes a single word, not even to copy from the board, never looks at me

12

even, and he never listens to a word I say. And he never does a jot of homework. How am I supposed to discipline the rest of the class when he just gets away with everything?'

Other teachers regularly sent him out of their classroom, presumably out of anger or frustration. When I or the Deputy Head discovered the boy ejected on the corridor and challenged the teacher for a reason, the stock answer was that the boy had disrupted the lesson by his dumb insolence.

The war-cry of the French teacher was taken up by other colleagues. After one case-study meeting about George, Frank Wilson, the Second Year Tutor, came to see me. There were calls from staff for the boy to be transferred to another school. His view was that too much of his own energy and that of colleagues was being expended on him, in vain, as he was making no progress either educationally or socially. I refused to give up on George and have him transferred. I told Wilson I would not be browbeaten by teachers who wanted a quiet life. The following morning, I made an announcement in the staffroom: George was no longer to be ejected from classrooms, unless he was a threat to either the other pupils or the teacher. I knew this would lose me friends on the staff. It was my second year in the post. So far I had prided myself on managing to build good relationships with all my colleagues, but the honeymoon period was now definitively over. There were no more formal complaints about young Campbell, but the Deputy Head, Bill Rodgers, told me that there was an undercurrent of discontent; allegations of not giving staff my full backing, the cardinal sin in the eyes of teachers, were being levelled at me privately.

Some of the staff discontent was gradually dissipated because George was so often absent from school. Despite all the efforts of truancy officers, his attendance eventually diminished to one day per week, Wednesdays, and so the clamour to 'do something about him' diminished correspondingly.

There was one bright note: George liked drama lessons, and drama was on Wednesdays. Our drama teacher was a young woman in her probationary year, appointed the

13

previous summer, my very first appointment at Harry Brearley Comprehensive. She went by the unfortunate name of Doris Day, her father being a fan of her Hollywood namesake, as she averred without any evident embarrassment. Despite her semi-permanent worried frown, I had liked the look of her, her energy, enthusiasm and effervescence, from the first moments of her interview. I admit that I was also swayed by her promise to revive interest in the school's moribund chess club, a hobby-horse of mine, and I had battled for her appointment against a panel determined to select a more experienced candidate. I had finally got my way.

'You're the boss,' conceded the chair of governors reluctantly.

'I suppose I am, aren't I?' I agreed. Young Miss Day was appointed.

It seemed that George liked her too. I discovered this whilst conducting her half-year appraisal in February. I knew that George was in one of her classes, as she taught all the second year pupils.

'How do you get on with George Campbell?'

'Oh, he's a little poppet! Absolutely no problem at all, sir.' She always called me 'sir'.

She told me George took a full part in all the lessons, although he never spoke. She had soon found out that it was pointless assigning any speaking roles to him. I congratulated her and later that week spied on one of her lessons through the glass door of her classroom, making sure that George did not see me. He was clearly enjoying himself. I assumed that drama was the reason that he graced us with his presence on Wednesdays of all days. Doris corrected me:

'I don't think it's just the drama, sir. It's Chess Club that he really likes. After school, on Wednesdays. I don't allow him into Chess Club unless he has attended school that day.'

'You mean he has actually come into school just for Chess Club?'

'He's tried it on a couple of times.'

I mentioned that George was thirteen years old and I asked her if she thought that he might have a crush on her; she seemed surprised and blushed crimson:

14

'On me, sir? Oh, no!'

I looked at her. She wasn't pretty. Perhaps she had a point. I apologised for my insensitive suggestion and congratulated her on her success with the boy. She was the only teacher who had built any sort of relationship with him.

I had had no inkling that the boy was interested in chess. From our conversation I discovered that quite early in the autumn term he had taken to turning up at the chess club, and for the first three or four weeks had stood in the background watching proceedings. She had then seen him sneak a book on chess for beginners from her desk into his satchel. It did cross her mind that he might be stealing the book, but she had decided not to challenge him. The following week he had returned the book covertly to her bookshelf and played out a game of chess against himself in the corner of the room. She had watched him from a distance; he clearly knew all the rules. By the end of the autumn term he was silently taking on all the lower school members and trouncing them. At last week's club she had played against him herself and had been unable to beat him within the hour.

It still rankled with me that I had made no progress with this troublesome little boy and I resolved to try a new tactic. I should explain that during my degree studies I played number one board for my University for three years, attaining Candidate Master status, and so I am a more than respectable chess player. After University, I started out on my teaching career, met Marilyn while working at my first school, fell in love and married her. There was soon no time for chess. In any case, I had a nagging suspicion that I was not quite as good as other people thought I was. I was rather like those sportsmen who are not quite good enough to play at the very top level and give up their sport because they are unwilling to accept anything but the best. For mental relaxation in those days, I turned to bridge, where I didn't have a reputation to maintain.

I buttonholed George one Wednesday lunch-time and took him to my office, as I explained, 'for another little chat'. Waiting on my coffee table was a chess board with the pieces laid out ready to play. The ensuing scene is etched in my memory, in every last detail.

We sit opposite each other, George with his customary blank expression, me all avuncular and smiling. The white pieces are on his side of the board. I invite him to play white and wait for him to begin. Nothing. I turn the board around and move white king's pawn forward two spaces to e4, the standard opening move. George reciprocates with his king's pawn, moving it to e5, the standard reply. I continue with bishop to c4 and he mirrors the move with his king's bishop. I thrust my queen forward to h5, and George responds by moving his king's knight to f6, presumably to chase off the white queen - a beginner's error that all of us have made at one time. I snaffle his bishop's pawn and declare checkmate. He stands up and makes for the door. I call him back. I explain to him that he lost the game by what is called 'Scholar's Mate'. There is no shame in it – it happens to every beginner, but he must learn not to fall into that trap again. I am pleased that I have been able to teach him a valuable lesson. I sit him down once more. This time he is white. He plays pawn to f3, and immediately I know what he is doing. He is trying to lose as quickly as possible, so that he can get out of here. I play the standard king's pawn to f5 and wait for the inevitable pawn to g4. This little boy is messing with me; he doesn't want to play and he's telling me so in no uncertain manner. I play the required queen to h4 and it's all over in two moves: Fool's Mate.

'Okay, George. You've made your point. Off you go.'

He stands and hurries out of the door without looking back. For a third time, this little boy has left me feeling totally impotent.

My next encounter with George Campbell was also across the sixty-four black and white squares of a chess board. One late Wednesday afternoon towards the end of the public examination period, Doris knocked at my door. After I had enquired about her well-being and, remembering it was Wednesday, how Chess Club was going, she explained that she wanted to further raise the profile of chess in the school, and had arranged a match, pupils versus teachers. Four other teachers had volunteered to play on the staff team, which left just one place.

'I know you're very keen on chess, sir, and I wondered if you would like to play. It would make a big difference if you would turn out. It would make it a really big event.'

I looked at the pile of work on my desk. Preparations for the next school year were not going well. Bill Rodgers was having problems creating the timetable and had called on me to resolve several issues. We were hoping to make four new appointments before the end of the summer term and there were almost a hundred letters of application to be waded through. For the past three weeks I had not left my office before eight o'clock in the evening. I couldn't afford the time.

'It's a great idea, Doris, but I'm afraid I just don't have time at the moment.'

'I thought, you know,' she stammered, 'seeing as you played in goal in the football team against the first XI, you might want to turn out in the chess as well.' Her voice tailed away; she was clearly disappointed with me.

'I'm sorry, Doris. Any other time, but . . .'

'That's a shame, sir. Never mind.' The semi-permanent worried frown had returned to her face.

'Keep up the good work, anyway. I'm very impressed with what you've done.'

I mentioned the invitation to play on the staff chess team to Marilyn that evening in bed and quickly wished I had not, as this seemed to put her in a particularly obstreperous frame of mind. She also seemed disappointed in me. I was always bleating on about heads' needing to have the human touch, to be seen around the school, to interact with pupils as well as teachers. Surely it was no skin off my nose to turn out for ten minutes and polish off some spotty youth before going back to my paperwork. After all, didn't I used to be some kind of Grand Master or something? I argued that, apart from my heavy workload, it would be unfair for me to play for the staff team, as I would be far too good for any of my young opponents. She accused me of being yellow, and although I didn't believe she was entirely serious, this still rankled. Having rebuked me soundly, Marilyn turned over and was instantly dead to the world. As for me, exhausted though I was, I found it oddly difficult to sleep.

The next morning I left home at 7.15, as usual. Marilyn walked to the front door with me to wave me off. I turned to her and kissed her.

'I've changed my mind about the chess. You're right. I should play in the team.'

'If they'll still have you.'

My wife was not a morning person.

I had a message sent to Doris asking her to see me immediately after assembly. She ambushed me as I was leaving the stage after giving my homily on 'beauty is skin deep'. It would have to be quick, as she had a class waiting. I said I wouldn't keep her and explained about my change of mind. She beamed. It was worth changing my mind just for that smile.

'Fantastic, sir! I'm so glad. George Campbell's playing, you know. Isn't that wonderful? I was going to tell you this morning. I thought it might change your mind.'

'Is he up to it? I mean, he wouldn't say boo to a goose, would he?'

'Oh, yes. He's a really good player. He'll be number one board. Playing against you, sir.'

A second-year boy on number one board! I was amazed to hear such confidence in the boy's chess prowess, but concerned that it was I who had to perform the delicate balancing act of beating him without humiliating him. I protested that she should be number one board, as I hadn't played for years. She insisted that I should not be so modest. She knew all about my chequered history. I said I hoped that was a pun, and she laughed and went off to her class.

I was preoccupied during our management team meeting that morning, and Bill Rodgers asked me afterwards if I was all right. Was there anything he should know? I reassured him, fobbed him off with a concern of mine about the standard of teaching in the sixth form, an issue of which he was already aware. In fact, I had been wondering about young George Campbell. Would playing chess for the school team be a bridge too far for him? On the face of it, this was a long stride forward in his development, but it could be a dangerous one. I thought

18

back to my other chess encounter with the boy. Would he behave in the same way? Why were we failing so miserably with him? I could not recall coming across another such case in my teaching career. I did remember a boy a year older than I at school, to whom something similar had happened, but only temporarily. Paul Rutter, Chatsworth House Captain and all-round good guy, whom I had admired for years, suffered the trauma of his parents' separating and was struck dumb for the last six weeks of his school career. We lost touch, but I met him the following year on a train from Newcastle to London. He was a national serviceman returning on leave from Catterick Camp. He was back to normal. Perhaps George would be cured too. Eventually. Perhaps this was step one of a return to normality.

Two weeks later, I was in earnest discussion with Bill Rodgers at the end of the school day, when there was a light knock at my door and my secretary came in:

'They're waiting for you in the Hall, Mr York.'

'Oh yes, your chance to show off your genius,' grinned Bill.

It was the chess match.

'I shan't be long, Bill. You can make that call to Leopold Street.'

'Oh no, I'm coming with you. I wouldn't miss this for the world!'

The Hall was unexpectedly full. The general hubbub dropped to a murmur, as Bill and I walked down the steps into what could only be described as an arena. Six tables, each with a chess board and clock, were set out in the centre, at intervals of three to four metres. Around the perimeter were at least fifty pupils. I have seen smaller attendances at Scottish Football League matches. Doris Day's publicity machine had been effective. Six pupils, all bar one from the Fifth and Sixth Forms, sat waiting for their teacher opponents, waiting for me. Little George Campbell sat impassive. I wondered how he was feeling. Was he nervous? It was impossible to tell. I sat down opposite him and offered a handshake. He did not meet my gaze, looking directly at the chess pieces, ignoring my greeting. What would he do? Would he commit hara-kiri

19

again, deliberately succumb to Scholar's Mate or something of the kind?

Doris stood and cleared her throat:

'Those of you who are Chess Club members will know how to behave, but for those of you who are not, here are one or two guidelines. You may stand close, but not too close, to the competitors' tables, so as to follow individual matches, but you may not talk within their earshot.'

I wondered if 'in earshot' was within the vocabulary range of some of our children. Doris continued:

'Chess is a game which requires the utmost concentration. If you wish to talk, you should go to the far corners of the Hall and whisper. Each player will have a maximum of forty minutes' thinking and playing time, as measured on the chess clocks. This means that games could take up to a maximum of one hour twenty minutes. Individual matches still unfinished will be sent for adjudication. Teachers will play white on Boards 1, 3 and 5, pupils will play white on Boards 2, 4 and 6. If the players are ready, we shall begin.'

I marvelled at her self-possession. She was quite a girl. Some of the spectators gradually shuffled towards the tables, choosing the match they wanted to follow. I was conscious of quite a number gathered behind me, fidgeting. I started my clock, played pawn to e4 and pressed the buttons to switch over to my young opponent's clock. The first moves followed the pattern of my first game with George. This time I was resolved not to let him have the easy way out, if he chased my queen and opened himself to Scholar's Mate. He did not. Instead he played a solid defensive opening and had soon established a sound basis for a tight match, where either a mistake or a piece of inspired attacking play would determine the outcome. As white, by the mid-game I had the usual small advantage conferred by playing first. As in the simple game of noughts and crosses, the first to play, white, should in theory never lose.

Young Campbell was taking an unusually long time to respond to my twelfth move, which had put me in a strong position, from where I would be able to line up my queen and rook against pieces standing in front of the black king, unless he took the correct precautions. I looked across at

20

Doris, diagonally opposite me at the next table. She was surrounded by admirers, most of whom I recognised as Chess Club members, who evidently adored her. Her concentration was total, her eyes shone and her face glowed. She had drifted into a haven of relaxation. Gone were the worry-lines of the overworked young teacher. She actually looked quite attractive, damn it! I scolded myself inwardly for my un-headmagisterial thoughts and turned my attention back to the board. My opponent had made his move and my clock was ticking again. Oh dear, Georgie boy, you've made a bit of a blunder there, haven't you? He had ignored the potential threat from my queen and played an irrelevant move, offering me the cheap capture of a knight into the bargain. Let's get it over, was my response. I ignored the knight sacrifice, lined my queen up against the black king and leaned back in my chair. I looked at my watch: twenty to five – still time to phone the Education Office. The crowd around our table had grown. They must have sensed the end was nigh. Bill Rodgers came over and glanced at the board. I signalled five minutes to him with my hand.

I looked further down the hall. The matches on Boards 5 and 6 had already ended, and the looks on the faces of the staff and pupils indicated that the teachers were two boards up. A pity, as the humiliation of a whitewash would do nothing for pupil morale. From a quick glance at her board, Doris looked certain to beat Philip Hargreaves, the Head Boy, but perhaps one of the two sixth-form girls on Boards 3 and 4 might at least force a draw. I hoped so.

I doodled on my pad, where I had made a note of all the moves of the game, a habit ingrained in me through years of competition. George Campbell's pad was untouched. A little boy behind me spoke very low: 'It's your move, sir.'

I looked at the dial of my clock. It had moved on by three minutes. George must have played his move 13 immediately. The boy had read my mind! He knew I would ignore the free knight so as to gain the easy winning position. What I had not seen, in my patronising dismissal of his move as foolhardy or incompetent, was that his next move of the knight would not only plunge my bishop and rook into jeopardy with an attacking fork, but also reveal a pin by his bishop on my queen. He had risked everything on a mind-game. If I had taken the knight he had offered, he would have been lost. From there on, he took the upper hand and savaged my pieces with a series of pins, forks, skewers and discovered attacks. At move 23, my time rapidly running out, I conceded. The other matches were over and the players and remaining spectators, all gathered around our table, burst into a spontaneous round of applause, as I toppled my king. My opponent stood, wriggled through the throng and ran out of the hall without a word, avoiding as best he could the congratulatory slaps on the back.

Doris was standing by my side now.

'Where's he off to in such a rush?' I asked.

A little girl answered for her: 'I think he has to look after his brother and sisters a lot.'

'Thank you, sir,' said Doris, with that winning smile again. 'That was very magnanimous.'

'Magnanimous? What was?'

'What you did there, letting him win. It will mean so much to him, I think.'

To my eternal shame I did not contradict her. The best I could manage was: 'Well, he's a very good player.'

'Yes, he regularly plays all the best players in the club, and he's never lost yet. I daren't play him anymore!'

I wondered why she had not told me that before, and felt a tinge of resentment. The teachers had won by four boards to two, but it would be all around the school that the Head had lost. I retreated to my office with Bill. It was too late for any phone-calls to Leopold Street and I was no longer in the mood in any case. I told him we'd call it a day and drove home through the rush-hour traffic.

If I thought that George Campbell's participation and success in the chess match would be the first step out of the silent world he inhabited, and I did, then I was totally wrong. I suppose I dreamed that the generous sacrifice of my dignity in losing the chess game might be the first helping hand on his road back to normality, and that one day he would come to me and say:

'Do you know, Mr York, that the day you allowed me to be beat you at chess changed my life? It gave me the confidence in myself that I had been lacking. I shall be forever grateful to you.'

It did not change his life. Nothing changed, except perhaps for the worse. At the beginning of the next school year, George's third year at the school, his attendance improved initially, but then he began to have squabbles with other boys in class. Some teachers reported that other boys were bullying him, whilst some suggested that he was encouraging and inviting bullying by other boys through his refusal to interact. He was involved in several fights after school, on and off school premises. Soon his attendance was back to the bare minimum of one day per week. He had still not uttered a single word in any class, had never yet completed a piece of homework and refused to report for detentions unless physically taken to the detention room.

Matters came to a head when George was accused of pushing his science teacher during a lesson in the chemistry laboratory. The teacher refused to have him back in class, and a governors' disciplinary panel, chaired by me, was convened to deal with the matter. The evidence against the boy was flimsy, and I suspected that the teacher in question, well-known for his proclivity to tease and victimise individuals, had provoked him. However, I agreed that we suspend him from school for three days, Friday until Tuesday. As the boy was in the habit of only attending school on Wednesdays, this seemed an acceptable compromise, although I left the meeting with a sickening feeling that the system was failing him, that the school was failing him and that I in particular was failing him. It was not for the want of trying. We had repeatedly called for the aid of the psychological service, with no positive outcome. I personally had conducted several interviews with George, interviews which had consisted of frustrating monologues, during which I at times came very close to losing my temper in the face of the boy's stubborn silence and total lack of response. The only positive note was his continued attendance at Chess Club, where he was now quite a star performer, would play simultaneous boards against three or four other members and was never known to lose.

23

In July of this his third year in the school, George was accused of attacking a female RE teacher, swinging an arm at her and hitting her on the shoulder and neck. I asked Bill Rodgers to investigate, which he did in his typically thorough manner. From interviewing the teacher and pupils in the classroom, Bill established that there had been a scuffle between George and two other boys which had developed into an angry exchange of blows between them. The teacher had intervened and George, continuing to hit out, had made contact with her, perhaps on purpose, but more likely accidentally. Pupils not involved in the scuffle maintained, possibly out of solidarity, that George had not been in any way aggressive, but was merely defending himself from the other boys. Bill talked to George's mother and discovered that the boy had ceased to communicate even with his siblings. He had been totally silent at home for several weeks, a period coinciding with the return of his father after a month's absence. There was clearly a deeply rooted problem behind the boy's mutism, on the face of it probably concerning his father. I enquired from the first year tutor, Angela Davis about George's sister, Nancy, of whom I had heard nothing.

'So far, there's no sign of any problem. Academically, she is way below average, but her behaviour is impeccable. She's as quiet as a mouse.'

'Not as quiet as George, I hope.'

'Oh no! She does speak when spoken to.'

'Are there any more Campbells on the way?'

'There's one coming up next year, as a matter of fact. Ryan Campbell.'

'Any reports on him from the primary school?'

'He seems okay. They say he can be a bit cheeky, but we can handle that. Par for the course these days.'

'I think we should be looking out for signs of bullying at home.'

'Oh?'

'By the father.'

'I'll keep my eye open.'

But during the rest of my seven years as headteacher at Harry Brearley, I received no report of any concern about members the Campbell family. It seemed my fears were unfounded.

Bill reported his findings to me and to the union representatives. He concluded that an apology from the boy and a promise from all three not to repeat the behaviour, along with a detention for fighting in class and a letter home to parents, would suffice. However, the teachers' unions were adamant that a heavier sanction must be applied. The three main unions had resolved, in a joint meeting, that no teacher would allow the boy back into class. It was a matter of principle. The boy must be removed, permanently suspended, transferred to another school. The old-fashioned word 'expelled' would have been more appropriate.

I met the three union representatives, in an attempt to persuade them to adopt a more reasonable stance, but they were not to be budged.

'Is that your final word, gentlemen?' I asked.

There were shrugs and nods of assent from the three wise monkeys opposite me.

'Then our discussion is over.'

I was boiling with anger that these so-called professionals seemed not to possess an ounce of charity between them. I would have thrown them out of my office like a night-club bouncer, if I had been capable.

The following afternoon, Bill slipped quietly into my office without knocking, which was not his style at all.

'We have a visitor from Leopoldstrasse, David. Ralph Keane. I cut him off on his way to reception – told him you are with a parent. He's in my office with a pot of Lapsang Souchong and a chocolate digestive.'

Keane was the Deputy Chief Education Officer. He and I did not get on, and I suspected that my appointment had been against his advice. We had already clashed earlier in the year over what I considered an unfairly low allocation of funds to the school.

'My cup runneth over. What does he want, I wonder?'

'Take a wild guess,' said Bill, with an exaggerated grimace.

'Wheel him in. And I want you present.'

Keane marched into the room, followed by Bill carrying the tray of tea and biscuits. I stood to greet him, resisting

25

as best I could his attempt to crush four of my fingers in his bony grip. He wore his usual country gentleman style, three-piece tweed suit, with the chain of a fob watch dangling from a waistcoat pocket. His short, dark hair was immaculately brilliantined, with a centre parting, and he carried with him a faint aroma of floral perfume that reminded me of Parma Violets. Like many small men I have known, he was aggressively self-important. He walked across the room to sit with his back to the window. Bill sat to his right, and I formed the third point of the triangle, squinting against the sunlight streaming through the window. I was about to stand, to close the venetian blind, when Keane began.

'No need for you to stay, Bill.'

'If you don't mind, Ralph, I like Bill to sit in on any meetings with Leopold Street.'

'Well, if he has nothing better to do, and the school is running like clockwork . . . Is that the case, Bill?'

'Like a Rolls-Royce, as a matter of fact.'

'Then I'll get straight to the point. There's a rumour going around the office that there's trouble at t' mill,' enunciated Keane slowly, with an unsuccessful attempt at a northern accent. 'T' natives are restless. The Chief has asked me to have a word, to smooth things out with the tribal elders, so to speak.'

He paused, for effect, waiting for some response from me, some signal that I was quaking in my boots before this ambassador from headquarters.

To be perfectly honest, I was. I gripped my hands together in my lap, so as not to show them shaking.

Bill spoke:

'I presume you mean this business about the unions refusing to accept one of our pupils in class?'

I found my voice: 'It's a storm in a teacup. It will all blow over. We can handle it.'

I saw Bill pull a face and look down at his feet.

'I'm afraid the Chief doesn't agree. You see, we have a contact at NUT headquarters, and with a new pay round coming up, they are willing to back their members to the hilt, make a martyr out of the poor lady teacher who has been so brutally assaulted whilst carrying out her professional duties, blah blah blah. There is nothing they

26

would like better than a national scandal, a few headlines in *The Sun*, the *News of the World* and co.'

He was enjoying himself. He bit into another chocolate biscuit, sipped on his tea, and smacked his lips.

'Excellent tea, Bill.'

'So, what you're saying is that you would like me to sacrifice this one little boy?'

He swallowed the mouthful of biscuit, put down his teacup and gave me a condescending smile, as though I were a backward pupil in his maths class, who needed only a little encouragement to realise that the calculation was very simple.

'It is one boy. One boy, who, if I understand it properly, rarely graces the school with his presence, anyway.'

He formed his hands into two sides of a weighing scale. His left hand floated, light as a feather, chest high, his right hand down below his thigh, as though bearing a heavy weight.

'On the other hand, if union action is taken, the school's work will be interrupted and the education of nine hundred others disrupted. I say nothing of the damage locally to the school's reputation, and the standing of its leadership.'

He waited for me to respond. I said nothing.

'It's your decision, David. The Chief is confident you'll get it right. On reflection, I think there's no need for me to speak to your union people. Whatever you decide, we shall of course back you. Thank you for your time.'

Keane stood, managed to crush only three of my fingers this time, and left, without turning his head.

Bill and I watched him disappear from the car park in his brand-new, red TR7 convertible, scattering a flock of avian visitors from the neighbouring council refuse dump.

'Take a seat, Bill,' I said, feeling and no doubt looking very glum. 'What's your advice? What would you do, if you were Head?'

He shook his head.

'Which question do you want me to answer?'

What did he mean? The question was clear enough.

'I am in the last stages of my rather undistinguished career, David. I've spent most of my life as a secondary modern. maths teacher, cajoling reluctant kids, boys

27

mainly, to gain a few basic skills in arithmetic, making sure they behaved themselves, while we tried to turn them into decent human beings with the right values, into self-respecting, worthwhile members of society. All in all, I've done okay. What I would do, if it were up to me, and what I'd advise you to do, at this stage of your career, are two different things altogether. But you're the boss. This is what they pay you that big salary for.'

I understood him all too well.

'How are we going to tell the lad?'

There was a long silence, before Bill spoke.

'I'll do it, if you like.'

The upshot was that the boy did not come into school for the rest of term and was transferred to a school at the other side of the city as from September.

Should I have resisted the threats of the unions and the admonishments of my superiors and risked certain strike action? Could I have fought harder for that fourteen-year-old boy? Would it have made any difference to his future? We shall never know. All I do know is that I had a sense of failure more acute than at any time during my career. Integrity, once sacrificed for expediency, is impossible to re-establish. From that point onwards, I had lost the respect of the staff at Harry Brearley; in their eyes, I was weak. When the opportunity to leave eventually offered itself, several years later, I took it without a second thought.

I did discover later that there had been one dissenting voice at the staff union meetings, that of Doris Day. As she no longer taught the boy, the views of this junior teacher had carried no weight whatsoever.

A headteacher in his first post has many concerns to occupy his mind, but for months the thought of that little boy alone in his silence returned to unsettle me. It was such a grievous waste of a young life, a waste of a childhood – a waste of an outstanding talent too, if his ability at chess were any indication. Gradually, however, he receded from my thoughts until, during the week before February half-term of 1981, Doris Day came to see me, ostensibly to talk to me about her plans for the next dramatic production. As she left my office, she turned, rubbing her hand across her mouth:

'Sir, what are your feelings about ex-pupils coming back to visit staff at the school? Is it okay?'

'I look on it very positively. It reflects well on us if our students want to come back to see us.'

'It's just that a boy has been coming back regularly, to join in Chess Club. Every Wednesday, in fact.'

I knew straight away who it was: 'That's good. A feather in your cap, Doris.'

'Don't you want to know who it is, sir?'

I smiled my most benign headmagisterial smile and pretended to be absorbed in my paperwork: 'I don't think I need to know every detail, Doris. Keep up the good work, though.'

When she had gone, I phoned my headteacher colleague at George's new school to check on the boy's progress, the very least I could do, I thought. It was not good news: George rarely attended school, seemed to have made no friends and was silent and uncooperative in the few lessons he attended. They had discovered that he often spent whole nights away from home and feared he was becoming almost feral and beyond the reach of social services. They were in the process of transferring the boy to the city's special unit for excluded pupils. It was likely too that George would soon be taken into local authority care. A few weeks later, I dropped in on Chess Club. George was there, apparently playing three boards simultaneously. I pretended not to notice him.

Doris left the school in the summer of that year to take up a post at another school, in the East Midlands, and with her departure presumably ended George's visits to the school. I heard nothing more of him until one late autumn morning in 1998, when, in my office at the British School in Berlin, I opened a letter marked personal. It was from an old Harry Brearley colleague.

It contained a newspaper clipping denouncing George Campbell as a patricide.

III

GAMBIT

(A sacrifice during the opening, made in order to gain an early advantage.)

2011

How do you solve a problem like George Campbell? What do you do with a houseguest who neither speaks, nor responds when you speak to him, nor shows any clear indication that he has even heard you? George is that houseguest who seems unwilling to take any initiative whatsoever. How do you keep him occupied? How do you entertain him?

For the first two days I resolved to do nothing, to observe him without being too obvious and to allow him to settle into strange surroundings. As it was wintertime, I was not even able to get him out of the house and into the garden, sit him in a chair and give him a newspaper. I took the *Guardian* up to his room the first morning; he accepted it from me but instantly set it aside, even before I had closed the door. It seemed he had no interest in either news or sport. On reflection, this was not surprising; he had lived outside society for almost thirteen years. What was surprising, however, was that he took no interest whatsoever in the world around him. He sat, staring into the middle distance, eyes blank, face free of expression.

Marilyn continued to treat him as if he were my friend Jürgen, asked about his family's health, remarkably remembering all their names and personal details, making polite enquiries in her own curious version of German about their progress at school. When speaking foreign languages Marilyn always had the knack of combining toe-curlingly inaccurate grammar and excruciatingly idiosyncratic pronunciation with the confidence of a tightrope-walker. If I had not known that Jürgen would have been almost eighty, were he still alive, and that his children were in their forties and fifties, her overtures would have made perfect sense. George remained unperturbed by any of this, silently accepting the cups of tea and cake offered by my wife and maintaining the same blank expression. It was high farce.

On the third day, I had the brainwave of setting out my chess board and pieces on the dining room table and leaving two or three books on chess lying around. Tuppence came to sit on the chair opposite me and looked on disapprovingly, as I set out the pieces with a white square in the bottom left corner, a deliberate error – it is the convention to have a black square on the left of the first rank. I left the door wide open, so that the board was visible. Two hours later the pieces had been correctly reset. A reaction! Perhaps I had found the only way in through the blank wall of silence. At the weekend I opened the *Sunday Times* at the page displaying the weekly chess puzzle and placed the pieces on the board as shown in the newspaper. He looked at the board for thirty seconds or so, and then made four moves with each colour, ending up with an obvious winning position for white. His face and body language betrayed neither satisfaction at solving the problem nor contempt for the triviality of the task. I solve about one in three of these puzzles and then only after half an hour's trial and error. He had succeeded in thirty seconds. I knew I was in the presence of a master.

I took George along to the local chess club and introduced him as a deaf mute, to avoid complicated explanations. That evening he beat six of the members consecutively in under two hours. I suggested that the following week he might play three or four members simultaneously, in order to stretch him a little more. He did so, playing against the clock and four opponents. He beat them all. The club secretary, embarrassed, suggested George enter a chess tournament with a higher standard of play. There was one such two-day event the following weekend in Leeds. He could provide the contact details. With a note of recommendation from the secretary, I succeeded in entering both of us. Summoning up all my remaining powers of concentration for the contest, I was pleased to emerge having won six and lost six, whilst George won eleven and drew one of the twelve boards in the Swiss system tournament. We returned to South Yorkshire with a silver trophy.

We settled into a routine of sorts. George, adopting Tuppence as his role model, moved silently through the house, sat on whichever chair was offered to him, consumed whatever food was set before him, all without any trace of pleasure, irritation, gratitude or any other emotion. On our weekly outing to the chess club I began to feel increasingly that we had outstayed our welcome. Members had begun to turn away and find an urgent need to be somewhere else, to go outside to smoke a cigarette, to visit the toilet – anything rather than participate in the mangling that George inflicted on his simultaneous board victims.

'It's not so much that he doesn't speak; you don't get anything from him. He never looks you in the eye, never acknowledges your existence. He's a robot!' complained the secretary, after we had spent our ninth or tenth evening at the club.

I had already sensed the undercurrent of discontent among members. Some were chuntering that George's presence ruined the whole atmosphere at the club. They clearly no longer enjoyed their Wednesday evenings.

I sympathised entirely with the secretary. His description of George's behaviour was accurate. For him also the original delight of hosting a player of such outstanding ability was now wearing a little thin. We did not return the following week. I explained to George why we were not going to the club:

'The club members think you're far too good for them, George. You need stronger opponents.' Then as an afterthought: 'How about me giving you a game?'

There is of course no response, but I set out the pieces, gesture to him to sit at the dining room table and place myself opposite. I do not give him the option of choosing a colour; I open with king's pawn to e4, George responding with pawn to e5. I continue with bishop to c4, and he follows suit with his bishop. No movement from his face, but already I know what to expect. I play queen to h5 and without hesitation George plays knight to f6. I capture the bishop.

'Very amusing, George. Scholar's Mate, again. No need to take the Michael. If you don't want to play, don't bother.'

I think I spot a movement in his left cheek, the merest flicker and perhaps pure imagination on my behalf. But is this the first hint of a response from George? He has signalled that he remembers our first encounter across the chess board, in my office 33 years ago. That is something, at the very least, a form of communication. I reset the chessmen and turn the board around. We play two further boards. We are not using a chess clock, and so I cannot tell you precisely how quickly George plays, but his speed of thought is dazzling. He sits opposite me, clear-eyed and relaxed, but set to swoop immediately I make my move, like a cat toying with its prey and ready to pounce at any sign of movement. That evening I am sure that I play better than I ever remember playing before. But whatever move I make after running through all the possibilities over and over in my mind, however surprising or inspired a stratagem I think I have dreamt up, he is always ready to make his next move instantly. And however long I ponder, he sits waiting patiently, with no hint of annoyance at my slow play. As he delivers the coup de grace for the second time, I look at my watch. We have been playing for well over two hours. I am exhausted. I thank him and offer a handshake, but George's hands remain motionless on the table in front of him. I bid him goodnight.

33

That night in bed I convinced myself that, at last, I had made something of a breakthrough. I had been close to giving up on George, as had everyone else in his life. I did not know how much longer I could tolerate the total silence and absence of response from this refugee that I had taken under my roof. Furthermore I no longer felt that I had any time for myself, for my own pursuits. Even a trip to the theatre or the cinema was now a trial, encumbered as I was with a demented wife and this perplexing houseguest. Was I clutching at a very flimsy straw in believing it significant that he recalled a trivial but secret episode that happened between us three decades ago? At any rate, I resolved not to give up on him yet. Fate had flung us together again in 2006. I had taken our chance meeting in Wakefield Prison as a prompt to my conscience, an opportunity to atone for my cowardly withdrawal of succour to a helpless lad of fourteen years at the very moment when he needed it most.

•

2003-2010

It is my experience that retirement from a post of comparative seniority in public life rarely results in a life of gentle golf and holidays in the sun. I was resolved to be the exception, and I confess that I did embark on this way of life for the first year of my retirement. I resisted all attempts to involve me in 'good works', in membership of committees and local pressure groups. For several months I enjoyed a life of stress-free relaxation: I loafed along the links of Lerma, La Manga and La Cala; I basked on the beaches of Bermuda, dozed in deckchairs in Dubai.

And I was bored. Bored with reading airport novels under a sunshade in tandem with Marilyn, bored by the interminable anecdotes of the dull clique of retired golfing chums about the birdie they made on the seventh at Lindrick or the putt they missed on the last on the Old Course. In any case, golf is a game you can only enjoy to

34

the full if you play it well, and my average of one majestic shot per round was no longer enough to provide the required satisfaction and to maintain an adequate level of enthusiasm. Marilyn at least had her voluntary work for Amnesty International and her weekly bridge evenings, in which she no longer included me. I cannot think why not, unless it was the way I would occasionally grimace when she played a card, or sigh when she revealed dummy.

There had to be more to life than this. I needed more.

It was opportune therefore that I bumped into Julian, an old Round Table friend who was a prison governor. He asked me how I was enjoying retirement, and I bemoaned my boredom. He smiled knowingly, and before I could say 'Jack Robinson' I found I had agreed to volunteer to be an OPV, an official prison visitor. I would be doing him a favour, and the few hours per month befriending a poor unfortunate prisoner would give a point to my existence. I visited a prisoner in Julian's establishment near Manchester, an Open Prison with 'Category D' inmates, for two years or so, until my man was released. Julian suggested I might take on a more demanding assignment at HMP Wakefield, a 'Category A' inmate serving a life sentence. At least it would spare me those tricky winter crossings of the Pennines, over the notorious Snake Pass.

The new prisoner that I befriended at Wakefield Prison was a fascinating young man who exploited his wealth of spare time to study for an Open University degree in politics. I should dearly like to tell you more about him, but relationships formed as a prison visitor are entirely confidential. At any rate, it was he who alerted me to the presence of George Campbell at Wakefield Prison. One afternoon when I had arrived rather later than usual, he curtailed my visit, explaining that he had to leave at three o'clock to attend the prisoners' weekly chess club. He didn't want to miss the fun. When I asked him what, specifically, was the fun to which he referred, he answered:

'Oh, I mean Boris, of course. He's so damned clever, we've decided he could play us all at once and win every game. Today we're taking him on, eight of us. There's a lot of money riding on it.'

I told him I would have liked to meet Boris, given my own interest in chess. I looked forward to hearing the outcome of the Boris challenge on my next visit.

'Everyone calls him Boris,' he went on, 'but we only call him that because Russians are supposed to be good chess players. I think his real name's Jim or George or something.'

My ears pricked up: 'Not George Campbell, by any chance?'

'That rings a bell, yeah, George Campbell. You know him, then?'

I knew George was in gaol, but had not expected to find him here.

On subsequent visits to my protégé I took to quizzing him about Chess Club and the exploits of 'Boris'. It was no surprise that he noted my curiosity and asked me to explain. I fobbed him off by saying how much I regretted giving up playing. The outcome was that a chess game became a regular feature of my visits.

My curiosity about George grew as the months passed. Eventually I could bear it no longer and arranged a meeting with the governor. He was expecting me to have come on some matter concerning my protégé and was surprised when I told him of my interest in George Campbell. He took out George's file.

'Campbell is a baffling fellow. He's never uttered a single word during his, let's see, eight years here. At first he attracted some unwelcome attention from the bully-boys, but he seems to have taken it all on the chin. We put him in solitary for a while, and that solved the problem, apparently. Perhaps the chess prowess has earned him a strange kind of respect from the other inmates.'

I asked what steps had been taken to cure him of his mutism.

'We've had, as I recall, three psychologists working on his case, but none has come up with a successful approach. He remains a mystery. They are not even any closer to knowing the reason why he committed the murder.'

I asked what techniques had been tried to coax George out of his silence, but he declared himself 'not privy to the methods of the shrinks'. In any case, he said, it was not just a question of silence. George Campbell did not communicate on any level.

'Except perhaps through chess,' I suggested.

'Except perhaps through chess,' acknowledged the governor.

As I left, I said that I was surprised to find George here in the 'Monster Mansion'. From my personal knowledge of him as a youngster, I found it puzzling that he could be categorised as such a high-risk prisoner.

'You haven't seen the pathologist's report on his father's body,' said the governor, shaking his head. 'If you had . . .' His voice tailed away.

I thanked him and took my leave, determined to take a closer look at the records of the 1998 murder case, which I had not followed at the time, being midway through my five year contract at an International School in Germany.

I found out that George had simply returned no plea, had offered no defence and had even refused to communicate in any way with the defence team assigned to him, to the extent of offering no response to questions which required a nod or shake of the head only. Throughout the trial he had stood silent and impassive in the dock, even in the face of the horrifying details of his crime presented in police evidence and the pathologist's report. The defence had called two of George's former employers as character witnesses; they declared him to be a reliable worker, if annoyingly uncommunicative. A picture was painted of his blameless, solitary existence in a rented attic room, surviving on earnings from casual work in the building trade, not once in trouble with the police and without ever resorting to financial help from the state. No mention was made anywhere in the trial record of his mother or his siblings. Perhaps they had disowned him. His second lawyer – the first had resigned her commission – had offered a plea of guilty to manslaughter but with mitigating circumstances, on the grounds that the balance of George's mind had been disturbed at the time of the crime. However, given the total absence of response to the psychologists assigned to report on his state of mind and with no evidence of remorse from the accused, the trial judge directed the jury to return a verdict of guilty of murder, to which he added a life sentence.

I wondered what had driven the mild little boy whom I had known to commit such a crime, and I resolved that, even in the face of such lamentable failure by the professionals, I would find out. I began to visit him, not as an official prison visitor, as that would have been against regulations – all OPV visits must remain strictly anonymous and the two parties unknown to each other. No, I visited George as a friend.

He had previously received only two visits, the first shortly after his incarceration, from a woman, the second, six months later, from a young Australian, whom the governor remembered particularly because George had refused to leave his cell to see him. I wondered if the woman might have been his mother.

'No, it was a certain Ms Day,' the governor informed me. 'Ah! Doris Day! But I think it's unlikely to have been the real one!'

He laughed. I didn't tell him that I knew her.

'Who was the Aussie?' I asked, mildly curious.

He looked down at the records on his desk.

'A chap called Shane Thompson. Mean anything to you?'

I shook my head.

I continued my visits to Wakefield as an OPV, until my protégé was transferred to the South of England, and began to see George once a month on visiting days. At first my visits felt like a total waste of time. My attempts at conversation with a silent interlocutor were clumsy and embarrassing. I brought him books and articles on chess, which he took from me with little or no evidence of interest. I would talk to him about my views on those articles I had read, again without response. Nor did I ever discover whether he had read any of them. Eventually, I learned to speak very little during these visits, to overcome the discouragement I felt at the evident disdain with which my comments and my offerings were received, and my hours with George began to resemble the silent communion of a Quaker gathering. Nevertheless, from time to time when the inspiration took me, I would recall

38

stories from our time together at Harry Brearley and relate them to George. It made me feel better, at least, but in none of my visits did George speak a word or blink an eyelid.

I concluded that the real obstacle between us was that George was incarcerated, and that only when he was free would there be any real chance of interaction. I began to make official requests for my friend's release on parole. I say my friend, because curiously, against all logic and the evidence of my own eyes and ears, I had now begun to consider him as such. After all, this gentle, silent man was self-evidently no danger to society. His rehabilitation would never be achieved by his continued imprisonment.

Eventually, my repeated questions about the possibility of parole bore fruit. I had rashly agreed to act as mentor to him on the outside, and at his second appearance before the Parole Board, in 2010, it was approved that, on the basis of his perfect prison record, a still silent George be released on licence, under my guidance and with strict conditions of probation. One side of me silently rejoiced, while the other side of me wondered in deep trepidation just what had possessed me, a retired schoolmaster with a sick wife, to take on such a challenge. I learned to ski late in life and consequently was always a poor skier. I marvel at the number of times I lost control on a steep mountainside and flew into a reckless, hurtling schuss. And survived. This was one last schuss, but for once it was voluntary. There was nothing for it but to lean forward, keep my head low and pray.

IV

ZUGZWANG

(German: forced move. When a player is disadvantaged by being forced to make a move which weakens the position.)

2011

One day in mid-February, Marilyn decided she would take George shopping with her to Sainsbury's. This was something of a surprise, as she had not been to Sainsbury's for over a year. She put on a coat and brought along George's anorak:

'Komm, Jürgen, du immer gern Sainsbury's. Komm mit mich.'

As always, George was compliant and dutifully put on his anorak. The supermarket was a mere quarter of a mile away from the house, and Marilyn set off walking in the right direction, gripping George firmly by the arm. I decided to follow them in the car, to keep an eye on Marilyn and to save them from having to carry the bags of shopping back home.

In the shop I watched the pair from a safe distance. All seemed to be going reasonably well. Admittedly, Marilyn was piling up an enormous quantity of party food in her trolley, presumably in preparation for a special occasion of some kind. Well, we did have a freezer and we could run to that expense just for once, if it made her happy, which it appeared to be doing. She was laughing and joking with George, who had been assigned the task of pushing the trolley and was keeping pace with her in his usual phlegmatic manner. Suddenly Marilyn grasped him by the hand and took him off in the direction of the wine counter. I watched them walk hand in hand, like two lovers. It was quite touching. She was pointing out the champagne shelf and obviously soliciting George's opinion on which to buy. He was not helpful. Eventually she settled on a bottle of Moet. I grimaced.

I joined them as they reached the checkout. I had confiscated Marilyn's credit cards some time ago, and someone would have to pay. George did not seem surprised to see me, but Marilyn looked a little uncomfortable, as though I had discovered a guilty secret.

'Oh! I see you're having a party tonight,' said the young lady at the checkout. 'Someone's birthday?'

'No, we're just celebrating the visit of our friend from Germany,' chirped Marilyn.

I noticed that there were two packets of tampons in the trolley, an item that Marilyn had not required for some time. I discreetly put them aside and murmured to the cashier that we would not be needing them.

We drove home in silence and Marilyn duly forgot all about the party, although she insisted on sitting side by side with George on the sofa that evening. If he was embarrassed, he did not show it. It was all mildly amusing.

What followed a few days later was less amusing. I woke one night with a start to find that Marilyn was not in the bed next to me. I thought she must have got up to use the toilet or to fetch a glass of water. When she had not returned a few minutes later, I went to investigate. She was nowhere to be found; neither in the bathroom, nor kitchen, nor any other of the rooms was there even a light burning. Eventually I knocked gently on George's door to

41

ask if he had seen her. In the light from the hallway, I saw her lying in bed next to him. I switched on the light. Both were wide awake. Marilyn grabbed hold of George protectively.

'I'm sorry about this, George. Come on, Marilyn, back to bed.'

She pulled back the covers, walked meekly towards me and followed me back to our marital bed.

I knew there was no point in talking to Marilyn about the incident. She was far past the point where she would understand. I did however find a quiet moment to have a word with George, who seemed completely unruffled by the whole thing, but gave no sign of acknowledgement of my explanations. I hoped that the matter was closed.

It was not. The following night, I woke again to find Marilyn gone. After taking a moment to check that no lights were burning in the house, I knew where she was. I went to George's bedroom, opened the door and switched on the light. Her nightdress lay abandoned on the floor by the side of the bed. Marilyn was entwined around George, who lay with his back to her. I lost my sang froid.

'For God's sake, Marilyn! Get a grip! And you, George, don't you have any damned common sense?'

George did not turn over or look in my direction. I grabbed Marilyn by the shoulder and pulled her out of the bed roughly, ramming her nightdress over her head and pulling it down. I led her back to our bedroom, where she fell asleep like a baby. I, of course, remained awake for the rest of the night. The following day, Marilyn behaved as though nothing had happened. Of course she did; she probably did not remember anything about the incident. That night too I was unable to sleep, for fear of her new proclivity for nocturnal peregrinations. It is a shock to the system, after almost fifty years of marriage, to find your wife naked in bed with another man, whatever the circumstances.

The next night I lay awake for a while and then pretended to be asleep and snoring gently. Marilyn was cunning. She had waited for the right moment to make her move. She crept quietly out of bed, and I watched her tiptoe out of the door, closing it gently behind her. I jumped out of bed and fielded her on the landing, to prevent the embarrassment of the previous two occasions.

I knew in my heart that something would have to be done about this new problem, but I decided I would wait and see for a while. Perhaps Marilyn would not wander again, if she knew I was keeping an eye on her. Who knows what had got into her disturbed mind? Even so, I began to have dreadful thoughts about a possible relationship between her and my friend Jürgen many years in the past. I tried to remember any occasions when they had been left alone together. It was madness! Even if it were true, what did it matter? How could I be jealous of a dead man and a demented woman? Nevertheless the evil thought had wormed its way into my subconscious, and my peace of mind was shattered.

After several more sleepless nights, I persuaded the neighbours' son, Jack, who is a handy lad, to fit a stout bolt on the inside of George's bedroom door. He did not actually ask me why I wanted the bolt fitted, but he gave me one or two odd looks, which vanished when I handed him the twenty-pound note for his help. George was not slow to get the message and secured his door that night. I slept soundly in the knowledge that Marilyn's perambulations would be thwarted, but woke to hear her sobbing bitterly and banging on George's door.

Embarrassed, I explained my predicament to George's parole officer, who reluctantly agreed that he be transferred to a halfway house, secure lodgings for newly released prisoners, overseen by the probationary service. In view of my promise to the Parole Board, it was not ideal. And it did not solve my problem with Marilyn, who took to sleeping in the bed where George had slept and weeping through the night. I could see that it was all so heart-breaking for her, as it was for me.

After a month or so of nights like this, during which neither of us enjoyed a deal of sleep, Marilyn lay in wait for me in the kitchen. She assaulted me with a hail of crockery and glassware and followed up by beating me around the head with a saucepan. You cannot imagine how difficult it is to pacify an elderly woman in such a state of aggression, without damaging either her or yourself. I was finally rescued by Suzi, who arrived to do

43

her housekeeping stint; she was able to calm Marilyn down, then take care of her and clear up the mess in the kitchen, whilst I, exhausted, wounded and defeated, spent the morning in A&E.

I telephoned the gerontology consultant at the Royal Hallamshire Hospital to explain what had happened and to ask her advice.

'We knew we should come to this point one day. There is no alternative; your wife has to go into a care home straight away. I can recommend a couple near where you live. My secretary will give you the details when I put the phone down. And make an appointment for you and your wife to see me. We'll find you the earliest possible date.'

When I had summoned up the courage, I telephoned our son, Michael, to tell him the news. To say that he was dismayed is to understate the effect of what I told him.

'How could you do that? I'll never forgive you for this!' was all he said, before cutting me off.

I tried calling him back several times, but I discovered later that he had already left to drive the one hundred and eighty miles from Bristol. He arrived hot and angry on my doorstep less than three hours later, having presumably broken every speed limit on the way. There had been rows between us before, but this one reached new levels of vitriol and abuse.

It is always a surprise when we discover how others really see us, perhaps from overhearing a conversation not meant for our ears, or at those moments when our friends make unguarded comments that reveal their true feelings about us. These discoveries, if we are fortunate or unfortunate enough to make them, are particularly poignant when they reveal the true opinions, favourable or unfavourable, of our children about us and our parenthood.

That evening's conversation with my son was such a moment. I have rarely seen anyone so angry, as he was with me. Why had I allowed his mother to become so ill before informing him? He could have done something about it. He knew people. I pointed out angrily, and I fear loudly, that there was a regular train service from Bristol to Sheffield, and why hadn't he used it if he had ever been able to spare his precious time in between sailing and skiing? He countered by claiming that on his rare visits he had never felt welcomed by me, that I had always excluded him from any important part of family life. I had never had time for him – I was too busy being that wonderful teacher and wonderful headmaster! I had sent him away on summer camps in America, on cricket and tennis weeks, on exchanges in Germany and France, all to get him out of my hair. Why did I think he had never married and had children? Because he was scared that he might be half as bad a father as me! I had neglected his mother and now I was just shunting her aside because she was inconvenient, she was interfering with my life as a do-gooder! That was what I did with people, used them and threw them away!

There were many more accusations concerning my unjust treatment of him, which all added up to an explanation of why he could not wait to leave the family home and had so rarely returned.

I was in shock. I told him I had no idea that he had felt this way and protested my good intentions in all these matters. As he stood to leave to find a hotel for the night – I did not invite him to stay – he turned on me once again, but quietly now, the anger simmering in his trembling voice:

'You wouldn't even let me go to Harry Brearley. You even excluded me from that part of your life. You were probably afraid I'd tell everybody what you were really like. Once when I was about fourteen, on the bus into town I heard some kids from Harry Brearley talking about one of their teachers, what a fabulous bloke he was, how he would always listen to you if you had a problem, always listen to your side if you were in trouble, always had time for you, you could always count on him to be there for you. I listened very carefully. Who was this paragon? I asked one of them who they were talking about. I thought it might be useful information that I could use to impress you for once. Do you know who it turned out to be?'

There was a long pause, but I knew what he was going to say.

'Man York, they said. You. I didn't recognise you.'

45

Tuppence is a stray tomcat who came to live with us in the winter of 2006, deigned to stay on condition that we regularly feed him raw meat and, after a trial period, agreed to adopt us. He is entirely black apart from the last inch of his tail, which is purest white, and the scar tissue on his face and head. When it became obvious that even the sternest of rebukes was ineffective, I attached a loud bell around his neck to afford the garden birds an even chance of surviving his murderous ambushes. Tuppence spends the hours of darkness engaged in the Viking activities of raping, pillaging and skirmishing. When I remember, I remove his bell at night, so as not to disadvantage him in his nocturnal battles against local parvenu challengers. He has a habit, which I have grown to respect over the years, of disappearing mysteriously for two to three weeks at a time and then returning nonchalantly, without explanation, to take his accustomed seat in my favourite recliner. 'Never apologise, never explain' is his watchword. On the occasion of his first two disappearances, Marilyn and I were convinced that we had lost him for good, and while we did not go as far as to post reward notices on every lamppost, we did miss him.

Tuppence had chosen this moment to embark on one of his walkabouts.

And so I was alone in the house, only a few weeks after I had been forced to evict George. I knew that, according to my agreement with the Parole Board, I should invite him back, but I needed time alone to lick my wounds, and frankly I could not bear the thought of his returning to sleep in the bed where Marilyn had spent so many nights weeping for him.

In recompense for turfing George out and to salve my own conscience, I continued to spend time with him, play chess games, go on walks, take him on visits to the cinema, but there was no improvement or change in our relationship or in George's condition. I realised that my mission had always been to cure him, a task which I had arrogantly dreamed was within my capability. The problem was that the more time I spent with George, the less progress I felt I had made. Chess had been a kind of breakthrough, but even that was not down to me. It had always been his sole way of communicating ever since I had known him and, it seemed, all the way through his time in prison.

Whatever I was doing it was not enough, and it never would be. I had seldom felt so miserable. I had very little contact with my son, and had no desire for contact with my sister, who was little more than a malicious old bat. I had given up my volunteer prison visits, when Marilyn had become ill, and I felt that I was no longer of any use to anyone. I realised that I had fallen into a deep slough of despond. I looked up the symptoms of clinical depression on Wikipedia. I had them all. I arranged the following evening to see my GP, who listened to my story with interest. He fiddled with his half-moon spectacles and delivered his verdict on my case:

'You don't have clinical depression, David. You're just miserable, unhappy, and with good reason, it seems to me. On your way home, call in at the fish and chip shop, the one on the corner near the football ground, and get yourself a large cod and chips, with mushy peas and plenty of salt and vinegar. Put them on a tray, make yourself a mug of tea, sit down in front of the telly and watch something funny. I suggest Seinfeld, or Dad's Army, or Laurel and Hardy. Have a nice stiff whisky before you go to bed, then get up bright and early – put the alarm on – and take yourself off out for a brisk walk in Derbyshire. If you're not as right as ninepence by then, come back and I'll give you some happy pills. But I don't think you'll be back.'

When I got back to the house, I found Tuppence curled up in my recliner, still wearing his bell. He had been gone for exactly five weeks and looked none the worse for the experience, if a little thinner. I shared my fish with him in celebration.

Call it the old-fashioned pull-yourself-together method, if you like, but the prescription seemed to work. I even sent an e-mail accepting, at somewhat late notice, an invitation for the following Friday evening to a reunion disco organised by alumni of Harry Brearley, 'The 1981 Harvest', as they had wryly christened themselves. The invitation had been forwarded to me by the OPV organisation, and I admired the ingenuity of my former students in tracking me down.

47

Always on these occasions there is the embarrassment of not recognising ex-pupils who know all too well who you are. Even some of the teachers who turn up are unrecognisable after almost thirty years. An hour into the evening, just when I was beginning to think up excuses to make my escape, a woman in her fifties approached me:

'You don't know who I am, sir, do you?'

I looked at her closely, and then the penny dropped. She called me 'sir'. And she was probably a little too old to be a former pupil of the school.

'It's not Doris, is it?' I offered hesitantly.

It was. We talked for almost an hour. I wanted to know all about what she had been doing for the last three decades. She had worked in several schools, had ended up in charge of the drama section at a North Derbyshire college and lived in Chesterfield. She had been married for ten years and was now divorced. Encouraged by the fact that she had been George's only other visitor in Wakefield prison, I told her of my involvement with him over the past five years.

'I'm so glad that someone has kept in touch with him. It was such a shame. And you say he still doesn't speak? And the murder – I so often wondered about that. He was such a gentle boy. You know,' she hesitated and blushed a little, 'I really wouldn't mind meeting him again, if you think it's appropriate, if we could perhaps arrange it . . . '

Frankly, I was ready to jump at the suggestion of someone else getting involved in looking after my intransigently silent ward. In any case, I remembered the special relationship that Doris had built with the boy during his schooldays. We agreed that the three of us meet the following weekend, to have lunch together, as a sort of excuse for re-introducing George to her.

I didn't tell her about turning him out of the house, nor my reasons for doing so. I had in any case resolved that very evening, having imposed some perspective on the incidents concerning him and Marilyn, to take him back under my roof.

Doris had proposed, her sense of drama I suspect, that we meet in the amphitheatre behind the Sheffield railway station. At five minutes to one on the Sunday lunchtime,

48

George and I stood in silence in the middle of the green expanse of the amphitheatre stage, waiting for her to emerge from the station. It felt like we were characters from a John Le Carré novel, waiting to exchange spies at Checkpoint Charlie. It was mid-June, and a handful of university students, dotted around the semi-circles of tiered stone seats, their end-of-year exams over, sat laughing and chatting in light summer clothing, drinking from cans of beer, cider and cola. I looked out over my home city and beyond to the Derbyshire hills, the air clear and still. My thoughts drifted back to my boyhood, Sunday family bus-rides out to Longshaw, with Mum and Dad, aunties, uncles and cousins, primus stoves, cheese and tomato sandwiches and paddling in the brook, and I wondered how many happy days George could count among his childhood memories.

The train from Chesterfield was late, and Doris came dashing out of the rear exit of the station, out of breath and her scarf flying behind her as she ran across the tram-lines and up the steps towards us. I thought I noticed a flicker of interest in George's eyes, but it was probably my imagination.

We all shook hands, amazingly even George, and then sat chatting on the front row of seats, Doris breathlessly attempting a précis of what she had been doing in the twelve years or so since she had last seen George. Her eyes never left his, and I have to confess to feeling somewhat excluded. We strolled into town and I treated us to a pub lunch. A pint of real ale helped Doris and me to relax – I can't speak for George – and the conversation was still going strong at three, when I had to leave to meet my sister-in-law for a prearranged visit to Marilyn at the care home. Doris promised to deliver George back home, after taking him to the cinema, a plan which she seemed set on. She embarked on a detailed explanation to George of the theme of the film and its main actors. I left her in full flow.

That evening at my house, she finished the cup of tea I had insisted on providing, placed the cup and saucer on the tiny coffee table beside her chair and sat upright, with her hands folded in her lap, like a child about to recite a party-piece.

'I just wondered . . .'

49

She turned to look at George, as if weighing up whether to include him in the conversation.

'I just wondered – it's been such fun, it would be rather good to see George again. Does he like walking? Do you, George?'

There was no answer.

'Or we could try the theatre, couldn't we?'

She turned back to me and spoke in a hushed, confidential tone.

'I could sort of take some of the pressure from you, sir.'

It was clear that I was not included in her plans. I put her out of her misery.

'That sounds like a wonderful idea. I'm sure George would love that, eh George? And, Doris, call me David, please. I think we're past the point where you have to call me "sir".'

And so, over the first two months of that summer, their friendship blossomed, or at the very least their meetings became frequent, regular, twice weekly. Doris delivered George back to me one Sunday evening after their usual ramble and picnic. As I waved her off on her way back to her car, she turned, and from her backpack she produced a crumpled magazine.

'I almost forgot! I saw this in the *Observer* colour supplement a few weeks ago. It's a piece about a Harry Brearley old boy, who apparently is doing great things in the world of . . .' She hesitated. '. . . in psychiatry. His name is Paul Morgan. Do you remember him?'

She handed me the magazine. I did remember. I was hardly likely to have forgotten him.

V

ANALYSIS

(The scrutiny of a position to determine best play.)

I confess that I have often followed the progress of some of my star ex-pupils, perhaps in the hope of gaining extra job satisfaction from basking vicariously in the glow of their success in life. It was quite surprising therefore that I had not kept up to date with the dazzling advance of Paul Morgan through the ranks of the medical profession, as I should have retained a particular interest in a boy whose future career I had once held in the palm of my hand.

Paul was a gifted sixth form student at Harry Brearley, on the point of sitting his A-level examinations in sciences, when during one of my periodic trawls of the school during lesson times I heard the sound of what appeared to be a scuffle or a struggle coming from the boys' toilet. I investigated and found Paul passionately engaged in a homosexual act with another sixth form boy. The incident was, to say the least, embarrassing for all three of us, and the two boys were devastated to have been discovered *in flagrante delicto*. I sent them both home and arranged to interview them the following morning.

I did not discuss the incident either with Bill Rodgers or with Marilyn, the two people I considered my closest confidants. The problem was knotty indeed. This was 1981, and whilst homosexual activity was now legal in private between consenting adults, neither of these boys was over twenty-one, and the school building could hardly be said to be private property. As far as I knew, the usual route taken in these circumstances was for offenders to leave the school quietly of their own volition, and for the matter to be hushed up, in order to protect the good name of the school. Of course, the parents had to know the reason why. It would mean, in this case, that the boys would neither be able to sit their A-level examinations nor take up their places on university courses. I explained this to the two boys, but assured them that I had not yet made my decision. Paul cut a particularly pathetic figure that morning. Squirming in his seat, wringing his hands, a caricature of Uriah Heap, he pleaded with me not to tell his parents, as it would break his father's heart. He would find an excuse for suddenly leaving the school. He was prepared to give up the scholarship he had won to study medicine at a prestigious university. I sent them both away and slept on the matter a further night.

Even having taken into account the considerable risk to my own position, the decision was easy. I resolved that, for the sake of the future professional and personal welfare of both boys, I would neither inform the parents nor anyone else and would allow them to stay on and complete their A-level examinations. It would have been inhumane to do otherwise. In return, I asked them to go out into the world and make the school proud of them.

Paul in particular could not thank me enough: 'I won't let you down, sir. I promise.'

He had gone on to become a distinguished psychiatrist, who ran a private clinic in Waltham Forest, to the north of London. I took the article in the *Observer* as a kind of sign, a message in a bottle, guiding me in the right direction in my quest to help George. I rang the clinic and left a message for the great man to call me.

He telephoned that very evening. I explained who I was, and there were a few seconds of uncomfortable silence, until he spoke again.

'I wondered if it might be you, although it's a fairly common name. What was it you wanted to talk to me about? I'm not much of a Prize Day speaker, if that's what you are going to ask me.'

I told him George's full history, about the silence, the murder, the gaol sentence and, not least, the chess. Curiously, Paul remembered him from school, as the 'little chess genius'.

'Elective mutism they called it? Well, we haven't used that term for over twenty years - too many connotations of choice or guilt and of the patient being in control of the mutism. Child psychiatrists would use the term "selective mutism" nowadays - inability to speak in certain environments. This hardly seems to be selective, though. I don't want to prejudge the issue, but the murder of his father seems to be a big fat hint. Why don't I meet him? See what I can find out.'

'I should be so grateful if you would.'

He must have detected the hope in my voice.

'Above all, Mr York, you must remember that many patients, too many, cannot be cured. All we can do is manage their condition.'

We arranged that I would take George down to Paul Morgan's London consultancy the following week. George complied, as always. As I feared, however, he was no more talkative with Morgan than he had been with anyone else. I spoke with the consultant after this initial meeting, whilst George sat outside in the waiting room.

'This is an intriguing case, unlike anything I've come across. I'm going to delve deeper into his medical record, when we've tracked it down. I have a brilliant young psychologist colleague, who I am convinced can help us get to the root of the problem. If you don't mind, I'd like George to come into the clinic for a spell, where we can investigate his condition more intensively. Do you think he would agree to do that?'

'Frankly, he doesn't protest much about anything, so I think he would agree.'

'He would have to sign. From our first brief encounter I doubt whether he would do that. What do you think?'

'Ah! Yes, that could be a problem.'

'In that case, we should have to section him.'

'Section him?'

'If he isn't capable of signing, we could detain him under the terms of the 1983 Mental Health Act.'

I think my jaw dropped and my mouth fell open.

'That wouldn't be fair. I can't do that to him.'

'You started off by telling me he wouldn't mind coming into the clinic. So, what harm would there be?'

'I suppose I was thinking of the stigma.'

Paul Morgan leant back in his chair and laughed out loud.

'This is a murderer, a father-killer, who hasn't spoken a word for thirty-odd years, and you're worried about the stigma? We all want the same thing here, to get to the bottom of the mystery of the poor man's silence and give him back his life. It would only be for 28 days – can only be. And it might just help us to assess the extent of any mental disorder and administer the necessary treatment.'

'And sectioning, detaining, how is it done? Do you just write a certificate?'

'It needs the signature of two doctors and a social worker. I can set that up. No problem.'

'As easy as that. I suppose what's really bothering me is the morality of it. Do I have any right to decide what's best for George?'

'Medical professionals, especially in the mental health field, wrestle with these ethical questions every day of their lives. Whether we like it or not, sometimes we have to play God. But the patient's interest *must* always come first. That's the touchstone.'

'The patient's interest? Or what *you* think is the patient's interest? I mean, look at us, sitting here deciding his fate, while he sits outside no doubt wondering what the hell is going on in here.'

'I can see that you need more time.'

'I'm sorry. It was so good of you to see him – us. Give me a couple of days.'

We shook hands and I drove George back to Sheffield, my mind in a whirl.

54

I had rarely felt so uncomfortable and apprehensive about any decision I'd had to make. It had been far easier to decide to sign the document committing Marilyn to live in the care home. I tried to put myself in George's place, isolated in his world of silence, incommunicado with the rest of the world. I remembered the decision that I had made all those years ago, under pressure from the staff and the local authority, to eject him from my school. Should I let sleeping dogs lie this time? Or should I cast him into the doubtless confusing and disorienting world of the psychiatric clinic in the company of a bunch of rich, mad people?

Back home that night, George and I sat in my kitchen with a mug of cocoa each, and I poured out my heart to him. I apologised to him for the shabby way he had been treated at Harry Brearley and for throwing him out of the school into an even more unwelcoming world. I apologised to him for throwing him out of my house, for no fault of his, when I had promised to look after him. I promised I would never do it again, that there was always a place for him in my home, and that I would look out for him and do my best for him as long as I lived. I told him about Paul Morgan's plans for him at the clinic and asked him to give me a sign of some kind, a clue as to whether he approved or not. I looked him in the eyes and took both his hands in mine; he did not resist, but there was still no hint of what he was thinking. I gave up, and we went to bed.

I slept well, and the following morning I woke knowing that I had made up my mind. But somehow I needed to confirm what I had decided with someone else. I looked up Doris in my phone book and dialled her number. She was about to leave for work, but said she had five minutes to talk. I filled her in about the consultancy with Paul Morgan and asked her opinion about my decision to sanction George's sectioning. She understood my reservations.

'I'm not sure I have any right to an opinion here, but I'm flattered that you've asked me. For what it's worth, I think you're doing the right thing. Sometimes we just have to place ourselves and our loved ones in the hands of the experts.'

I thanked her for her support and told her I would keep her posted. I telephoned the clinic immediately, before I could change my mind, and left a message for Morgan. Half an hour later he called me back. He was surprised and pleased to learn my decision. We arranged for George to spend 28 days in the clinic for observation and treatment, from the first Sunday in September.

'What about fees? Could this be done under the National Health Service?'

I needed to know what I was letting myself in for. Financially.

'I do work two days a week for the NHS, but in London. I can't, I wouldn't pull strings for George to be admitted to a hospital ward there. It would have to be my private clinic.' He paused. 'There will be no question of fees, though. This is far too interesting a case for me to miss out on.'

I thanked him.

'No need to thank me. After all, I owe you one, don't I?'

There were initial problems in convincing the Probation Service to allow George to be released from my personal mentorship and the supervision of his probation officer for such an extended period. Although an original requirement for George to wear an electronic tag had been rescinded at the request of the prison psychologist, one of the principal conditions of his licence was that he live at the same address and that any change of abode, even for one night, had to be approved beforehand. In the end, Morgan stepped in with his personal guarantee that George would remain under close supervision, and permission was granted.

During the month of September, whilst George was at the Waltham Forest clinic, except in the case of dire emergency I was neither to visit nor try to make contact with him or the clinic. I would hear from Paul Morgan or one of his colleagues if they needed to consult me. Doris phoned me at least twice a week, eager for any snippet of news I might have received. She was anxious, but then so was I, both of us hoping for a miracle cure and for George to emerge from the clinic communicative and fully restored to the normality he had not enjoyed since he had been a small child. We were to be disappointed.

On the fifth of October, I went to pick George up from Waltham Forest. Doris had asked to drive down with me, but I had put her off. I wanted to be fully in charge, and deep down I confess I resented her insinuating herself into what I considered my private crusade to find a cure for my silent protégé. On arrival I was shown into Morgan's office. I was trembling as we shook hands, whilst his face and body language displayed no emotion whatsoever. Coffee and biscuits appeared before me as if by magic, brought no doubt by an assistant or secretary, although I was in too much of a daze of nervous expectancy to notice. I opted to let the coffee go cold, as my hands were shaking far too much to risk picking up the cup.

At this point I feel I should pause in my narrative to issue a caveat. I have done my very best to recall the details of my conference with Paul Morgan, but it is more than likely that I have missed out important elements, or perhaps misunderstood or misinterpreted what he was intending to convey. I throw myself on the mercy of the reader and ask to be excused any ineptitude, or any unscientific language or reasoning that I may have attributed to Paul Morgan.

He greeted me warmly, using my first name, a modern day practice which I abhor when it comes from professionals who do not know their client personally. But in this case it solved my problem of how to address Morgan. I was now at liberty to call him Paul, as my memory of our former pupil-teacher relationship inclined me to do. After what seemed an eternity of small talk about the drive down south, the weather and my own health, intended no doubt to set me at my ease, Morgan launched into his professional manner to report back the results of their investigations.

'If you don't mind, David, I'm going to bring George in on this discussion.'

'Doesn't it depend a great deal on what you're going to say to me, Paul?'

'You're right in that there is a risk that what I say may frighten him. On balance, however, my colleague and I think we should keep him fully informed. He probably could not be more frightened than he is now inside that silence. What's more, we warned George what we were about to do at every stage of the process, and we are fairly sure he understands, even though he never responds. Shall I proceed?'

I nodded, and Morgan asked for George to be brought in. I was anxious to see him and wondered if his appearance or demeanour would have changed at all. I was surprised to find him shaven-headed, the stubble on his scalp just beginning to grow back. I looked at Morgan questioningly, as I stood to greet George. The psychiatrist raised a reassuring hand to stifle my question.

'Take a seat, George, and we'll begin. As you are both aware, the problem George has is deep-seated and long-term. These four weeks have been essentially of an investigatory nature. It is unlikely that you will notice any modification in George's behaviour. He still does not speak or communicate in any way, with anyone.

'You are a highly educated man, David, and from what you tell me about George's talent for chess, then he is every bit as sharp as you or I. So I shall go into some detail in reporting our investigations.'

'I'm not highly educated scientifically, and nor is George.'

'Very well. As far as I can, I shall try to paint a broad-brush picture, but there will inevitably be some technical detail. OK?'

He waited for me to shrug my assent, and then continued.

'Routine blood and urine tests showed no abnormality, in particular no sign of recreational drug or alcohol abuse. All George's organs appear to be working well. We began our investigation with an MRI scan, which showed no evidence of a tumour or other brain lesion of any kind, confirmation that George's condition is psychological rather than neurological in character. We conducted an EEG, an electroencephalogram, to ascertain whether the part of the brain required for speech is still theoretically functional, with positive results. We checked the voice-box. As we expected, all the working parts are in place, if somewhat atrophied. George can still cough, for instance. So, no problem with the mechanism, then.'

'Did you really need to do all those tests? I mean, they are intrusive at best and could have been quite alarming for George.'

'Yes, we did. We may be mental health clinicians, but we never rule out the possibility of a physical element. Having established this, we observed George's behaviour, both when alone and in the presence of other clients, medical staff and other employees of the clinic, using unobtrusive cameras and microphones.'

'Is that ethical? I don't think I would like that done to me.'

'It's not a secret. Clients coming here agree effectively to submit themselves to any investigative procedure we see fit to use. Unsurprisingly, even when alone, George never speaks, attempts to write, or even shows interest in any of the books or magazines left for his use in his room. With one exception – a chess magazine.

'In an attempt to penetrate the walls George has erected around himself, my psychologist colleague tried various methods to relax him. We found him totally immune to hypnotism, even in combination with various drugs, for instance Valium.

'George has no hair because we had difficulties establishing the excellent contact with his scalp that we needed for optimal results from our EEG investigation – we shaved his head and fitted him up with a custom-made skullcap with all the electrodes built-in. We used the EEG machine to record the electrical signals from his brain when we applied a variety of stimuli - images, words, sounds, photographs and of course questions.'

'What sort of questions? What sort of images?'

'I'm coming to that. Broadly speaking, our conclusions were that George is heterosexual, has a normal warm reaction towards small children, has no interest in sport, politics or music, but loves chess – you knew that, of course. There was always a strong reaction to pictures of men he does not know personally. We obtained pictures of his family from newspaper archives, and the photo of his father provoked an especially strong reaction. No surprise there, given that we know why George spent twelve years in prison.'

'What exactly do you mean by a strong reaction?'

'The EEG is a somewhat blunt instrument, but so far it's been our best way of getting behind the screen of silence. It helped us to penetrate the mask blocking our view of his emotions. We asked questions about his childhood, his relationship with his siblings and his parents. Pictures of or questions about his father sent George's EEG recording off the scale, an indication of very strong emotion. It could be guilt, but we suspect fear or hatred.

'I would add that he was connected to the EEG skullcap for two nights during sleep. It's clear that he suffers a lot of nightmares, which was already evident from our observation of his sleeping body movements and the frequency of his rapid eye movements. Strangely enough, these bad dreams never seem to wake you up, do they George?'

He stopped and looked closely at his patient for a few seconds.

'Sorry, I was just checking your pupil dilation. Habit.'

He looked back in my direction.

'You are both no doubt wondering when I'm going to get round to giving you some kind of diagnosis or action plan.'

Morgan had read my mind. I was becoming impatient to hear what the expert proposed to do to cure my ward. He looked from me to George and back again, like a story-teller building up suspense, and then resumed his analysis.

'We are fairly certain that George's original muteness and refusal to communicate in any way at school was a response to some trauma in his childhood, originally when he was about nine years old, but possibly continuing through his teen years. Questions of child abuse are sadly no stranger to the headlines in our newspapers these days, and it does not take a Sherlock Holmes or a Sigmund Freud to point in that direction as the source of the problem. As George won't tell us anything, we can only try to get a reaction by asking direct questions, by speculating. Even then we have needed an electronic device to find any evidence of his emotional responses. We have had to be careful, as we don't want to alienate the poor man completely. We want him on our side, and we need him to accept us on *his* side. You have to remember

60

that he is silent for a reason. Try to imagine the total isolation inside George's mind.'

I turned my head towards George sitting beside me.

'I have tried to. You can be annoying and frustrating, George, but I know it must be hell in there.'

Morgan steepled his fingers.

'We have here a man who is unable, or unwilling, or too paranoid to communicate in any way. There is a strong possibility that his speech organs have by now lost their function, not having been used for thirty-odd years. Your hands certainly wouldn't work if you hadn't used them for that long. But the physical problem is not the real one, clearly. Our problem is a psychological problem, although almost certainly with an articulatory disorder to boot. The murder of George's father is a strong link to the original trauma, and in itself must have been a further trauma.'

I turned to look at George, feeling his hurt at the mention of the murder and his father, but half hoping that Morgan's statement might have provoked some reaction from him.

Not a flicker.

Morgan went on.

'I see from his medical history that George was treated for clinical depression whilst imprisoned, with no appreciable improvement in his behaviour or well-being. In fact he was judged to have deteriorated and the medication discontinued. One doctor seems to have diagnosed him as suffering from LIS, that's locked in syndrome, or a specific version of that condition. This diagnosis has to be discounted, as LIS invariably results in quadriplegia, and George's bodily functions seem perfectly normal. So, we are left with our original diagnosis of traumatic or hysterical mutism.

'We believe, however, that there is more to it than this. We know that stressful or traumatic events can trigger schizophrenia. George has indeed developed symptoms of schizophrenia.'

He paused, seeing my expression of horror, and waited for his statement to sink in fully.

'Schizophrenia? You mean . . . split personality?'

Morgan looked disappointed with me, and took a deep breath.

'I'm afraid that's a poor description of the condition. Basically the schizophrenic has problems distinguishing his own thoughts, ideas, perceptions, imaginings and fears from reality. As in my field even we so-called experts and specialists can't agree on the definition, cause and treatment of schizophrenia, it's a fairly loose term to attach to George's condition. I'm afraid we don't have a better. But even in terms of schizophrenia his condition is unusual. And we're still guessing, weighing in the balance rather flimsy evidence.'

He looked at George and smiled. 'What would you say to us, George, if you could talk? Are we barking up the right tree?'

He turned back to me. 'We did not rule out catatonia.'

I almost leapt from my seat at the word. 'Catatonia? Isn't that where patients go into some kind of coma? Catatonic state, that's . . .'

'Calm now, David. Catatonia is not really recognised as a disorder in its own right these days, but rather more as being part of other psychiatric disorders such as schizophrenia, or post-traumatic stress syndrome, or depression. One of the five main test symptoms of catatonia is mutism, as is the extreme apathy that George appears to display, but appearances can be deceptive here, of course. Agreed, there is no catalepsy or stupor, nor any of the extreme mobility or immobility of the body that is usually evident. So, again we don't have quite enough for a diagnosis.'

He leaned back in his chair and continued, almost under his breath. 'It's very tempting, on the other hand, to call George's condition catatonic schizophrenia.'

'My God!' I gasped. 'I don't know what to say. What can you do?'

He rubbed one hand over the balding area on top of his head, then leaned forward and folded both hands under his chin.

'We think - we're guessing admittedly, but it's an educated guess - we think that inside George's mind there is a huge fear and mistrust of other human beings, triggered by traumas of childhood. These fears have made him incapable of trusting another human being with his own private thoughts and emotions, and have concentrated themselves not in a physical fight-flight reaction of his body, but in a total shutdown of communications. He may be having hallucinations, may see, smell, or hear things that others don't, may hear voices giving him instructions or advice, or telling him he's worthless. It's quite likely that he believes himself personally responsible for his own condition, even personally guilty of causing the traumatic event or events that first plunged him into this state. He may have delusions that everyone is out to get him – there have probably been quite a few life events which would have reinforced this delusion, if it exists. Even what we have done over the past month, ostensibly to help him, could be adding to his isolation. My colleague and I considered whether it could be simply a matter of all this fear and paranoia sending danger signals to the amygdala, which results in George shutting down all communications. In some patients it can simply be a matter of too much dopamine being produced – dopamine, as you know, is the chemical which carries messages between brain-cells. We try to counter this by administering neuroleptic drugs, which you may know as antipsychotics.'

I shook my head. I didn't. I was out of my depth.

'We considered neuroleptics, but NMS is a significant danger here, we feel, in the light of our possible diagnosis of catatonic schizophrenia.'

'NMS? Should I know what that is?'

'Apologies. That's neuroleptic malignant syndrome, a side-effect of antipsychotic medication in some patients. It results in fever, possibly delirium, unstable blood pressure, Parkinson's-like symptoms. Not nice.'

His eyes were half closed now and he seemed to be almost talking to himself, rather than addressing us.

'There is no physical damage to the brain, George has not abused cannabis or other recreational drugs as far as we know, and so we are left almost certainly with an unidentified trauma as our trigger. If we could find a way to get George to communicate, in any manner whatsoever, we might find a way in. Psychotherapy or CBT might normally be a route, but without any communication from the patient, both are impossible.'

'CBT?' I said, somewhat forlornly by now. I felt blinded by science.

'Cognitive behavioural therapy.'

I was no wiser, but did not pursue the matter. 'So, what do we do next?' I asked.

'This is where I should issue a health warning about the medical profession, David. We don't know everything, but one thing we have in common is that we always want to cure our patients. Once we get our hands on you, we're very reluctant to let go. The surgeon wants to cut you open and remove the offending part; the physician wants to give you drugs or send you off to the surgeon; the homoeopath wants you to believe in fairy tales, and the psychiatrist wants to give you drugs or therapy, or both. Sometimes we're not sure, and sometimes we get it wrong.'

We sat in silence, as I watched the second hand tick round at one second intervals on the wall clock above the door. It completed one lap of the circuit, then two. It felt like two hours. Morgan spoke again.

'I'm a psychiatrist. In the absence of therapy, I should like to prescribe drugs. That's what we do. But as we are not certain of our diagnosis, we are not certain which drug to prescribe. Do we treat depression, post-traumatic stress, catatonic schizophrenia? Do we bombard him with anti-depressants or antipsychotics? Prescribe the wrong one and we make the problem worse.

'There is one catch-all treatment we could try, which might just be effective short-term, might provide a kick-start to George's recovery. It has been found effective for a wide variety of deep-seated psychiatric illnesses, including depression, catatonia, schizophrenia, although use with schizophrenics is frowned on by the authorities in the UK. It's usually indicated when drugs have proved ineffective, or as an emergency measure where it's considered there is a risk of patient suicide.'

'OK,' I interrupted him. 'You're selling it well, but let's stop there, shall we? We don't want to frighten the horses. You'd better tell us. What is this treatment?'

'ECT.'

More initials. I did not have to ask the question.

'Electroconvulsive therapy,'

64

We both turned our heads to look at George, Morgan no doubt checking on the size of his pupil dilation, I looking for any sign of the shock I myself was feeling at hearing those words. Nothing disturbed George's features. There was no flicker, not even the merest hint of emotion in the sphinx-like visage.

'You mean like in *One Flew over the Cuckoo's Nest?*'

'That was a work of fiction. That's not how it is. It is true that ECT was abused back in the day and got itself a bad name in the seventies and eighties. It's now conducted under anaesthetic and with great care to protect the patient.'

'It's still like hitting the brain with a sledge-hammer, though, isn't it?'

I felt my anger rising.

Morgan said nothing. I had the bit between my teeth now.

'And if it works, you don't know how, do you? And what about the side-effects? What you do is the equivalent of giving the patient a huge epileptic fit, isn't it? Scrambling the brain! I studied the film and the book years ago with a sixth form group, and they did some interesting research on electric shock therapy - its effect on the patient's memory, for instance.'

'I see you're quite the expert on ECT, David. I have my reservations too, but you're wrong, you know. It's now considered very respectable treatment, and a number of research projects have demonstrated its effectiveness. Some patients, it's true, have suffered a degree of memory loss, but this was probably due to clumsy administration of the treatment. Admittedly, we're still not certain, either, of the long-term effects. There's not been enough research so far. Also too many patients relapse a few months after the treatment, even when it's been effective. But my feeling is that if we could just get George started on the right road to recovery, communicating even minimally, we could find the answers.'

I shook my head slowly.

'You can rest assured that we should only administer ECT with the voluntary consent of the patient, or the patient's next of kin when the patient is incapable of consent. Voluntas aegroti suprema lex.'

He waited for a reaction, either to his proposal, or to his ostentatious piece of Latin. I said nothing.

'I can see you're not convinced. And we don't know what *you*'re thinking, do we, George?'

He looked down at the papers on his desk.

'I did warn you that we doctors like to find solutions.'

He opened both hands and showed his palms, as if in supplication.

'There is, of course, one other way I haven't mentioned.'

'Oh? What's that?'

'TLC.'

'What?'

'Something George has probably never had from the day he was born, something you're trying to give him now, it seems to me. TLC, tender loving care. A very powerful medicine.'

He stood up and reached across the table to shake my hand. He nodded to George.

'Let me know what you decide. The offer's open. You can come back any time. You know that, George, don't you?'

The drive back up north was for once trouble-free. A silver Toyota was parked outside my house when we arrived at around five o'clock. Doris scrambled out of it and followed us up the driveway at an undignified trot. She hugged us both, as we got out of the car. She could hardly wait to hear the news.

VI

CRITICAL POSITION

(A position in a game where the next moves will determine the outcome)

During the autumn months leading up to Christmas 2011 Doris became an ever more frequent visitor to the house. George always spent at least two weekday evenings in her company, and whatever the weather, Doris would arrange outings for the two of them each Saturday and Sunday, outings on which I was usually invited but gradually began to feel like an unwanted chaperone. I began to find excuses not to accompany them. On three of the weekends, Doris had entered them both for two-day chess tournaments, each of which George had won convincingly. His success had attracted a good deal of interest in the chess world, and he was expected to be competitive at the British Championships in August of the following year.

From time to time I would quiz Doris about George's progress towards normality, when he was out of the room.

'You're seeing a lot of him, Doris. Either you're very fond of him, or you are an extremely kind and generous woman. Perhaps both,' I smiled.

Doris looked down and blushed scarlet. I waited a moment for her to recover some composure and then continued.

'Does he ever . . . Has he ever spoken to you?'

She shook her head.

'A pity. The two of you seem to be getting on so well. If he ever talked to anyone, it would no doubt be you.'

I would have liked to tell her that George seemed to like her company, that because he never raised any objections to any of her plans, he must approve. But on the other hand George never objected to anything, and so how could we know what he liked and disliked? Doris seemed to have read my mind.

'We get on very well. He's easy to be with. He doesn't speak, but he does . . . communicate.'

'How do you mean? How does he communicate? Does he . . .?'

I hesitated, wondering how to phrase the question delicately. Did he touch her? Were they intimate in any way? I feared I had strayed into private territory. Doris helped me out.

'It's nothing specific. No smiles, no touching my hand or my arm, or any of those things you might expect, but there is something that I can feel telling me that he's happy to be with me. And I am . . . I like being with him. Since my divorce, I have felt myself getting angry with any man I come across, colleagues, my boss at the college, male students even. With George it's different. There is no excuse to be angry with him. And a man who plays chess like an angel . . . God! You have to admire him!'

Her bottom lip turned white where she bit into it. She turned her head towards the door through which George had left the room, her eyes filling with tears.

'He's so clever! Such a mind, a brain the size of a planet! And he's locked in there, alone. You have to feel for him.'

I was taken by surprise. It was the most Doris had revealed about herself since we had met again the previous summer at the student reunion. I considered raising the question of George's further treatment at the clinic, in the light of this new openness from Doris, but decided not to approach such a delicate matter at a moment when she appeared so vulnerable. When I had first reported back to her on Paul Morgan's conclusions that evening in October and had tried to open a discussion on possible further treatments, she had been horrified at the prospect of electroconvulsive therapy for George and had burst into tears. I had reassured her that I would take no such drastic step, without first thinking long and hard and certainly not without consulting her.

I did not confess to her my own similar reaction to the suggestion of ECT. Rather I used her fears and sensitivities as a convenient excuse to defer any decision about George's future therapy. As the weeks went by, and George and Doris appeared to grow closer, or at the very least to monopolise each other's time, I began to feel less and less that the decision was mine and mine alone. It was a great weight from my shoulders, for my confidence in the infallibility of the medical profession had been shaken by Morgan's apparent uncertainty over George's diagnosis. I remembered Gordon Peck's remark about the emperor's new clothes all those years ago and wondered if there might not be just a grain of truth in it. At any rate, my uncertainty and indecisiveness led to inertia, in the hope that TLC was perhaps the best solution after all.

One Saturday afternoon in early December, Doris and George returned from a Christmas shopping expedition and Doris announced to me that she was to be interviewed the following Wednesday for a post at our old school, Harry Brearley. She had used my name as a referee – she hoped I didn't mind, as she hadn't thought to ask me in advance – and I should be hearing from the school in the next couple of days. She was effectively applying for her old job, her first appointment in teaching. I pointed out to her that she would be facing a sharp drop in salary and seniority, to which she replied that she had decided that it was time to slow down and to shed all the management responsibilities involved in her present post. I reminded her that a full programme of classroom teaching was young persons' work and hardly represented slowing down, but she was resolute and determined to land the job, for which with my recommendation she would scarcely be turned down. It seemed a fait accompli, but I was suspicious of her motivation. It was as clear as day that she wanted to be geographically nearer to George and to be able to spend even more time with him. This was confirmed to me when she revealed that her house in Chesterfield was already on the market, and that she and George were to inspect some local properties for sale the following day. Would I care to join them?

That evening I observed the pair, as they sat on my sofa watching a romantic comedy on a film channel. Each, in his or her own different way, was a picture of serenity. The lines of worry etched into Doris's face by the long years of persistently anxious frowning were eased away in the dim light of the sitting-room, as she laughed at the inanities and sentimentalities of the film, feeding George chocolates and teasing him for his permanently serious expression. Both looked younger than their years, Doris especially. And once I thought I caught the merest hint of a smile at the corner of George's mouth.

The logistical problems of family diaspora that each Christmas poses should have been minimal in my case. After all, there was only my son and any possible partner of his to be taken into consideration. Marilyn's sister had her own children and grandchildren to enjoy; my own sister was fortunately not the slightest bit interested in sharing my company on festive occasions, and I would have found her presence and that of her curmudgeonly husband burdensome, if not irksome.

Michael had taken surprisingly little persuasion to spend Christmas with me in Sheffield. He had suggested that it would be 'rather nice for Mum', if we fetched her from the care home on Christmas morning and included her in the ritual Christmas lunch celebrations and whatever followed naturally. With reasonable luck and a following wind perhaps she could stay overnight in the family house. After all, there would be enough of us to look after her. I realised what he had meant, when he told me later that his new partner, Claire, would be joining us for Christmas. Her 'people', as he put it, were in Wiltshire and he and she would spend New Year with them. I did not mention George, assuming that Michael would realise he would be here with us and wishing to avoid disturbing the temporary *détente cordiale* between us. I was pleased that

Claire was coming, as she might turn out to serve as a buffer zone between Michael and me, to preserve the peace.

Another assumption that I made was that Doris would be joining her family in Leicestershire for the festive season. I discovered my mistake when she informed me at the end of the school term that she had invited George to spend Christmas and New Year at her house in Chesterfield, 'to celebrate my last Christmas there', she added as an excuse. She had assumed, from some careless, self-pitying remark that I had let slip a few weeks before, that I would be spending an uncomfortable Christmas with my son in Bristol. I was cross with her for inviting George 'behind my back' and, I suppose, also because I resented the central position she had taken up in George's life, at my expense. I convinced her that it was far too late to obtain permission from the Probation Service for such arrangements. Instead I invited Doris to join us for Christmas, a compromise which she accepted with good grace, but with the proviso that she help Suzi with the cooking and preparation for the big day. I am scarcely a New Man, being particularly useless in the kitchen, and so I had engaged Suzi to do the housekeeping for me over Christmas. I had invited her and her small daughter, Alicia, to join us for lunch and the other festivities.

If I had thought that this hotchpotch of guests would lead to us all playing happy families around a festive dining table, I was sadly mistaken. Michael and Claire arrived late on Christmas Eve and, exhausted from the hectic drive up from Bristol, went straight to bed after a nightcap. On Christmas morning, I was sitting with the two of them over breakfast at the kitchen table, when George appeared. Michael exploded.

'You didn't tell me that psychopath would be here! Aren't there places they can go to, hostels or something?'

I had to restrain myself from hitting him, for the first time ever. Claire looked alarmed. Michael clearly had not told her about George. I swallowed my anger.

'George, I think you've met my son once. This is Claire, his girlfriend. I should explain, Claire, George doesn't speak. He's an old student of mine and a friend.'

Claire reached out her hand to shake George's, with the now predictable lack of response from him. Michael shoved away his coffee cup and plate and left the kitchen without a word. In the uncomfortable silence which followed, Claire finished her piece of toast and made her excuses. Poor woman!

I made fresh toast and closed the kitchen door to shut out the muffled sound of a heated conversation coming from upstairs.

Michael behaved badly all day. He greeted Doris's arrival with 'how many more strangers have you invited?' I explained to him and Claire that Doris was an old colleague and a valued friend of both George and myself, and that she had volunteered to help Suzi in the kitchen. At that point Michael and Claire went to fetch Marilyn from the care home. When they came back an hour and a half later, it was evident that both he and Claire had been crying. Claire took me aside to explain that Marilyn had stubbornly refused to leave with them, and it had taken the combined efforts of themselves and two carers to persuade her into the car. As for Marilyn, she now seemed calm enough. The only person she appeared to recognise was Suzi, whom she treated to a smile and a warm hug.

Lunch was a catastrophe. The tension in the air transmitted itself to Doris and Suzi in the kitchen, who served up overcooked vegetables along with an undercooked turkey. Michael made mumbled remarks about not having expected to be eating with the employees. If Suzi heard him, she hid it well. The rest of us certainly heard it. I saw Claire place a restraining hand on Michael's forearm. I wondered what she saw in him. I had begun to heartily dislike my own son. Marilyn ate very little and climaxed the occasion by tipping over her plate of food like a spoilt toddler. Claire and Doris fussed a little over the mess that she had made, and Suzi told her that she was very naughty. The little girl looked on in amazement. Claire tried to make a joke to lighten the atmosphere, but none of us was in the mood to smile.

Even the expensive burgundy that I had bought for the occasion tasted sour.

Michael and Claire skipped the dessert course, and while the rest of us nibbled at Suzi's excellent Christmas pudding, they took Marilyn for a walk in the fresh December air, before it went too dark, Claire explained. The presents that I had so thoughtfully selected for everyone lay untouched under the Christmas tree. Only Alicia showed any interest. I was relieved that she was there to lighten the atmosphere.

It was five o'clock before my son and his partner returned with Marilyn. They had found a jolly pub, Claire explained, had stopped off there to give Marilyn a rest and had not noticed the time. Michael thought it best they took his mother back to the care home now, and we abandoned any plans for her to stay overnight.

'We shall get straight off to Bristol when we've taken Mum back, if you don't mind. If she's not fit to stay over, there's no point in us staying either. It gives us the chance to call in on Claire's people after all.'

Claire thanked me for all I'd done, for all the thought I'd put into the day. I think she wanted to say that it was a pity that everything had gone so awry, but she said nothing more, out of loyalty to Michael. We all stood in the driveway to wave them off as cheerfully as we could, but my throat was dry with emotion and there was a deep, empty hollow in the pit of my stomach. I wondered how my other guests were feeling, but could not bring myself to apologise for the whole awful mess I had concocted for their Christmas Day. Despite their presence, I felt as lonely as Robinson Crusoe. Nevertheless, I was grateful that they were there. I sought consolation in the Glenmorangie that Doris and George had bought me for my Christmas present.

The three of us, and perhaps George in his own way, worked hard to make merry for the sake of little Alicia. I performed some simple magic tricks, we played at Pass the Parcel, Black Magic and Escalado, and some of our laughter was genuine.

Claire called me the following afternoon, with what I interpreted as an apology for their part in the calamitous Christmas Day. She had asked Michael to explain to her who George and Doris were, and she thought it was an admirable thing that I was doing, and that he was wrong to disapprove. She told me that Michael was under a great deal of strain at work, and had been very tense over this whole Christmas business, that he hated the fact that his mother was confined to the care home, regretted bitterly having seen so little of her over the years and blamed himself for neglecting her. She said nothing of how he felt about me. She thanked me once more and hoped we would meet again very soon in better days. She would love to introduce me to her son, Greg, who was in the first year of his A-level course and a keen golfer. She was sure we would get on famously. I had no idea that Claire had a son. Neither she nor Michael had mentioned Greg, but then there had been little opportunity for small-talk. I appreciated her well-meant attempt at reconciliation, or mediation, but if she was trying to deflect some of the rancour I felt towards Michael, she was unsuccessful. Some things once said cannot be unsaid.

A couple of days later, Doris called to pick up George at about 1.30. They were going to a local football match, the visiting team being Doris's hometown club, Leicester City. She asked me if I wanted to join them.

'We can get you another ticket, I'm sure, David, although it may not be next to us.'

I thanked her and declined the offer.

'That's very kind of you, but I think I'll just put my feet up and read the paper, if you don't mind.'

'Okay. Perhaps we can all go to the cinema together one night this week.'

She stirred the cup of tea I had given her, over and over.

'About New Year,' she said eventually, 'I've been thinking that I'd like you and George to come over to Chesterfield on New Year's Eve. I could cook us a special meal, and you can both stay over, so that we can celebrate properly.'

'There's still the problem with the Probation Service – the conditions of George's licence.'

'I was afraid you would say that.'

'Oh, to hell with it! Just do it, Doris. Who's going to know?'

Doris grinned: 'I won't snitch if you don't.'

She turned to look at George and squeezed his shoulder.

'That's settled, then. You up for it, George?'

Whether George was 'up for it' or not was not at all clear, but settled it was. In the end, I made the excuse that I was feeling off-colour and stayed home. Doris hid her delight well, when I told her I should not be coming, but inside I knew she was dancing a jig at the prospect of having George all to herself.

I walked into town on New Year's Eve in an attempt to enter into the party spirit, but the pubs were all jammed with drunken people and the restaurants fully booked. I took a taxi home, watched television until midnight, toasted the New Year 2012 alone and fell into bed to toss and turn well into the small hours. There had been years when invitations to New Year parties had flooded in, and refusing so many had been embarrassing. Sometimes Marilyn and I would have loved the opportunity to spend New Year's Eve quietly at home for a change. This year I had received one invitation and had turned it down. I do not recall actually entertaining the possibility of suicide, but in retrospect I believe that such black thoughts were never far away from my mind.

•

The man consults his list one final time. He has all the items that the woman has written on the list, save one, the special face cream that he has been unable to locate, even with the help of the teenage shelf-stacker who so diligently conducted him to the pharmacy section of the supermarket. Otherwise the trolley contains all the items listed, plus certain impulse purchases of his own, a bottle of Gordon's gin, a box of Maltesers, and a die-cast model of the James Bond Aston Martin DB5, which the boy has already opened and dropped into the trolley with the rest of the shopping, along with four items that he has randomly plucked from the shelves unbeknown to the man: a multi-pack of KitKat chocolate bars, a box of muesli, a tube of toothpaste and a bottle of methylated spirit. The boy, two years and one month old, sits in the seat at the back of the trolley, sucking Fredbear, his constant companion, without whom he refuses to eat or sleep and will venture not one step. Fredbear lives up to his name, having had most of his original features sucked and chewed out of recognition by the boy.

The man pays for his shopping at the checkout and belts the boy into his car seat for the drive home. The boy is crying, but the man considers this normal behaviour for a small child, and does not enquire the reason for his distress.

When the man arrives home, the woman comes to take the boy out of the car. The boy is now sobbing. Fredbear gone, Mummy, he says. The woman is inordinately angry with the man; he does not understand an anger so disproportionate to the triviality of the loss of a worn-out cuddly toy. The woman tells the man that he thinks only of himself, is a useless parent, and has never had any real interest in his child. She has asked him to do one little thing and he has fallen short of satisfactory performance in every important detail. Even his failure to obtain the essential face cream is glossed over in comparison to the negligence exhibited in the loss of Fredbear. The woman questions the man's capability to be responsible for the basic care of a small child and asks him if he would have allowed the boy to eat ground glass. The man points out that the woman is exaggerating and tells her not to be stupid, adding one or two strong adverbs to emphasise his point. The woman tells the man that he will be in charge of putting the boy to bed and staying with him until he goes to sleep in future, escalating as she does so the battle of the adverbs.

The man returns to the supermarket, retraces his steps, and searches the car park and the supermarket interior. Fredbear is nowhere to be found. In the toy section of the supermarket, the man is relieved to find a replacement bear, equal in every respect to Fredbear, including size and colour, and superior, the man considers, in terms of hygiene, aesthetics and utility.

This is Newbear, he says to the boy. Newbear has brought you some sweeties. The boy does not speak, goes to the bathroom, drops Newbear and his sweeties into the toilet bowl and pulls the flush.

VII

DESPERADO

(A piece that seems determined to give itself up, or to sell itself dearly.)

The inauspicious start to the new year left my spirits at an unrelieved low ebb throughout the rest of the winter. My unhappy state of mind was aggravated by my deteriorating relationship with Doris, as I continued to refuse all invitations to join her and George on their outings, including one designed to celebrate my own birthday. Eventually she ceased to invite me, and our exchanges became limited to 'hello' and 'goodbye'. The reader will have noticed that I have made little or no mention of other friends and acquaintances during this narrative, all of which is indicative of the atrophy of all my social connections during my single-minded quest to atone to George for my part in his descent into wretched isolation. Whole weeks would go by without my making or receiving a single phone call or personal email message. I was becoming, by design or otherwise, as lonely as he.

Finally my mood was lifted, temporarily at least, by the unusually sunny and warm March, which inspired me to

77

accompany George on one or two revitalising walks in the Derbyshire countryside. In tune with my depression, my resistance to temptation had weakened, and early in January I had begun once more to smoke cigarettes; the fresh air on the rambles breathed life into my jaded lungs, and I began to feel again the old urge to live.

The year 2012 was to provide us with the worst summer weather I remembered in my entire life. It was to be England's wettest year on record. But meretricious March lured us into a false sense of well-being that brought a smile to everyone's face, including mine. Pubs, cafes and restaurants dusted off outdoor tables and chairs, as their customers spilled out onto the pavement each weekend. Suburban gardens filled with the aroma of barbecued meat. A state of drought was officially declared. However, it is not for the abysmal weather of its summer, nor for the promise of that sparkling March that the year 2012 will remain so memorable for the rest of my days. A series of cataclysmic events were to send my life spinning out of control.

Towards the end of the month I decided to treat Marilyn to a picnic at Padley Gorge, a few miles from the city. I took George along for company. Marilyn too had responded to the sunny weather and was full of smiles, greeting George once more as my old friend Jürgen.

'Oh Jürgen, so wunderbar von dich zu kommen. Und dein Bruder ist hier!'

For some reason she had assumed that I was George's – or Jürgen's – brother, Markus, although he had never had a brother. By now I was used to this kind of strange response from my wife, and at least under my new alias I was being welcomed rather than rebuffed.

Marilyn was highly animated that Tuesday, that last day in the country, flitting from one topic of conversation to another with surprising mental agility, slipping easily from lucid reminiscences of past times with Jürgen to confused accounts about what were obviously recent dreams. The old Welsh lilt, once almost erased by a lifetime's exile, had returned to her voice, and in her light, floral summer dress, she looked almost a young woman again, her cheeks tinged with pink, her eyes clear, her laughter girlish. Her appetite was eager, and she ate more than her share of the picnic that I had provided courtesy of Marks and Spencer. She would even have drunk a second glass of wine, had I not distracted her and moved the bottle to safety. On the way back to the car, I took her hand to help her over a stile, and she offered no resistance when I did not relinquish it. As we said our goodbyes, I kissed her gently on the cheek. Her skin was as smooth and soft as a baby's.

•

The young man, at 22 still a boy, stands fidgeting nervously outside the chapel of Merton College, waiting for his senior colleague, Mr Twyford, 'The Colonel' to the boys. The young man is in his first post in a grammar school in the city of dreaming spires and remains as yet star-struck. The history and grandeur of the colleges are thus far too much for his northern industrial soul to comprehend. Mr Twyford, master of junior maths and French, whom no boy has ever seen rise from his seat behind the oak desk on its podium at the front of the classroom where he teaches, or, more accurately speaking, supervises boys' work from afar, is an alumnus, many moons ago admittedly, of Manchester Grammar School and understands that the young man's northern industrial soul yearns for the nourishment of high culture. Therefore, his wife being indisposed and unable to attend, Mr Twyford has offered her ticket to the young man, who willy-nilly dare not refuse.

The young man knows from the ticket that Handel's Messiah is an oratorio, but this is where his musical expertise ends, as he has no idea what an oratorio is and does not know anyone he can ask without feeling a complete fool. His school Latin is of some help; he remembers the phrase 'orationem habere', one of many on the list set by his Latin master 'to be learned and inwardly digested', and meaning 'to make a speech'. He is fairly certain that the theme will be religious, given the venue and the season of the year. Perhaps there will be a series of bible readings interspersed with solemn church music.

Important people, serious men with grey hair and expensive suits, accompanied by women wearing fur stoles and long evening dresses, sweep past him, in their element. Groups of giggling undergraduate girls in their gowns, each and every one pretty, gay and confident, dance down the gravel driveway and disappear into the chapel. No one sees him. He is invisible.

Mr Twyford arrives at last, dawdling myopically towards him, and then greeting him heartily with his great bass drum of a voice.

'There you are, young fellow! Smart suit! I like to see a young chap in a smart suit. Come on, now. We'll be late! Best seats in the house, by the way!'

How Mr Twyford has managed to wangle tickets on the front row, among college worthies and invited dignitaries, is not a question the young man asks himself. He is rather more concerned with the sheer exposure of his position. He is unsure whether or not to cross his legs, whether to sit knees together bolt upright, or to slump a little so that people in the row behind can see. His collar is tight, and he already feels uncomfortably hot in the close atmosphere of the packed chapel.

The music that follows is a revelation to him. He has never heard such beautiful sounds. The choir is a heavenly chorus, the orchestra mellifluousness personified. There is a dark-haired girl, small and slim, in the front row of the sopranos at the end nearer to the audience. Her hair is cut short, pageboy style, with a coquettish, triangular tuft peeking out over each ear onto her cheek. Her mouth opens inordinately wide as she utters each note, allowing him to dwell on her perfectly regular teeth. His eyes are unwilling to move away from her. He thinks she has the prettiest face he has ever seen. For hours and hours the young man lets the music wash over and through him, never for a moment releasing the dark-haired girl from his gaze.

But the climax is yet to come. The dark-haired girl steps forward and begins to sing a solo, accompanied by a single violin. 'I know that my Redeemer liveth' soars to the rafters from that small mouth and fills the chapel. How can such a tiny body make such a glorious sound? The young man is in raptures of joy. At the end of the solo he leaps to his feet, *begins to clap vigorously and is quickly pulled back down into his seat by his senior colleague.*

'Not done, old chap. Wait till the end,' whispers Mr Twyford.

But the dark-haired girl has seen him and met his adoring gaze for a split second.

Two weeks later, one late afternoon during the last week of term, the young man is in Russell Acott's music shop, choosing a suitable thank-you gift for Mr Twyford. He has in mind a recording of Handel's Messiah, but is uncertain which to choose from the several on offer. He is conscious of a conversation between a female customer and the male shop assistant. The customer has her back to him. She is small, is wearing a duffel coat and a crocheted woollen hat like the one his mother wears. Her voice is distinctively Welsh. The lilting tone of her sentences is somehow alien to Oxford and refreshing to his ear. He grins and imitates her inside his head, before returning his attention to the six different versions of Messiah.

The assistant has now walked over and directed the female customer to an adjacent shelf. The young man turns to look at her, curious. She sees him.

'Hello,' she says. 'It's you!'

And smiles the broadest of smiles.

It is the dark-haired soprano from Merton College chapel.

•

On the Friday morning of that week I received a phone call from the care home with the news that Marilyn had passed away during the night. The cause of death was not yet certain, but the doctor suspected a cerebral haemorrhage. I called Michael immediately on his mobile phone. He was driving in to work and answered my call against a background of city traffic. He answered, but I discovered that I could not find the words to tell him. I pretended that we had been cut off and sat with my head in my hands, trying to regain a semblance of composure. At any other time, the news would not have surprised me. I had been warned that the state of Marilyn's arteries was poor. But on that Friday, emerging as I was from my long winter of torpor, I was deeply shocked. An hour or so later, I had built up the courage to tell him and called again.

'Oh no! When was it? She looked so well when I saw her.'

He was distraught. He had been to see Marilyn once since Christmas, two or three weeks previously, although he had not mentioned his visit to me. Our conversation was short, and I told him that I would let him know about funeral arrangements, as soon as I knew more.

I replaced the phone and turned away. George had been standing behind me, listening in on the conversation. For once he looked me straight in the eye; then he went into the kitchen and returned minutes later with a cup of tea, which he handed to me. Tea and sympathy, I thought to myself and thanked him.

Later that day, after I had made all the emotionally draining calls to relatives, old friends and groups that Marilyn had belonged to, I found George waiting for me in the sitting room, in front of the chessboard laid out for play, at the small table we used for our games, opposite a tumbler of whisky that he had poured ready for me along with the pad that I always used to record our games. I sat down facing him, nodded and moved my king's pawn forward two squares. I would probably have slumped in an armchair or lain wretched on my marriage bed, but instead I played the game of my life, and although I lost as always, it took every last iota of George's genius to defeat me.

As had long since been agreed and was confirmed in her will, it was arranged that Marilyn be buried alongside her parents in the family grave, in the Welsh mining village where she was born and brought up. I decided to drive down and back on the day, as I wanted to take George and Suzi along with me to the funeral. After all, in the last year of her life they had spent as much time with Marilyn as anyone else. The long journey from Sheffield to South Wales meant that, although I received over a hundred cards of condolence from my own and Marilyn's friends and associates, apart from three stubbornly loyal old women friends and half a dozen local people who must have known her family, the funeral was attended only by close relatives. Cousin Ivor, a contemporary of Marilyn, who had lived his whole life in the village, spoke warmly of her from the front of the chapel. He told stories of their wild pre-teenage years, their joint escapades running free in the local countryside, 'during those childhood summers that seemed to last for ever'. He recited, faultlessly by heart, what he told us was Marilyn's favourite poem, Dylan Thomas's *Fern Hill.* Although I could not recall her ever expressing a partiality either for the poet or for this particular poem, I found the hypnotic notes of Ivor's mellifluous baritone very moving. I was not alone. Looking around I saw several members of the congregation in tears, not all of them women.

As always seems to be the case whenever I visit Wales, it was raining hard on the afternoon of the funeral. The grave was on steeply sloping ground, and, as the coffin was being lowered, I was pleased that I was standing on the lower side of the trench excavated by the gravedigger. I watched Marilyn's sister, in high-heeled shoes and supported by her husband, struggling to maintain her footing on the high side. There followed a moment of pure slapstick, which could have been extracted straight from a Buster Keaton silent movie, when the funeral director, a young woman, fell awkwardly and slithered down the bank halfway into the grave. She was rescued by Michael, who hauled her up and out, her tights in holes and her solemn black suit sullied. No one spoke. No one smiled.

The Reverend Colin Davis read the final words of the funeral service, and Michael and I tossed our handful of earth, now turned to slippery mud, down onto the coffin. I was grateful that my tears were concealed by the rain running down my face. We stood as the vicar prayed for Marilyn's immortal soul, and I felt a hand slip into mine and grip it firmly. I turned to see who it was. It was George.

The landlady at the village pub, where I had booked an upstairs room for the funeral buffet, took pity on us and lent us a couple of towels to dry off. The vicar had turned down my offer to join us, and so we were barely a dozen, and our voices echoed around the austere, dingy room.

'I see you did Mum proud, Dad,' said Michael, his facial expression grim. 'No expense spared. Well done.'

That was the limit of the conversation between us. At least Michael was polite to George and Suzi, thanking them both for coming.

'She is my good friend,' said Suzi. 'I must come for her. In Hvratska funeral for good friends is important.'

Michael hugged her, I think to hide his embarrassment.

Claire had accompanied my son for moral support, although she had met Marilyn on just that single occasion at Christmas. She and I did our best to hold a conversation, with limited success. I discovered at least that she worked for the same charity as Michael in the West Country, and that that was how they had met. She was a few years his senior and a widow. A nice woman, I thought. In different circumstances we might have got on well together.

I escaped on the pretext of going outside to smoke a cigarette. I stood in the yard behind the pub, between the outside toilets, the dustbins and the empty barrels and crates of bottles. I stared out at the green mounds that used to be spoil heaps from the nearby colliery and remembered the first time that Marilyn had brought me here, at October half-term in 1966, a few days after the disaster at Aberfan, a few short miles up the road towards Merthyr, when 40,000 cubic metres of shale and rock had slid down onto the village primary school and obliterated the lives of 144 children and teachers. The nation was in mourning, and here the whole community had turned out to lend a hand during those early days, digging, comforting or doing whatever they could find to do, helpful or not, anything rather than stand idly by while others suffered. It was impossible not to be caught up in the emotion of that tragedy.

Beyond, through the mist and the thin drizzle, lay the Brecon Beacons, Marilyn's favourite place. 'The loneliest place in the world', she called them, but my days of tramping the Brecon Beacons with a young Welsh lass had been amongst the least lonely in my life. I spoke out loud.

'If you want real loneliness, Marilyn, then take a look.'

I turned to go back in and found George standing behind me.

'I didn't see you there, George. Time we left for home I think, if we want to be back before bedtime.'

He disappeared into the toilet.

The funeral had hardly been a roaring success, although the landlady had fed us royally, catering for thirty, as I had instructed her. She told me not to worry, as the darts team were in later and would eat the rest, no problem. But there had been none of the festive atmosphere that lightens these darkest of days, as slightly tipsy relatives and friends renew old ties and laugh together over their memories. It was merely another chapter closed. Marilyn was gone now, once and for all, buried far from my home under two yards of her native Welsh rock, and the faint hope, revived that last afternoon together in the country, of rediscovering some tiny part of the old friend and lover I had once known, was buried with her.

On the drive back, I knew what I had to do. I would equip myself properly and return to the Brecon Beacons, to walk and camp in the emptiness. It was what I needed most. George I could safely leave in Doris's hands. He did not need me anyway. I had been clinging on to my duty to him as a way of justifying my existence. I should let go.

The search for my lost youth in the Brecon Beacons, for I now admit that that was what it was, ended in ignominy. I stayed the first night, ironically Sunday April 1st, at a fixed campsite in Trecastle, and arranged to leave my car there for a small fee, until I returned. On the second day I struck out into the hills on a warm, sunny morning, something of a rarity even for April in South Wales. From the outset I was in difficulties. Even though I took the bare minimum of clothing – two T-shirts and two changes of underwear and socks – I soon discovered that I was carrying far too much weight, despite the state-of-the-art tent and cooking equipment and the freeze-dried high energy expedition food, which weighed very little. After a couple of hours of tramping I was exhausted, and I remained so for the rest of the day, until I fell into my sleeping bag at dusk, having no energy left even to eat.

85

The following day, Tuesday, I awoke refreshed after ten hours' sleep, rustled up a breakfast of powdered egg and energy bars and felt comparatively good for the rest of the morning, despite the cold, thin drizzle. When I stopped to rest at midday, I took off my boots to rest my aching feet and discovered that they were severely blistered. I dressed the blisters as best I could and forced myself to eat an apple and an energy bar and to drink a litre of water. When I reluctantly stood up to press on with my hike an hour later, I found that my hips and one of my knees had seized up. I did the stretching exercises recommended by the masseur that I visit from time to time and managed to carry on for three hours or so. I stopped well before dusk and treated myself to a warm meal and a mug of Earl Grey tea. Refreshed, I inspected my feet. I shuddered at the sight. They were a mess. The strange thing was that I felt no pain. As I wriggled into my sleeping bag that evening, I wondered when I would have space for the quiet reflection and meditation I had promised myself.

On the Wednesday morning of my expedition I woke with a raging fever and a seriously bad cough. I decided that enough was enough, and I would head for home, my tail between my legs. At least I had the legitimate excuse that I had fallen ill. I would tackle the Brecon Beacons again in the summer, with the better weather, and after I had done some serious training in preparation. I consulted the map for the easiest route back to the campsite, looked around for landmarks and found none. I was lost, as, I discovered, was my compass! The sky was invisible through the thickening mist, and I was not skilled enough in countryside lore to even know which was north and which was south. I felt too ill to panic. With the presence of mind to know that I did not have the strength to carry it, I abandoned the tent and the rest of my camping equipment to the wilderness. I set out in what seemed to be a downhill direction and stumbled on through what was very soon a dead-still, clinging fog for goodness knows how long, until I was jumped upon by two squaddies. I had strayed into Ministry of Defence territory. The soldiers were part of a training expedition and mistook me for a foreign agent, real or simulated. They brooked no argument and dragged me, protesting my innocence, back to their superior officer, a young man with a cut glass accent, who immediately spotted the very obvious signs of my genuine exhaustion. The Army, bless 'em all, whisked me down to the hospital in Brecon, where I was looked after for three days and nights by kind nurses and a crotchety, disapproving female doctor, who gave me a daily lecture on knowing my own limits.

By the time I had driven back to Sheffield on the Saturday, having discharged myself from Brecon Hospital against the doctor's advice, I was pretty much exhausted once again. I had been away for a week. There was no sign of George about the house, which was in apple-pie order. Suzi had evidently passed through. There were ten messages on my answering machine. The first was from the NHS, an automated request to confirm my annual appointment at the ophthalmology department of the Royal Hallamshire Hospital. The second was from Claire, asking how I was after the funeral and the drive to and from South Wales. Of the other eight, one was from Doris, wondering if I was back from my expedition, the other seven from Michael, the last one from earlier that day, saying simply: 'Where the hell are you, Dad?'

I had not told my son of my plans for the expedition to the Brecon Beacons. Why should I have done? I didn't think he would be interested in the slightest, considering the present state of relations between the two of us. Perhaps Claire had worried that I had not returned her call and insisted that he call me. That was it. But by the fifth or sixth message he was sounding genuinely concerned. Perhaps he actually cared about me! Fingers fumbling with excitement at the prospect of reconciliation, I pressed the buttons of the speed dial to call him. He answered immediately. He must have been on the point of making or finishing another call, but I imagined him sitting impatiently by the phone waiting to hear from me.

'Michael?' I began, hesitantly.

'Dad, is that you? God! You gave us a fright! I was ready to ring the police.'

Not ready to come up and find out for yourself, I thought, unfairly I suppose, but thankfully did not say. I gave him a short account of my expedition to South Wales, somewhat sanitised, so as not to make me look the total

87

ass that I had been. He saw through my thin disguise of the facts and lambasted me mercilessly. It was typically selfish of me, to think of no one but myself, my own ego. What the hell did I think I was doing? At my age! What did I care if people were worried sick about me? I was just one of those irresponsible idiots who swan off and put themselves in danger and expect the rescue services to risk their own lives saving them! I just went my own sweet way and to hell with anybody else! Look at me, sitting on my fat backside and rattling around in that huge house with its two sitting rooms, two bathrooms, four bedrooms, an attic, huge cellars bulging with expensive wine, and a garden the size of Wales! While others were losing their homes, while the other half of the country were living on the breadline, having to resort to food banks, while handicapped people were having their benefits cut off, and millions of talented young people were isolated from the job market, Tory fat-cats like me were just coining it, living off the fat of the land.

An ice-cold anger gripped me. First of all, I pointed out how unfeasible it was for me to sit on my fat backside and rattle around at the same time. Secondly, I hadn't noticed him complaining about all this privilege that he had also enjoyed when he had lived with Marilyn and me. Thirdly, what the devil was it to do with him how I lived? Why did he suddenly think he had such a right to tell me how to behave? Fourthly, I had never voted Conservative in my life.

'Come on,' I said, 'what exactly is it that I'm supposed to do?'

'You want me to tell you? All right. You should sell that house and your big flashy gas-guzzling Jag for a start, buy yourself something more suitable for one person and give the rest of the money to people who really need it. What are you going to do with all that dosh, anyway? You can't spend it all, and you can't take it with you. You won't live for ever, you know.'

The unkindness of youth.

'I was thinking of leaving it to you.'

'Well you can stuff it! I don't want your money, Dad. Anyway, Claire's people are loaded, but in their case they put their money where their principles are! Unlike you! Walk the walk for once in your life, Dad!'

This was the last straw! I caught a glimpse of myself in the hall mirror, face flushed and veins twitching on my temple, as the anger pumped adrenaline around my body. I should have put the phone down, ended the conversation then, but I did not. He had dealt me a low blow and I needed to hit back, to hurt him as he had hurt me. The patience and forbearing that had served me so well with thousands of pupils and hundreds of teachers were exhausted. *I* was exhausted.

'Walk the walk, you say? That's rich coming from a waste of space who's never been able to stick to one job for more than five minutes, who's ended up in his forties, the prime of his life, working for a pathetic little charity for a pathetic little salary, who can't keep a girlfriend for longer than six months. Shall I go on? I'll tell you what, Michael, if that's how you feel, then so be it. I'll change my will tomorrow! You always were an ungrateful whinger!'

I ended the call and, the pangs of hunger I had been fending off for the last two hours of my drive home now submerged under a welter of emotion, I went to bed without supper, angry, insomniac and as miserable as the proverbial sin. Secretly I had always been proud of my career, of what I considered my substantial contribution to public life. I was shocked by my son's outburst, my amour-propre wounded by his accusation that I was wallowing in wealth whilst others less fortunate suffered poverty. I had never thought of myself as well-to-do or privileged; what I owned I had worked hard for. Like most teachers, members of parliament and civil servants, I was convinced that I could have earned far more money in the private sector and therefore imagined myself something of a martyr for public service.

But it was not my wounded pride that kept me awake that night. It was the knowledge that I had lost my son once and for all. Some things once said cannot be unsaid, and I knew that my own malicious and vindictive words, although uttered in anger, were unforgivable and almost certainly irredeemable.

89

VIII

CONSOLIDATION

(Moving pieces to better squares, thus improving a position which has been weakened by an attack.)

I woke late the following morning. When I finally came downstairs to the kitchen, I was surprised to find George there. He had heard me moving about upstairs, had made a pot of tea and was pouring a mugful for me. As he handed it to me, the phone rang. It was Doris. Could she come round to talk to me? Yes, it *was* quite important.

Ten minutes later, the doorbell rang. She was there already.

'My goodness, Doris! That was quick! Have you bought a Porsche?'

'Oh no, I'm in the new house. George has been helping me move in for the last couple of days, haven't you, George.'

Of course. I had forgotten that she was moving jobs and home. She would be starting at Harry Brearley the week after next.

I invited her into the sitting-room. I had an uneasy feeling that she was about to unburden herself upon me, at the moment when I was least open to sympathy for the troubles of another human being, reeling as I was from the effects of the catastrophic telephone conversation with my son. I waited for her to speak.

'Are you okay, David? You look worn out. How was your trip back to South Wales? Did you find what you were looking for?'

I had explained my return to the Brecon Beacons to Doris by telling her, somewhat enigmatically, even romantically, that I was going in search of the answer to certain questions I had always asked myself about Marilyn's birthplace. Her enquiry, whether I had found what I was looking for, triggered an entirely unexpected response from me. I told her the full story of my pitiful expedition in the Welsh hills, my rescue by the young soldiers, my recovery in hospital, my emotional and physical exhaustion. I must have cut a ridiculously pathetic figure.

Doris was sympathetic. She came over and sat by me on the sofa, taking my hand in both hers.

'You poor thing, David. What an awful experience! It must have been terrible for you! Why didn't you tell us you were going on some Outward Bound mission? I would have put you off, if I'd known. Or insisted that you take somebody with you. George could have gone. Right, George? Did you tell Michael? Did he know about this?'

I shook my head.

'Does he know now?'

I told her about the awful telephone conversation. I spared her, and myself, no detail. She listened in silence.

'We all say things we don't mean. You were exhausted. And angry. So was he. Angry. He was worried about you. He cares about you. You're his father, David! It will be okay. He'll come round, don't worry.'

She squeezed my hand, then stroked my arm and kissed me softly on the cheek. I was already at breaking point, blinking back the tears filling my eyes. The kindness that Doris was showing towards me, the knowledge that here was someone on my side, someone who cared about me, opened the floodgates.

Doris waited for me to regain some of my composure, then handed me a box of tissues from the coffee table.

91

'George and I are going over to the house. The wallpaper in the living room is pretty dire, and we're going over to strip it off. I don't know about you,' she grinned, 'but I find stripping very therapeutic. Why don't you join us?'

I did. And I felt better for it.

It was only when George and I were back home that evening, I in a healthier frame of mind, one of Doris's excellent meat and potato pies inside me, pleasantly weary, showered and ready for bed, that I realised she had not told me about the important matter she had come to discuss with me that morning. But I was not to remain in suspense for very long.

Doris rang as the pips on BBC Radio 4 announced that it was nine a.m.

'I'm sorry it's a bit early. There is something I need to tell you. George and I are driving down to Oadby to see my mum and my brother if he's around, and so we need to make an early start. I was going to tell you yesterday, but I thought that maybe you'd had enough shocks for one weekend. I'm just warning you that I'm coming over now. I don't suppose George will have told you much – haha!'

She sounded in a jolly mood, and so at least it was not going to be bad news.

It was an hour and a half before Doris arrived, full of smiles. There was no sign of her routinely fretful look. She was sporting a new haircut, with striking blonde highlights. Even I, the most unobservant of men when it comes to women's sartorial appearance, noticed that she was wearing an entire new wardrobe. She wore a primrose yellow dress, belted at the waist, knee-length, with a matching cashmere cardigan. Her shoes were a sort of strappy Greek sandal, golden with a two-inch heel. Expensive looking golden-tinged tights completed the ensemble. Marilyn would have said she had 'made an effort'. I am no judge, but I thought the outfit worked rather well. I told her so. Her smile became even broader. I think I must have stared admiringly at her shoes for rather too long. She looked down at them too.

'Don't worry, my driving shoes are in the car. I shan't be tackling the M1 in these. I just wanted to show off the new outfit. Sheer vanity, I admit it!'

George came into the hallway and Doris greeted him with a peck on the cheek and a hug. She turned to me.

'Shall we sit down for this, David?'

'Do I need to break out the brandy?' I said, only half joking.

I sat in my usual armchair, while Doris and George sat together on the sofa facing me, looking like an interview panel.

'What are you doing on Friday?' asked Doris.

I did not have to rack my brains or consult my social calendar.

'Nothing special. Why?'

'We'd like you to be best man at our wedding. Wouldn't we, George?'

'Wedding?' I gasped. 'Are you sure? Is George okay with this?'

I looked at George. His face was as vexingly expressionless as ever.

'You don't see him running away, do you? He's a big boy, David. He doesn't need anybody else to help him make up his mind.'

I looked from one to the other, and then settled my gaze on Doris.

'But getting married, isn't that a bit drastic? How about a trial period? Living together for a while.'

'I'm an old-fashioned girl, David. It's this way or not at all, and I need George with me, living with me.'

'But why Friday? Why such a rush?'

'Because there's a free slot at the Town Hall. Several, actually. We could take our pick. It's Friday the 13th, you see.'

I could see the logic. In no way do I count myself as superstitious, but never in a million years would I have chosen Friday the 13th as my wedding date. I could not help questioning the wisdom of not only taking on an impossibly difficult marriage but also cocking a snook at fate.

Fortunately, I had long since learned that there is rarely anything to be gained and much to lose by being a wet

93

blanket. I congratulated them both, wished them luck, and said I would be delighted to be George's best man.

'Twelve noon on Friday, then. Make sure he's there on time! Reception afterwards in the *Sheffield Tap*. We've sorted the official bit, by the way. George's probation officer was thrilled. So thrilled that we invited her to the wedding! She says she can't come for long, but she will turn up for the ceremony in her lunch hour.'

The wedding party was small in numbers - Doris's mother, brother and sister-in-law, three colleagues from her last job, Marie, an old school-friend, and myself - but the day was as special as any I have known. The bride, resplendent in scarlet, and the groom, grave and distinguished in his designer second-hand suit bought from the Oxfam shop, were a most handsome couple. The registrar, schooled in advance by Doris, accepted George's silence as acquiescence and pronounced my two friends man and wife. We made merry for the whole of the afternoon, seated around a festive oval table in the lounge bar of the *Sheffield Tap*, relishing the excellent real ales, sandwiches and pickles provided by the bar staff. The magnificent old rooms, reconstructed lovingly from the Edwardian Refreshment Room & Dining Rooms on Platform 1 of the former Sheffield Midland railway station, were a perfect venue for our party. I had composed a few amusing sentences revealing how the two had first met and my amazement and delight at seeing them tie the knot so many years later. Doris's brother spoke warmly about her and George, and led us in a toast to their future in one of the local brews.

Like most people, I love a happy ending, and whether it was the exhilaration of the occasion, the good company, or simply the inner glow of being pleasantly tipsy, as I watched the pair climb hand in hand onto the evening train bound for their brief weekend honeymoon, I truly believed, was certain that here indeed I was witnessing a happy ending. On the platform, waving them off, Doris's mother wept tears of joy, and I comforted her, instinctively. I felt I was among good people. I was confident that George was in the safest of safe hands, and that, at last, his return to health and wholeness was assured.

In the euphoria of the day I had forgotten my own troubles. That night I slept like a baby.

The spring and summer of 2012 passed without any further life-changing episode, with no hint of the cataclysmic events that were to follow later in the year. Doris took up her new post at Harry Brearley and was busy finding her feet in a very much changed establishment, putting her own stamp on the drama work of the school. Her professional work and the business of settling into a new home left her little time for me. George, now judged fit for work, was employed four days per week by Nacro, an ex-offender support organisation, painting and decorating, in order to meet his obligation to carry out 300 hours of unpaid work before the deadline, which had already been extended from 12 to 18 months, because of his delicate psychological state and his periods of treatment at the clinic. So it was that my outings with him were less frequent. He had not abandoned me, though. On two separate occasions, when we had not seen each other for over a week, I answered my door-bell to find George standing on my doorstep. When I mentioned this to Doris, she laughed:

'He probably misses you, you idiot!'

Men of my generation were taught to hide their emotions, to swallow disappointment, to accept victory and defeat with equal good grace, and to maintain a stiff upper lip in the face of tragedy or heartbreak, the values of the British public school, the values of Kipling's *If*. I was twelve years old when my father died. The memory of my mother's words to me after his funeral remains crystal clear:

'Life goes on,' she said. 'We have to be brave and carry on.'

Michael did not contact me during these months, and although I was several times on the point of picking up the telephone to call him, I did not. For years Marilyn and I had coveted our friends' grandchildren, looking forward to the day when we would celebrate the arrival of our own. I had long since lost hope that I should ever have this link with the future. The bad blood between me and my son served only to aggravate this disappointment. But I was well trained. I carried on. And so it was, outwardly at least, with comparative ease that I relegated to a hidden recess of my subconscious the sadness of losing first my life's companion and then my only son.

Released as I was of my duty to act as mentor to George, I began to find time hang heavily on my hands. I tried to involve myself more in tending my large garden, but a year of neglect had permitted nature to take over completely, and even if I had possessed any horticultural talent, the job would have been far too much for me. I threw in the towel and restricted myself to mowing the lawns.

At a loose end, I decided to re-join the golf club and rekindle a few old acquaintances there. I was surprised to find how much I had missed my golfing chums and their easy companionship, and there is something about an English golf course on a fine day that, like sleep, 'knits up the ravell'd sleave of care'. Even on the wet days, and there was no shortage of those that summer, there was the solace that at least I had enjoyed a good walk, followed usually by a reviving hot shower and several fiercely contested frames of snooker. There are consolations to being a single man. For evening entertainment I had returned to the local chess club, where without George I was now welcomed rather more enthusiastically.

As for George, he continued his meteoric rise through the ranks of British chess players, winning each and every tournament he entered. In the run-up to the British Championship he had yet to lose a single game. I was excited for him and expected great things. Consequently, I was all the more disappointed, when I telephoned to offer my support in the preparation for the event and perhaps as analyst during competition days, only for Doris to tell me that he had withdrawn from the Championship.

'Don't you mean you withdrew him, Doris?'

'Put it like that, if you like. I think it's far too much to ask of him. We don't know what's happening inside George's head. We can't even guess at the strain the Championship would put him under. I need to spare him that. It would be cruel to put him through it.'

'I think he could have won, actually won! Wouldn't that have been a boost for him? For his confidence?'

'And what kind of stress do you think winning would have put him under? All the fuss, all the media attention! His mental illness, his prison record, trumpeted all over the gutter press!'

I was angry with her. Chess was the one field of life in which George could excel. It was, to my mind, the single factor that had kept him from the abyss during the last three decades. He needed these moments of success to have any chance of a full recovery. It was a matter of opinion, and both of us were on George's side, but I was sure that I was right. Nevertheless, in my heart of hearts, I conceded that my anger was spiced by the frustration of having to hand over the key to George's welfare to his new wife.

It was not until the end of the second week of the school summer holidays that I was invited to dinner with Doris and George at the new house. They had just returned from what Doris called their 'official honeymoon', their first one having been confined to a single weekend. During the meal Doris told me all about their trip to Norfolk, where despite the dreadful weather, they seem to have enjoyed themselves well enough, boating, camping and bird-watching.

It was after the meal, as I sat nursing a liqueur that I hadn't really wanted, that Doris exploded her bombshell.

'Listen, David. George and I have decided that it's time for him to go back to Waltham Forest.'

'To Paul Morgan? I thought you must have . . '

Doris interrupted me.

'Do you think he would still take George back? On the programme, I mean. It's been almost a year.'

'He did say come back any time, and I'd say he's a man of his word. On the programme? What do you mean?'

Doris spoke quietly.

'I mean ECT.'

There was a great deal I wanted to say, but I bit my tongue. It was no longer my business. When George had gone out of the room, I asked her what had decided them to take this drastic step. I used those words, 'drastic step'.

'We can go along like this for ever, David. But I need more. I need George, a complete George. I need a complete marriage. This is not enough for me.'

I considered telling her that she should have thought of all this before, but decided that it would be unfair. She had probably had the same thought. Love makes us all do things we regret at some point in our life. Against my better judgement, I agreed to use my contact with Morgan again and arrange for George's treatment. Afterwards it came to me that for once Doris's motivation had not seemed to include George's best interests. It was what *she* needed from him that had appeared uppermost in her thoughts. I was left with the uncomfortable feeling that she may not have given sufficient consideration to whether the outcome would be good for George.

IX

WILD

(An extremely confusing, baffling or complex position or move.)

I contacted Paul Morgan the following day. I half hoped he may have forgotten us by now, or have some excuse not to take George back into his care. It was far from the case. Morgan appeared to be in a surprisingly light-hearted humour.

'We haven't forgotten you, David. In fact, George is quite a celebrity in the psychiatric world! There's more than one of my fellow practitioners who would dearly love to snaffle him from me. I presented a paper on his case at the Geneva Conference a couple of months ago – I gave him a pseudonym, of course; he's Harpo in the literature, if you want to look him up on the Internet. He was the talk of the conference. Actually, I was all for contacting *you*, but my colleagues here thought it was a bit unethical to hunt a patient down, so to speak!'

I was not keen on the Harpo pseudonym, which was a little disrespectful, I thought. Morgan seemed quite pleased to hear about the marriage, if only because George now had a definite next of kin. I told him of Doris's decision to opt for ECT.

'I'm pleased about that. I think – we all think, here – that it's the way forward.'

'Have you thought of taking a second opinion? Didn't you say that using ECT on schizophrenics was frowned on in Britain?'

'That's probably true for the NHS, but as we discussed, schizophrenia is a rather vague term of reference. I assure you that there's been no shortage of second opinions - plenty of my colleagues have made their views known to me! Actually, there's plenty of support for ECT in the international community. You may have to bow to expert opinion on this, David.'

I asked him to explain exactly what the treatment would consist of. He told me they first determined the dosage of the electric shock, taking into account the severity of the patient's condition, along with age, physique and gender. A short-lasting anaesthetic was administered before each treatment, to minimise discomfort, and the patient's heart and brain activity were closely monitored at all times through EEG, ECG and blood oxygen level checks. In George's case, they would administer the treatment on alternate weekdays, for a period of three weeks.

I did not feel better for knowing the details.

The clinic contacted Doris directly, and it was arranged that George be admitted to Waltham Forest the following weekend. After the treatment he would stay at the clinic for an undefined period of time, during which the psychologists would attempt to make the required breakthrough that they expected to be triggered by the ECT.

On Friday the 7th of September, Doris phoned me with the news that George was coming home the following morning by train. She was thrilled to report that Morgan and his team had made considerable progress, following the therapy, that George was now capable of certain facial expressions and was writing brief answers to questions.

I rang the clinic immediately. I wanted to hear from Morgan first-hand. He returned my call half an hour later. He was somewhat less ecstatic than Doris, but confident that they had made a significant breakthrough in communicating with George. He and his colleague were more certain than ever that the origin of the mutism lay in his boyhood relationship with his father. However, George put up a solid brick wall of defence whenever they broached the question too specifically. Morgan felt it was unwise to push him too hard at this time, and that a pause in the treatment was indicated.

I thanked him and was about to put down the phone, when he continued.

'There is just one more thing,' he said, almost apologetically, and then paused for a few seconds. 'What we should really like to know is why he killed his father, and why so violently. For a man like him, who has always been so gentle and timid in every other respect, such a violent murder is totally out of character. We tried to talk to him about the trial, to ask him in particular why none of his family turned up to support him. The prosecution didn't push it - it was hardly in their interest to find excuses for George's behaviour – and his defence team don't seem to have been much cop. So we have no clue there.'

'I couldn't agree with you more. Every time I see George, I wonder what could possibly have made him so angry. Do you think it would still be useful to talk to them now? His brothers and sisters, I mean.'

'That's what I'm hinting at, David. I suppose I should come out with it straight. What you need is a private investigator. Find his family, and maybe they'll talk now. You know the sort of thing I'm thinking has happened, and all this business with TV personalities and Catholic priests being outed as paedophiles might just be enough to have loosened their tongues after all this time.'

'A private investigator?'

'Yes, but I'm assuming his wife can't afford to employ one. They don't come cheap. What about you, David? Are you good for a few quid?'

'I've been told I'm a stingy plutocrat, so why not? Do you know anybody?'

'We do have a good man we sometimes use ourselves, but he's London-based. What you need is a local man, somebody with local contacts. Have a sniff round in Sheffield. I'll leave it with you.'

Having long since recognised in myself a certain proclivity for procrastination, I decided that immediate action was required. I went to the Yellow Pages book that normally lies unopened from one year to the next in my bedside table drawer. Unfortunately, the section headed *Detective Agencies* presented me with 38 possibilities, what the French call *le délicieux embarras du choix*. I read through the names and addresses; some looked more promising than others, although most seemed to advertise themselves principally as agencies for trapping unfaithful partners. One large display claimed past police experience as well as thirty years as a local enquiry agent. On the face of it this seemed ideal, until I realised that any past police service from over thirty years ago might well be totally irrelevant. One or two claimed to specialise in locating missing persons, whilst others listed a whole range of investigatory activities. I was at a loss to decide how to choose. I decided to contact several of the more promising firms by telephone after the weekend.

I played golf on the Sunday morning and, serendipitously, bumped into Ray Broomhead, a former chief of South Yorkshire police, on the course. We were both searching for our balls among the trees between the 10th and 13th holes. Ray appeared to be in a black mood, and was thrashing about in the undergrowth with his sand iron. I spotted both our balls lying close together and called him over. I pointed out a wide gap in the trees through which he could see the green.

'You've got a good lie at least, Ray. A nicely struck four-iron should get you on the dance floor.'

He settled into his stance, wiggling his substantial buttocks unattractively, and although he did not hit his shot cleanly, perked up considerably when the ball landed short of the bunkers and skipped over onto the green, settling by the flag. It was an excellent moment to ask him what he knew about private eyes. I arranged to meet him in the bar afterwards to discuss it.

Over the pint of lager that I had bought him, he told me he had 'just the ticket' for me. Ray is very much old school, but straight as a die and a credit to his profession.

There should be more like him. He has the clipped tones of the army officer, speaks in short bursts of phrases which are usually not complete sentences, reminding me of the major in *Fawlty Towers* and making it difficult not to grin when listening to him.

'Les Bradshaw, former senior detective. Straight as a die, works alone, doesn't take on any old snooping job, has lots of current personal contacts in the force. Not in Yellow Pages, tough as old boots, red-hot, best officer in CID.'

There was no decision to make. Bradshaw was my man.

'Can't give you a telephone number. Try Hallamshire Golf Club. Les is a member.'

I resolved to contact Bradshaw the very next day. I would set the wheels in motion. I should have done it years ago.

On the Monday morning I phoned the secretary of the Hallamshire Golf Club. He was unwilling to give out Bradshaw's number or address, but promised to leave a message on the members' noticeboard. I wondered how often Bradshaw went into the club and cursed myself silently for not following my first instinct to simply wander into the clubhouse and look him up in the members' handbook. Why did I always have to behave so properly? Always so anally? Always like a headmaster for God's sake! It could be weeks before Bradshaw contacted me, if at all.

I had heard no more news from Doris, and after a few days I became impatient to know more about George's progress. On the Thursday evening I phoned and arranged to go over to see them at the weekend. Doris invited me to Sunday lunch. I was delighted when George greeted me with something resembling a smile and shook my hand.

After lunch, whilst George was busy with the washing-up, Doris took me for a stroll in the garden, ostensibly to show me how they had reshaped the beds and planted new shrubs and trees. She told me that George was having the most terrible nights, during which he woke several times in great distress, streaming in perspiration and uttering desperate howls of pain. She had never known him like this. He was normally a sound sleeper. She had had to resort to sleeping in the guest room, to be in a fit state for her taxing work. For Doris, this negative effect of George's treatment at Waltham Forest far outweighed the positive features. She welcomed his developing ability to communicate, but thought that the pain of the nightmares was far too high a price to pay.

'I'm afraid they've stirred something up from the past that's too much for him to bear, David. I'm afraid we may have done the wrong thing. We should have left things as they were. I bitterly regret it. He's in so much pain! It's heart-breaking to see him!'

She dissolved into tears, and I put my hand on her shoulder to comfort her, feeling like an awkward teenager as I did so.

'Don't blame yourself, Doris. You did what you thought right. We are all doing that. And who knows? It may all turn out to be for the best.'

'No, David, you were right. About the ECT, about the chess. The chess championship would have been a picnic compared to what he's been through.'

I asked her if she had told Paul Morgan about George's reaction.

'No I have not! I've totally lost confidence in him. All these people care about is their own self-aggrandisement, their own ego! He doesn't give a damn about George!'

I asked about George's part-time job. In her view there was no prospect of George taking up manual work again in the near future; she considered him in no fit state to share a work place with other offenders. She would, however, encourage him to enter more chess tournaments, in order to build his self-esteem. I was surprised at her volte-face in regard to chess, but I was glad to offer to be more company for George in the daytime, whilst Doris was at work. She accepted my offer gratefully.

It did not seem the right moment to broach the idea of the private detective.

At any rate, Bradshaw did not call me back. Was fate taking a hand here? Or was I merely allowing circumstances to prevent me from having to make a decision? After two more weeks, during which George and I enjoyed our long rambles whenever weather permitted, played chess, pottered about in our respective gardens, or went to afternoon cinema shows, on the last Friday of September I decided to call Paul Morgan.

He received the news of George's nightmares with the equanimity I had learned to associate with him. He was not surprised in the slightest at the effect of the ECT. It was encouraging, in that they had clearly 'woken hidden ghosts', as he put it. Just as in athletics, there was no gain without pain. I told him I thought he was being hard-hearted. He accepted that this might seem to be the case, but that a dispassionate approach was essential in arriving at a professional judgement.

'Everyone needs to keep a cool head now, David. Ideally, we'd like to see George again here as soon as possible. There are drugs that can eliminate the worst effects of the nightmares. Can I rely on you to speak to his wife about it?'

I pointed out, rather curtly, that that was his job, not mine. His certainty was beginning to irritate me. As one who has agonised over every single life decision I have ever had to take, I have always mistrusted people who are so absolutely sure about their own judgement. He asked me about my progress in engaging a private detective. I told him I was certain that Doris would not approve, and so I had not approached anyone.

'Have you asked her? It seems to me it's more important than ever.'

I suggested that he raise the matter himself, when he spoke to her, but added that I would still be prepared to foot the bill.

The following Monday Doris called me to tell me how angry she was with me about the private detective proposal. Why couldn't I just mind my own business for once? I considered reminding her that I was the one who had fought for George's release from Wakefield Prison and had taken him under my wing without counting the personal cost, but I did not. As I put down the phone, I asked myself why I had once liked this woman. Now I thanked my lucky stars that I was not the one married to her.

I saw nothing of George for the next fortnight, and as October half term approached for the local schools, I knew I should see no more of him until the second week of

November at the earliest, as he and Doris would no doubt be off on some jaunt during her week's holiday.

I was more than surprised therefore, when in the small hours of the Wednesday morning before half-term week my bedside telephone rang, summoning me from an unusually deep sleep. It was Doris, almost screaming down the phone.

'He's gone, David!'

My fuddled brain attempted to compute a meaning out of these few words. She must be talking about George. Gone? But where had he gone? Or did she mean he was dead? Please God, no! I put on my glasses and looked at the clock radio. It was 3:10 a.m.

'What do you mean, Doris?' I asked, dreading the answer.

'He's gone. He's not here.'

Thank God!

'When did you notice? Just now? Have you searched the house? He could be taking a walk in the garden. Perhaps he can't sleep.'

'He's been gone two days!'

'What! No explanation? No note?'

There was silence on the other end of the phone. I realised that I had said something stupid.

'Why haven't you told me before? Doris, answer me, why haven't you told me this before?'

'I know I hurt your feelings. I didn't want you to think me a complete fool. I just hoped he would come back on his own.'

'I'll come round. Give me half an hour.'

'David.'

'Yes?'

'He's taken the car.'

'I didn't know he could drive.'

'As far as I know, he can't. But he's seen me drive. And it's an automatic car.'

'My God! There's no knowing where he could have got to!'

It crossed my mind that with no licence and no insurance this escapade could at the very least land George in hot water.

I took a two-minute shower to wake myself up and drove round to Doris. We talked through the rest of the night. George and the car had already disappeared, when Doris looked out of her bedroom window on Monday morning. There was no clue as to where he might have gone. I offered to drive around the streets locally to see if I came across either him or the car, but we both realised that this was pointless. I reassured her that George would turn up soon enough. She told me that he had been spending a great deal of time in local libraries, but she had no idea what he had been doing. She had assumed it was something to do with chess and was more than a little ashamed that she had thwarted any chance he might have had to become national champion.

At 7.30 the doorbell rang. We both rushed into the hallway, bumping into each other in our haste. Two dark figures were visible through the glass door. The bell rang again. Doris ran to unlock it, fumbling with the keys. One of the policeman spoke.

'Is it Doris? Doris Campbell?'

'Yes,' panted Doris almost inaudibly.

'We've found your car, Doris. Did you not know it was missing? You haven't reported it stolen.'

'No, yes, I realised . . . just now.'

The second policeman, standing slightly behind his colleague, raised an eyebrow.

'We found it on Winnats Pass, near Castleton. It had been sitting there for at least a day. A member of the public who had passed it four times reported it to us. There was a man slumped over the steering wheel. Our good citizen knocked on the window to see if he was all right and woke him up. The man wouldn't answer his questions.'

'Was he okay, the man?'

'The Derbyshire police have him, down at Chapel-en-le Frith station. He's been fed and watered and the police doctor has given him the once over. He's okay. Apparently he refuses to say a word, and as he has no identification at all on him, we're a bit stymied for the moment. We would charge him with something, but were not quite sure what - car theft, taking a vehicle without consent, creating a hazard for moving traffic.'

'It's my husband, George. George Campbell. He's mute.'

'Well, that explains something, at least. What it doesn't explain is why you didn't notice either your husband or the car was missing.'

Doris invented a story that she and George had had a row and that she was too embarrassed to speak about it. She called in to work to explain that a family emergency would prevent her from coming in. I drove her the thirty miles or so to Chapel-en-le Frith, with a can of petrol in the boot, suspecting that George had probably run the tank dry. We collected him, dishevelled and blank-faced. The station sergeant seemed particularly pleased to get George off his hands, and providentially no mention was made of producing insurance documents or driving licence. As Doris was paying the £150 towing and storage fee at the police compound, George walked towards me. Was I mistaken, or was he trying to speak? I leaned forward, my ear close up against his mouth. He was so close now that I felt his lips brush my earlobe, silently at first, and then I swear I heard the faintest of hoarse whispers.

'It's done.'

There was nothing further. I looked him in the eye. It was almost as if I could see straight through those clear grey orbs into his brain. Nothing.

'What's done, George? Where have you been? What were you up to these last two days?'

Nothing.

We drove home in our separate vehicles.

During the next three weeks George and I spent four weekdays together, silent days during which I tried repeatedly and in vain to persuade him to speak to me. We went to the horse races, to the Yorkshire Sculpture Park and on two of our familiar circular rambles in Derbyshire, and so were alone together for extended periods. I also accompanied him to a weekend chess tournament in Blackpool, a prestigious tournament which George won comfortably, and we shared a hotel room there. Either I slept too soundly to notice them, or George's nightmares had completely disappeared. I was looking for the merest hint of what he had been doing during those two lost days

108

at the end of October, but the closest he came to communicating with me was a nod or a shake of the head. I felt that our relationship had taken an abrupt step backwards. The trust I had built up so painstakingly seemed to have evaporated. What was he thinking? Was I his headmaster again? Was he scared of me? How could I know what was in his mind? And how could he know what was in mine? I began to doubt whether I had actually heard him speak that day in Chapel-en-le-Frith, or whether it was my imagination, stirred by the euphoria of finding him safe and sound.

But the whispered words still echoed in my head.

'It's done.'

X

STRATEGY

(Analysis of game positions and creating long-term plans for future play.)

It was on my return from the Blackpool chess conference that I found the text message on my mobile phone from Les Bradshaw. I worked out that it was ten weeks since I had left the message with the golf club secretary. His message was brief, asking me to call him back at my convenience and leaving a mobile phone number. I had totally given up on hearing from Bradshaw, and in the meantime Doris's anger at me for even contemplating the idea of engaging the private detective to delve into George's past had rendered his lack of response irrelevant. Doris had effectively forbidden me from going ahead. I would telephone him to say that I had no further interest in using his services.

That night I could not sleep. Nagging at me ever more urgently was my need to know what was at the root of George's tortured existence for what was now more than three and a half decades. The words 'it's done', imagined or real, would not let me rest. What was 'done'? What had been finally settled during those two lost days when George had gone missing? Why did I so badly need to know? I threw off the duvet, went downstairs to the kitchen, turning on all the lights in the house.

I made a mug of tea and sat at my kitchen table. I knew why. It was for the same reason that I had taken George under my wing on his release from Wakefield Prison. My guilt, the guilt of having allowed a fragile teenager to slip from my care for the sake of a quiet life, for the sake of my own professional advancement, despite his desperate, if silent, cries for help.

I did what we all do. I rationalised a selfish decision. Doris had admitted that she had been wrong about the national chess championship, about the electric shock treatment, had admitted that I was in the right. One day she would admit I was right about this too.

I called Bradshaw back on the Monday morning. The call went straight to voicemail. An hour later I got a text message explaining that he had not been into the golf club for three or four months because of a persistent shoulder problem and had in fact decided to give up his membership. Another member had eventually passed on my message. Bradshaw suggested that we meet for lunch in *The Broadfield*, a pub on the Abbeydale Road.

I confess that I was expecting to meet a cliché, someone approximating to my image of the typical ex-policeman gumshoe, the jaded, paunchy, dissolute alcoholic, reeking of tobacco and body odour, wearing a shabby tweed jacket with leather elbow patches. I was to be pleasantly disappointed. There was no sign of any dissipated private eye when I arrived, a couple of minutes early. At the bar stood only a slim, good-looking man, no more than forty, smartly dressed in a light grey three-piece suit, with mid-blond hair expensively cut, and with a healthy glow to his cheeks. He was deeply engaged in 'chatting up' a woman who looked in her mid-forties, with black, shoulder-length hair, wearing a dark business suit and a purple silk Hermès scarf, who was giving him the cold shoulder. I saw her refuse his offer of a drink, at least. I presumed that he could not be my man and did a quick tour of the rest of the pub, scanning the tables for possible candidates. None.

111

I approached the bar and was about to order myself a drink, when the woman standing next to the grey suit spoke.

'Mr York, I presume. I'm Lesley Bradshaw.'

'Oh! I'm sorry. I was expecting . . . someone older, a retired police officer.'

'That's what I am, Mr York.'

'I must say you look well on it.'

'That'll be the swimming. For the shoulder problem.'

Between mouthfuls of my steak pie and chips and a pint of ale – Ms Bradshaw chose a salad and a fruit juice - I explained my commission. I wanted the private detective to locate all the members of George's immediate family. The investigation was to be entirely confidential, and under no circumstances was George, his wife or any of his family members to be approached, to know that the investigation was underway, or that I was behind it.

'So you don't want me to actually find any of these people. You just want me to find out where they are. Am I correct?'

'Yes, that's it.'

'Then this will be a purely paper exercise.'

'I suppose so.'

'Do you mind my asking why you want to know where all these people are? I assure you that I am very discreet. Unless of course you are intending to break the law.'

'For the moment, I prefer to keep my reasons to myself.'

She thought for a moment and then told me she was prepared to accept the commission. She detailed her charges, a daily rate plus expenses, asked me for George's date of birth, present address and number of siblings, and promised to come up with results within two weeks at the very latest.

The following day I dropped George at home after our Tuesday ramble. He was fishing his walking boots and backpack out of the boot, when Doris came to the car, opened the passenger door and climbed in beside me. My hand was resting on the gear lever, and she reached over and took it in hers.

'I had a good think while you and George were in Blackpool last weekend. You've been such a good friend to both of us, David, and I've been such a cow at times. It's because I love George so much and I want the best for him. I know you love him too and feel the same way. Thank you for all you've done for him, and for your wisdom and sound judgement. I don't know what I would have done without you when George went missing. I'm sorry. I've been taking your friendship for granted.'

'Please carry on taking it for granted,' I said, feeling the shame of betrayal colour my face, and hoping she mistook the blush for a sign of embarrassment at her compliment.

I was surprised to get a call from Ms Bradshaw as early as the following Saturday morning. Could I call round to her house before lunchtime? She had something for me. I was there in half an hour.

She lived in a stone-built detached house at Ranmoor, one of the more expensive areas of the city. Either the police had an enviable pension scheme, or her private detection business was thriving. She greeted me with a warm smile and showed me into her sitting room. Slipping into detective mode myself, I looked out for any sign of a Mr Bradshaw, large-sized shoes or wellington boots, jackets, hats. I found none. Lesley Bradshaw was wearing a rather more relaxed outfit of jeans and sweater and wore her hair in a pony-tail. The absence of a silk scarf revealed the incipient wrinkles around her neck and made her appear more vulnerable. She disappeared into the kitchen and reappeared five minutes later with a pot of coffee. An envelope file, labelled 'York', lay on the table waiting. She poured the coffee.

'Okay, let's get down to it. This is what I have. George Campbell has four sisters, or had, and one brother.'

'Four?'

'Yes. Let me go through them. George is the eldest sibling, then comes Nancy, born May 1967. Nancy died on her 23rd birthday. She threw herself from a railway bridge in front of an express train. Were you aware of that?'

'No, but somehow I'm not surprised.'

'Why is that, Mr York?'

'Oh, no particular reason. It seemed a problem family, that's all.'

'You didn't know her personally?'

113

'Not especially. No, not at all. She was a pupil at my school.'

Bradshaw frowned.

'Next is Ryan, George's brother, 43 years old, born January 1969. He has been tricky to track down. The last news I can find of him is that he was working on a farm in Devon eleven years ago. I have no address for him. I do have a photograph of him from police files, but only from the time he was cautioned for nicking a motor-scooter at the age of fifteen, in 1984. He has no further police record, and strictly speaking that file should have been destroyed.'

She passed me two grainy police mug-shots, one full face, one in profile, of a scruffy youth with dark hair. I could feel her eyes on me, as I inspected the photographs, presumably watching for my reaction. There was none. The boy's face meant nothing to me. He was like so many other teenagers I had come across. I shook my head. Bradshaw continued.

'You're familiar with portrait enhancement software? Removes all the blemishes and makes you look younger? Well, I've found it's also excellent for simulating how a person will look in ten or twenty years' time, which could be useful. Ryan was married by the way, to Natalie Smith, by a registrar in Crediton, Devon, ten years ago, and has two children, a boy and a girl.'

'That's good work, Ms Bradshaw – Lesley. May I call you Lesley?'

She nodded.

'Les, if you don't mind.'

'Do you think we could find Ryan? If we need to.'

'If he's still in the Crediton area, which he may be, as he seems to be in a stable relationship, then there's a good chance. Is he the one you're looking for? Or shall I carry on?'

'Go on,' I said.

'Sister number two, born April 1971, is Dana, aged 41. Dana is in a mental institution – a locked ward in the Northern General Hospital – and has been for most of her adult life. She's easy to find, but it depends exactly what you want from her.'

She took my silence as a cue to continue.

'Sister number three is Tess, born November 1975, not quite 38 years old. Tess moved to live with her grandmother in Lincoln in 1981, at the age of five, is married to Andrew Tyler, a schoolteacher, and has two boys aged ten and twelve. She lives in Spilsby, in Lincolnshire.

'Sister number four, Carly, born July 1981, is 31 years old. She has a daughter, Catherine, born July 1995, now aged seventeen. Social services in the London borough of Lambeth picked up Carly and her daughter in June 1998, but there is no trace of them after August 1999. I have no idea where they are now.'

'Carly must be the one I had not accounted for. Wait a minute! A daughter aged seventeen? Are you telling me she had a child at fourteen?'

'Fourteen years and one week, to be precise.'

'And the father?'

'Not registered on the birth certificate.'

'Poor kid.'

'She's not the first, and won't be the last. Shall I go on?"

I nodded, although in all my years as a teacher I had never come across a pregnancy in a girl that young. Ms Bradshaw continued.

'George's mother, born Marie Elizabeth Davies in March 1950, disappeared from her Sheffield address in Khartoum Street in August 1998. I can find no subsequent trace of her whatsoever. If she is alive, she is now 62 years old. And of course you know all about his father, Stuart Ian Campbell, born June 1944, died May 1998. You didn't think I wouldn't find out, did you?'

I squirmed a little and shook my head.

'I should have said something. That was pretty stupid of me.'

'Of course, I know quite a lot about George Campbell, too. I was not an investigating officer on his case, but I was on the force at the time. The lads talked about the Campbell murder for years after. Still do, I think. Frankly, I am surprised to find that he's been released so soon. And I hope you don't mind, I know quite a lot about you also, Mr York. That was pretty easy. You seem to have led a blameless life, though, not quite in the same league as your friend George.'

115

I muttered that I didn't mind. Of course she had to know something about me. I tried to digest all the information she had presented to me. I seemed to have lost my capacity to think clearly. I sat there for some time in silence.

'Are you going to come clean, Mr York? About your motives for this investigation, I mean. I can't go any further with this without knowing what you're looking for, what exactly you want to find out. You're going to have to trust me.'

My head was in a whirl. I picked up the papers that Bradshaw had laid back on the coffee table and tried to sort out a way forward. It might possibly be of value to locate Ryan, if only to find out why he had run away from home at fifteen, but he had not been in Sheffield at the time of the murder. Tess, the sister in Spilsby, was a most unlikely source of information, having left Sheffield and the family home at the age of five. I could try Dana, who at least had the virtue of being easy to contact. But what sort of mental state would I find her in? Perhaps her medical history would cast some light on what had driven George to such extreme violence. If we could find George's mother, she surely would be in a position to help, if only she were willing. The same could be said for Carly, but again we had no idea where she was. Had she been in Sheffield at the time of the murder? There was no mention of her at the trial. All we knew was that she turned up in London a couple of months later, and we had no idea when she had arrived in the capital.

I put the papers back in the file, closed the envelope and replaced it on the table. I looked at Bradshaw, leaning back in her armchair, relaxed but alert, a hint of a smile at the corners of her mouth. She had a face to trust. I could imagine criminals confessing all to Les Bradshaw and signing their statement believing she had done them a favour.

'Les,' I said, 'I am impressed by what you've done in such a short time. I should like you to take this further.'

She looked at her watch.

'I have two hours before I collect my daughter from the station. Take your time, Mr York.'

I told her the full story, from the first moment I had met George Campbell in 1978.

She listened intently without question or interruption to the whole of my account, her eyes never wavering from my face, as I meandered through George's story, stumbling over details of dates and times, repeating myself, backtracking, at times wandering down irrelevant blind alleys.

As I finished, I checked my watch for the first time. Ten minutes of the two hours remained. Bradshaw thanked me and laid out her plan for the next stage of her investigation. She had considered whether my visiting Dana at the Northern General, as a friend of the family, was of value, but had decided that it would be unethical. We should leave that area of investigation to the professionals. I should inform Paul Morgan immediately about Dana and leave the next step to him. It would be a waste of effort to look up Tess, in Spilsby, given that she had left the family home at the age of five and probably would have little or no recall of her early life. Our first task should be a trip to Devon, together, to track down Ryan. Meanwhile, she would 'spend some brownie points' by calling in a favour owed her by a former sergeant colleague, Jan Summerfield, at South Yorkshire Police headquarters in West Bar, to help us trace George's mother and his missing sister, Carly.

I realised that in the short period I had known Lesley Bradshaw she had gained my complete confidence. I was putty in her hands. I agreed with all her conclusions and fell in without hesitation with her plan to drive from Sheffield to Crediton on the following Monday afternoon. I left her house, excited and energised, clutching the file she had built up on George's family, and drove straight home to telephone Paul Morgan.

117

XI

PATZER

(German: bungler . A weak chess player.)

We drove the 250 miles to Devon in my car. Bradshaw
reckoned the Jaguar would be far more comfortable than
her VW Golf, and I would save money by not having to pay
her 40 pence per mile. We shared the driving; in fact
Bradshaw drove most of the way, whilst I sat back and
watched the miles fly by.

Crediton, home of some 7,000 souls and the birthplace
of St Boniface, lies seven miles to the north-west of Exeter
on the main trunk road to Barnstaple and North Devon, a
sleepy town nestled in the vale of the River Creedy. Once
famous for its woollen industry, it now relies for its main
source of employment on the manufacture of
confectionery. Whether this was responsible for the
uniformly chubby, ruddy-faced appearance of a group of
schoolboys kicking a ball around on Parliament Square,
when we arrived at our destination, *The Three Little Pigs,* is
open to question. We settled into our rooms, and I
suggested a stroll around the town to stretch our legs after
the long drive. I had read that the railway station at
Crediton had been designed by Isambard Kingdom Brunel

118

and was anxious to visit this architectural treasure, even in the dark of that November evening. Les Bradshaw turned down the offer to join me in favour of a 'G and T and a chat with the landlord'.

I made the pilgrimage alone and was disappointed. The station is a very modest affair, and even its award-winning Tea Rooms were closed at that hour. The goods yard, once famous for sending three milk trains per day from Devon to London, was also closed, in this case since 1967. In its favour, however, the station remains well used, and there is an hourly service to both Barnstaple and Exeter and thence to the rest of the outside world.

I returned to *The Three Little Pigs* to be greeted by the sight of a smiling Les Bradshaw and the landlord in fits of laughter. Whatever my woman had said had clearly tickled mine host. I joined her at the bar, where she declined my offer to buy her a refill. The landlord disappeared behind the bar, still chuckling.

'What was that all about?'

'Oh, just an old CID story. Always a winner. How was the railway station?'

'Don't ask. Are we on for dinner here?'

'I ordered one steak and one salmon. They are fresh out of turkey dinners. You can choose. I had to order, as the kitchen was about to close for the evening.'

I chose the steak. I had a feeling that Ms Bradshaw's healthy eating habits would favour the salmon. Judging by her body language, I had made the right choice.

'Do you want to know the good news?'

'No, I prefer bad news. Of course I want to hear the good news! What is it?'

'This was a good choice of B&B. The landlord remembers Ryan Campbell. He did the catering for their wedding reception. Even better, he's sure he still has the contact address and telephone number.'

'Les, you're a genius!'

I resisted slapping her on the back and shook her hand firmly instead. The landlord returned and handed over a slip of paper with a telephone number written on it in pencil.

'There's a pay-phone in the corner, if you need it.'

Bradshaw thanked him and tapped her mobile phone, indicating to me that she was going outside to try the number. She was back in five minutes, looking considerably less happy.

'It's the telephone number of a farm about ten miles from here, where Ryan used to work at the time. The farmer says that he and his wife lived for a while on the premises in a caravan, but that the job had only been temporary. He has no idea where Ryan Campbell is now.'

I cursed our luck. The disappointment was worse for having had my hopes built up so quickly. Optimism is a cruel mistress. I had lost my appetite and did not do justice to the rump steak provided by *The Three Little Pigs'* excellent chef.

'It's not all bad,' Bradshaw comforted me, over her ice-cream dessert. 'Devon is a big county. At least we now have a starting point. We'll go there tomorrow and sniff around, mention Ryan's and Natalie's names, show people the mock-up photos, leave some in the post office window, or the village shop, and local pubs. We may get a bite. And on Wednesday it's the livestock auction in Exeter. We can ask around there too.'

'If we don't find him that way we can always search for his wife's parents, can't we?'

'Mr and Mrs Smith? Good idea, David.'

I decided it might be better to keep my ideas to myself in future, or at least to think them through a little before I aired them, but I slept better for being reassured that Les Bradshaw knew exactly what she was doing. I contemplated how I might have tackled the search for Ryan Campbell myself, realised that I would have been totally clueless and that my private eye could well turn out to be worth every penny she would cost me.

We spent the following day, Tuesday, in Tiverton and the surrounding villages, carrying out Bradshaw's plan to distribute the leaflets and computer-aged photos that she had printed, leaving them in shop windows and pubs. We must have spoken to hundreds of people between us, but only four individuals had even the slightest recollection of meeting him. No one knew where he was now. I found the endless tramping from place to place more exhausting than I could ever have imagined. By the evening I was on my last legs, whilst Bradshaw, still spruce in her smartly pressed suit, looked as fresh as a daisy. I told her I would have to call it a day, and we returned to Crediton and the haven of *The Three Little Pigs*.

On the way back, Bradshaw admitted that she was fairly sure that we were barking up the wrong tree in the Tiverton area and was not very sanguine that our leafleting would bear fruit.

'Let's see what tomorrow brings,' she said, even she sounding a little less optimistic than twenty-four hours previously.

We arrived at Exeter livestock market after ten o'clock on the Wednesday morning, and the auction was already in full swing. It was my first experience of a livestock auction, and I confess I found it bewildering, even distressing. It seems I am not cut out for country life. The rank smells of farm animals and their excrement clung to the linings of my nose and throat; the sudden impact of the body heat from the animals and the packed throng of farmers in the covered auction ring brought me almost to the point of vomiting; half an hour of the incomprehensible, non-stop jabber of the auctioneer blaring through the loudspeakers in response to the imperceptible nods and winks of his clients rendered me almost brain-dead and incapable of carrying out my assistant detective role. No one was interested in my mock-up picture of Ryan Campbell or in the mention of his name. The fullest answer I received was 'never seen him in my life'. Most of the uniformly attired, capped, tweed-jacketed, wellington-booted clientele were too absorbed in the proceedings to grace me with more than a glance or a grunt.

I was relieved to see Les Bradshaw waving to me from the opposite side of the surly hemisphere of farmers. I made my way over to her.

'Any luck?' she said to me, out of politeness I assume, as the look on my face must have told its own story. I shook my head.

'Not surprising,' she consoled me. They're all too busy to talk to a couple of outsiders. Perhaps we'll catch one or two of them in the pub later. These two old-timers, though,' she continued, nodding towards two ancient characters leaning against the front rail, each sucking on an unlit pipe, 'I bet they've been coming here for donkey's years; I bet they know everybody in the county.'

She motioned me to come with her. I followed her down to the front and stood for twenty minutes silently watching a consummate professional at work. First of all she engaged one of the old men in small talk, saying that she would wager that the pair of them had been coming here for a year or two, that they had seen some changes, not all of them for the better, told them that her grandfather and great-grandfather had been farmers in East Devon, near Chard, and had been driven out of the dairy business by the low prices and the drought of '76. This set the two of them off on a trail of reminiscence about past droughts and other scourges of the farming community, which I could only half follow because of the strong Devonshire dialect, and during which the detective merely listened, contributing the odd sympathetic nod or murmur. When she finally introduced the question of Ryan Campbell, the three were already old friends.

Nevertheless, Bradshaw's question was greeted with some suspicion.

'So you're vrim the police then?'

'Private investigator,' said Bradshaw producing her business card.

'Like what us zees on the television then?' said old-timer number one, impressed, screwing up his eyes to scrutinise the card before passing it to his friend. 'Is this feller Ryan in trouble then?'

Bradshaw assured him that Ryan was in no kind of trouble. It was a client of hers trying to trace a long lost relative.

'There b'aint many Ryans around these parts,' muttered old-timer number two, holding the photograph that the detective had handed over. 'I only know of one, but ee's nort like this chap yur.'

'Arry Burrows's Ryan? Is ee Campbell, then,' said his friend. 'B'aint zactly the daps of ee, be it?'

'Tis nort like eem at all. Don't think 'tis Campbell anyway. Cack-handed lad?'

Number Two nodded.

'That's Arry Burrows's Ryan. Arry reckons ee's a vitty pigman. A dab hand, ee reckons. Worth ees weight in gold.'

'B'aint ee married to that maid vrim Hookway?'

'Right enough. A comely bowerly woman. What was her name?'

Number Two shook his head.

'Not ee though. Picture don't look nort like eem at all.'

Bradshaw thanked them, asked for directions to Harry Burrows's farm, just in case, and flashed me a wink and a broad grin. The old-timers agreed that it was between Broadclyst and Ashclyst Forest, and then embarked on an argument in almost unintelligible dialect about the best way to get there. I worked out that Number One favoured the Honiton Road and a left turn at the airport, whilst Number Two argued a strong case for driving straight through Whipton and Pinhoe on the B something or other which would take us straight to Broadclyst. We left the argument about the best route to Broadclyst unsettled, and the two agreed that we must then take the North Road out of Broadclyst, we might or might not see a sign on the right for Burrows's farm, as it was merely a farm track and not a made up road. Number One added that if we got to Rattlecot, we would have gone too far, should turn around and go back down to Moor Lane, which would now be on our right, turn back on ourselves until we reached the *Coach House Farm*, which was a hotel, and where they would be sure to give us directions. Number Two disagreed:

'They posh 'otels b'aint vur me, I don't trust 'em one little bit. I won't go aneest en!'

'I hope you got all that,' said Bradshaw to me, including me for the first time in the conversation. 'I shall be relying on you for directions.'

'Your kin, this Ryan feller?' asked Number Two.

It was easier to agree. We said goodbye and I shook the horny hands of our informants.

'Doesn't say much for the portrait software,' said Bradshaw, when we were back out in the clammy but reviving November air, 'but I'm confident this is our man. Hookway is in Crediton, near as dammit, where they got married.'

I almost hugged her.

'All that stuff about your grandfather and great-grandfather – was that true?'

Bradshaw laughed: 'Does it really matter, David? It worked, didn't it?'

I drove back to Crediton and we checked out of *The Three Little Pigs*. We were going north, and Bradshaw had decided there was no sense in driving back again. Our business in South Devon was done. Over our sandwich lunch she borrowed the landlord's telephone directory, and I dialled the number for Burrows' Farm. I had felt like a clueless amateur at the livestock auction and wanted to do my bit. A woman answered. I asked to speak to Ryan Campbell.

'Speak up a bit. You're crackly. Ryan, you say?'

'Yes, please. I thought lunchtime would be a good time to catch him,' I almost shouted down the phone.

'That's better now. No, ee's out with Arry, tining the shords. Back before dark, though.'

'Does he have a mobile?'

'Arry makes en switch en off.'

'Will you tell him I'll drop by and see him around five?'

'What's it about? What shall I tell Ryan?'

'It's about his brother.'

'Didn't knaw ee had any brother. Right 'nough, my lover. Five o'clock, then.'

Mrs Burrows, as I presumed she was, ended our conversation. Bradshaw looked at me and swallowed her mouthful of beef sandwich.

'Five o'clock it is, then. I presume Ryan wasn't there waiting impatiently for your call.'

'No, he's out tining the shords with Harry.'

'You don't say. I wonder who's looking after the pigs.'

XII

EN PASSANT

(French: in the act of passing. The rule that allows a pawn that advances two squares to be captured on the next move by a pawn on the same rank and adjacent file.)

My satnav took us back down the Exeter Road and then through Pinhoe, which I am sure would have delighted Number Two. We had left plenty of time for the short drive and arrived almost half an hour early, having put the suspension of the Jaguar through a severe test on the half-mile long farm track, which I feared would never end. Mrs Burrows told us that Ryan was feeding the pigs. We thanked her and, leaving behind what illumination there was from the farmhouse window, we followed the smell towards a large barn and the single outside bulb above its doorway. A balding man, probably in his early forties, emerged at that moment from the barn, where, from the grunts, squeals and sounds of animals squabbling over food issuing from that direction, the pigs were housed.

I had insisted, against Bradshaw's advice, that I do the talking this time.

'Is it Ryan?' I asked.

The man peered through the darkness towards us.

'Yes, that's right. Are you police?'

I detected a northern accent, but more West Yorkshire than Sheffield. Bradshaw cut in.

'I'm a private investigator, but David here's a friend of your brother.'

'Peter in trouble again?'

'Peter?' I said. 'I didn't know you had a brother called Peter.'

This was a surprise, a family member we had not discovered.

'Well, he's my stepbrother as a matter of fact. I thought she said you're a friend of Peter's.'

'We're talking about George,' said Bradshaw, seeing the look on my face.

Ryan sniffed, took off his right work-glove and rubbed his hand slowly across his nose.

'I have no brother called George.'

'I take it, then, that you are not Ryan Campbell.'

A buxom, fair-haired woman in working overalls and a headscarf appeared suddenly out of the gloom on our left. Number One's description of her as a 'comely bowerly woman' was apt.

'What's happening, Ryan? Who are you?'

'It's okay, Sarah. A mistake, I think. I'm Ryan Lowe. You've got the wrong man.'

We apologised and withdrew from Burrows' Farm in a far less ebullient frame of mind than when we had arrived.

Bradshaw and I held a brief and rather sullen conference before deciding to continue north and head back to Sheffield. I felt the trip had been a complete waste of time. Bradshaw tried to put an optimistic gloss on our efforts; we had covered a lot of ground, left a very important paper trail and in effect done the very best we could in the circumstances.

I am afraid that I sulked like a thwarted teenager, so great was my disappointment at our failure to find Ryan Campbell. I took the wheel and drove the Jaguar far more quickly up the M5 than was good for our safety. I calmed down eventually, and when I saw signs for the Bristol exit, the idea occurred to me to call in on Michael and Claire, who I knew lived in Henbury, a couple of miles from junction 17, the exit for North Bristol. At least I might get something out of the trip after all. I told the detective of my intentions, and she had no objection, as long as I dropped her off at a service station or pub, where she could reply to some of the phone messages that had been filling her voicemail box over the past three days.

The Henbury address led me to the front door of a substantial, ivy-clad, detached house, which stood thirty or forty yards back from the road. I arrived at exactly six o'clock and rang the bell. After a few seconds, unsure whether the bell was working, I rang it again and then knocked loudly. Somewhere in a distant part of the house, I heard Michael's voice.

'Okay! I'm coming! Hold your horses!'

He opened the door, and his mouth fell open on seeing me.

'You! What's happened?'

'I was passing. So I thought . . . Aren't you going to invite me in?'

'Claire's not here. There's only me. What are you doing here? Why didn't you phone?'

Eventually he stood aside to let me come in and led me into an airy, high-ceilinged sitting-room, of even more generous proportions than my own. In the hallway I passed an ancient umbrella stand and a grandfather clock. He had some gall accusing me of living in the lap of luxury, I thought. I explained my abortive mission to find George's brother and why I wanted to find him.

'Private detective? My God, Dad! You're not half spending some energy on this George chap! You seem to devote half your life to him!'

I had no answer to his implied criticism. It was too complicated to explain my ancient guilt, my quest for atonement, to justify my fervour for helping George to regain some vestige of the normal life to which we are all entitled.

Thankfully I managed to change the subject, to ask Michael about his work, about Claire and her teenaged son. His answers were laconic at best, but this was the longest conversation the two of us had had for many years. After an hour or so, I explained that, reluctantly, I had to leave to pick up Les Bradshaw, who was waiting for me at *The Old Crow*. He followed me into the hallway. I stood grasping the door knob, uncertain whether to shake his hand, or hug him, or neither. He looked down at his feet.

'It's been on my mind to, to say I'm . . . to apologise, for that business last Christmas.'

I blinked in surprise, not least at the way he had skipped back eleven months, neatly side-stepping our almighty row the week after his mother's funeral.

'It's in the past, Michael. Let's leave it.'

'No. I'm embarrassed at how I treated your friends. And you. Claire and I nearly broke up over it, you know.'

I didn't know what to say. The silence was emphasised by the ticking of the grandfather clock.

'You mustn't let that happen. I really think you've found someone special there.'

'It's just that I'm so angry, Dad. I'm angry with the government, I'm angry with the way underprivileged people are treated in our country, the way disabled people have had their living allowance stolen, I'm angry that our health service is being dismantled, and I'm angry with the Lib Dems, those third-rate, self-seeking, unprincipled nobodies that sniffed a bit of power and dropped all their so-called principles. I voted for those weasels! I'm angry for all those kids, out of work and no future, while those arrogant Etonian cabinet ministers tell us we're all in it together! I'm angry with the Americans, with Tony Blair, I'm angry with men that use religion for spreading all that hatred, I'm angry with those gangs of animals that groom teenage girls and abuse them, I'm angry with myself, with everything, all the time. And, I can't help it, I'm angry with you.'

'Can you tell me why?'

'Just for being you, Dad. Just for being you.'

I would have hugged him, but he turned away.

'I'm sorry, Dad. I can't help it.'

I said goodbye and closed the door behind me.

I opened the door to the lounge bar of *The Old Crow* and looked around. Les was sitting in a corner under the window. She looked up from her newspaper, picked up her handbag and walked over to greet me. I was conscious of the envious glances from the men standing at the bar. She did not have to ask how my meeting with my son had gone. She suggested that she drive the rest of the way home, and I did not refuse her offer.

It was well after ten when we landed at Ranmoor. We both got out of the car, and I thanked her for her hard work. She acknowledged my thanks with a nod, and we stood there for a moment in silence, under the relentless November drizzle.

She smiled.

'Don't worry, David. We'll get there. I promise.'

I said goodnight. A handshake did not seem appropriate. I think I had fallen the tiniest bit in love with her.

There's no fool like an old fool.

•

The man looks at his watch, sees that it is after eight and groans a little, as he climbs out of the car in the driveway. He unlocks the front door, drops the heavy briefcase on the hall table and calls out the woman's name. She does not reply. She is in the kitchen, looking through the window out into the back garden. He does not notice the iced cake with eleven candles, as yet unlit. He joins her. She is watching the boy. The boy is some 50 yards away, facing them, practising his cricket shots in the gloaming. He is wearing pristine cricket flannels, snow-white cricket pads, top quality Adidas spiked boots and brand-new batsman's gloves, along with his school cap and, incongruously, his school tie. He has marked out a cricket pitch on the extensive, closely mown lawn. An open can of emulsion paint, a brush, and a measuring tape, all lying close by, are evidence of his work. Six gleaming new cricket stumps are perfectly positioned, three at each end of the 22-yard strip of grass that he has mown cruelly short. Four gleaming new bails sit ready on top of the two sets of stumps. By the side of the nearer set of stumps lies a shiny Duke's cricket ball, a 'new cherry, the ones they use in Test matches'. The boy swishes his brand new Gray Nicholls bat, made of the finest English willow, especially expansively, if inelegantly, striking an imaginary ball out of an imaginary Lord's cricket ground. The woman looks questioningly at the man, who consults his watch once more and shakes his head. Too late, he says. Too late.

XIII

CAÏSSA WAS WITH ME

(Caïssa: the goddess of chess, dispenser of good fortune.)

The following morning I heard a clatter at the front door. I investigated. Tuppence was dragging himself in through the cat-flap. He limped along the hallway on three legs and flopped at my feet. He was in a very sorry state. He had two deep gashes, on his nose and forehead, and had lost several chunks of fur. He opened his mouth soundlessly, and I noticed a bleeding gap in his upper gum where the long canine tooth should have been. Both his front paws were badly damaged and weeping blood. He had lost at least one claw.

I bent down and picked him up very gently and very gingerly. The only time Tuppence allows me to touch him is when he is injured. At other times he guards his personal space jealously and is not above lashing out at any unsuspecting adult who attempts to pet him. With small children he is more tolerant and merely makes himself scarce.

I bathed his wounds with cotton wool and warm water, dabbing gently at the scratches, cuts and areas where fur had been torn out. His left rear leg was especially sensitive

131

to my touch. Inside the house, Tuppence is as silent as a Komodo dragon and has never spoken to me since the day he arrived, although I have no doubt he howls with the best of them when he is out on the tiles. Today he uttered tiny mews of pain whenever I touched sensitive areas. It was the first time I had heard him make a sound of any kind. I talked to him quietly, as I worked my way round his battered body.

'You look as though you've done fifteen rounds with the number one contender, Champ. How did it go? Looks to me like you lost your title this time.'

Tuppence was noncommittal.

'I've been your cut man for over six years now, Champ. It looks like this was one title bout too many. It happens to them all in the end. Time to call it a day, I think. This time I can't patch you up. It's the hospital for you, my friend.'

He looked me in the eye. I should mind my own business. I was just a cut man.

The vet was a hard woman. She stitched up his wounds and encased his broken back leg in a light plaster cast. She looked at me accusingly.

'This is a very old cat. What on earth are you doing letting him out at night? In future please keep him indoors.'

Perhaps she was too young to empathise with the plight of a proud old prize-fighter who had taken on one challenge too many.

Back from the vet's, I covered Tuppence's favourite recliner with an old sheet, to protect the fabric from bloodstains, and sat him in the chair as comfortably as I could, next to him a litter-tray that I had bought from the vet. He began immediately to claw and bite at the sheet with his good back paw and remaining teeth, trying desperately to drag it from the chair. There was nothing for it, the sheet would have to go, and the upholstery would have to suffer.

I called Paul Morgan that afternoon. He had spoken to a consultant at the Northern General Hospital about Dana Campbell. Her mental illness was attributed largely to some unspecified abuse suffered during her childhood, but the consultant was unwilling for Morgan to probe any further into Dana's history, for the time being at least, as carefully balanced medication had induced an unprecedented level of stability in his patient. This was disappointing news, if not unexpected.

I resisted calling Les Bradshaw, impatient though I was to discover the outcome of attempts by her police contacts to trace George's mother or his sister, Carly. That evening I telephoned Doris to ask how George was, as I had not seen him for over a week. She seemed very pleased with his progress since the Chapel-en-le-Frith incident. He seemed more relaxed and was attempting to form words. She was considering whether to enlist the support of a professional speech therapist. I agreed that this seemed to be an excellent way forward. I explained to her about Tuppence's injuries, and that I was housebound for the next few days at least, but that she and George were welcome to come to me.

I did not mention my trip to Devon.

At five o'clock the following afternoon, Friday, the last day of November, Les phoned me to report back on the search for George's relatives. Her contacts had so far drawn a blank on the search for his mother, who seemed to have disappeared from the face of the earth. There was no trace of her on the record of any local authority in the United Kingdom, nor had her death been registered in the fifteen years since she had left Khartoum Street. It seemed she may have deliberately disappeared, which Les assured me was not difficult. Neither of us ruled out the possibility of her living somewhere else in the European Union, but from what we knew of her this seemed unlikely.

'What about Carly?' I asked, rather tentatively, by now not expecting Les to have made any further discovery.

There was a slight intake of breath on the other end of the line, a sigh perhaps.

'The good news is that we found a flight list with the names of a Miss Carly Campbell and a Miss Catherine Campbell, Carly and her daughter – the passport numbers match up. They left on a Qantas flight from Heathrow to Melbourne on August 17, 1999.'

'Australia! How on earth did she afford to do that? Was it a single ticket?'

'No, they had return tickets all right, but the bad news is that they weren't on the flight back three weeks later.'

'So, for all we know she's still in Australia.'

'I would think that's pretty likely. I spoke to a charming young man named Ranjit at the Australian Department of Immigration and Citizenship. His computer said no, our Carly Campbell was not on his list of legal immigrants. He would look into her further. The wheels of bureaucracy grind slowly, but he promised faithfully to get back to me by the end of next week.'

I was on the point of suggesting that Les and I meet to discuss the way forward, although I am not certain that this was my real reason for wanting to see her, when she told me that she would not be in Sheffield again until the end of the following week, as she had taken on another assignment. She would report back any further news then. It was a sharp reminder that, although I had been the centre of her life for three days, I was just another client for Lesley Bradshaw, private eye.

That night, from my bedroom, I heard the sound of a disturbance downstairs. I picked up my old tennis racket from the top of the wardrobe – what I intended to do with it, I have no idea – and crept as stealthily as I could down the stairs, avoiding the creaking tread halfway down. It was not an intruder. I found Tuppence with half his body through the cat-flap, thrusting feebly and futilely with his good leg. I eased him gently back inside. He did not resist. Once I had settled him in the recliner, I took out my electric drill and screwed the cat-flap shut. I went back to bed and, ridiculously, pathetically, I wept.

The following Tuesday George came to visit. I still did not feel able to leave Tuppence unattended, and so we stayed around the house for the whole day. George helped me tidy up some of the mess in my neglected garden, and after lunch we played a hopelessly one-sided game of chess. It cannot have been very satisfying for George, as my level of concentration was low, my mind very much on other matters.

After our game, I made coffee and we kept Tuppence company in the sitting room. I sat on the end of the sofa, with George close by at right angles to me in an armchair, the coffee table between us.

'George,' I began, and waited for him to turn his head and look me in the eye. 'Those two missing days, when the police found you in Winnats Pass, where had you been? What were you doing? Can you write something down for me? I'm really curious. No, not just curious. I think it might be important.'

George treated me to his newly acquired smile – not yet an authentic smile, more of a twitch, with the right side of his upper lip rising slightly and forming a crease in his cheek – and reached over to me, placing his hand on my forearm. He was trying to reassure me, but the message was not clear. Was he telling me that all was well, or that it was better that I didn't know?

'Have you told Doris?'

His answer was an almost imperceptible shake of the head.

'Did she ask you?'

This time I could not have sworn that George gave any response whatsoever, but I was convinced that the answer was again 'no'. Surely Doris must have wanted to know? How could she not have asked the question? Perhaps she was doing what we all do at some time or other in a marriage or other relationship. We sidestep the danger of hearing an answer we shall not like, of finding out what we do not want to hear.

On the Friday evening Les Bradshaw, returned from wherever her new assignment had taken her, called me as promised to report back on the information received from the Australian authorities. Her man Ranjit had called her back, in the middle of the night, Les told me rather sourly. Carly and Catherine Campbell had indeed arrived in Melbourne, Victoria in August 1999, and had stayed for a week in a youth hostel in the state capital, but the Australian immigration authorities regretted that they could now find no trace of them. There was no record of either on any public census. Ranjit's rather matter-of-fact justification of this administrative lapse was that Australia was an enormous country, where people sometimes simply disappeared. Frankly, illegal immigration of this nature was rife. Foreigners arrived as tourists or students and stayed on, disappeared into the shadows in the cities, or into the outback. Carly and Catherine Campbell were simply lost.

I had hit a brick wall. I agreed with Les Bradshaw that there was nothing further to be done and decided reluctantly to abandon my search for George's family. At this rate, all it would bring me was an ulcer or a heart attack, and even if I were successful I should get no thanks from Doris or George. I thanked Les for her diligence and professionalism, and immediately telephoned the clinic in Waltham Forest, where I left a message for Paul Morgan, explaining my decision.

It was by pure chance that I saw the article. That evening I had no enthusiasm for cooking and decided on a Chinese takeaway. I stood waiting for my order in the shop, along with two other customers. On the window-sill, lying on top of an untidy pile of back copies of *Hello* magazine and *Woman's Weekly*, was a copy of the local evening newspaper, *The Star*. I was disappointed to find it was from the previous day, and after a quick glance at the sports section, I flicked idly through the rest of the paper, from back to front. A familiar photograph, on page five, drew my attention. It was of the block of flats where an aunt had lived for many years. I read the accompanying news item.

GLEADLESS VALLEY PENSIONER

LAY DEAD FOR WEEKS

A PENSIONER who had lived in the same high-rise tower block on the Gleadless Valley estate for ten years lay dead for several weeks before his body was discovered.

Cameron Campbell, 70, died alone at his home in Callow Green. No one appears to have missed him, and his body was only discovered when police broke open his door, after caretaker

Mary Knowles alerted them about the unpleasant smell coming from his one-bedroom flat.

Police officers found the flat secured by a Yale lock. There were no indications of a break-in or any other suspicious circumstances.

Neighbours described Mr Campbell as polite and a man of few words, but said they only knew him slightly.

Single mother of two Bernice Simmonite said: "He was always very nice to the children. He would always stop to say hello and stroke their hair and give them a sweetie, but I have only been here for a couple of years and I didn't know him very well. I realise now that we hadn't seen him for a while.'

A female tenant from a neighbouring block, who asked not to be named, said: "It's a disgrace that nobody missed him or checked up on him. They just let him die on his own, like an animal. Who knows what the poor man suffered? It's a horrible way to go. Shame on all his neighbours!"

Mr Campbell, who was a bachelor and lived alone, was discovered on November 30th. An inquest into his death was adjourned yesterday.

Could this be George's uncle? He was about the right age, and just how many Cameron Campbells would there be living in the city? I cursed myself for not having thought of trying to trace him. Well, now it was too late; he was dead, and in all probability the world was none the worse for that. I tore the column out of the newspaper with a view to showing it to George and Doris, shoved it into my jacket pocket and tossed the newspaper back onto the window-sill. My pessimism was short lived. Just before noon on the following day, Saturday, the telephone rang. A youthful female voice greeted me. I confirmed my number and asked who was calling.

'This is Natalie Campbell.'

I tried hard to hide my excitement. I took a deep breath.

'Oh! Mrs Campbell. How kind of you to get in touch!'

'Are you the gentleman who is looking for Ryan, Ryan Campbell, my husband? Only, there was no answer on the other number, and so I thought I'd try this one.'

She had clearly tried Les Bradshaw's mobile, without success. She went on, anxious to explain herself.

'I went into Tiverton to see a friend, and Ryan's face was staring at me, everywhere, like a 'Wanted' poster. It was quite a shock.'

It seemed that Les's portrait software did work after all.

'I'm anxious to contact your husband, on a matter concerning his brother, George.'

'I'm afraid I don't know George. I've never met him. What is it about? A will or something?'

'No, that's not it. Could you put your husband on the phone?'

'Ryan's not here. He's got a job as a long-distance lorry driver. He's just been doing casual jobs before, but we saved up so he could pay for his own training, and he's got a good job with a local firm. He's not in trouble, is he? I don't want him to lose this job. He's in Sheffield today. Visiting his sister in hospital.'

It seemed that my luck had changed. Natalie Campbell was delightfully, blessedly garrulous! She eventually gave me her husband's mobile number, and I contacted him and arranged to buy him lunch in *The Red Lion* in the city centre.

I recognised Ryan immediately. Apart from the two-day stubble, he was the spitting image of the enhanced photo on our leaflet. The pub was noisy and crowded with office workers celebrating the approach of the festive season with the special Christmas dinner on offer, and so it was comparatively easy to hold a private conversation, without being overheard, in a corner of the snug.

Ryan told me he had been to see his sister the previous evening and would go again later that afternoon.

'I always need to go twice, whenever I come to visit, which is only two or three times a year, living so far away. T' first time I go she just screams at me and calls me everything from a pig to a dog. When I go t' second time, she's always calmed down a bit. She's all apologies, and we get on okay for an hour or so. I feel my visit's been some use, brought her summat.'

I explained to Ryan why I was trying to contact him, for George's sake. Over a ploughman's lunch and a pint of *Absolution*, he poured out his life story to me. He regretted losing contact with his brother, even though George had turned 'a bit weird' after he'd gone on to secondary school. After all, he explained, George had always tried to look after him when they were little. He had only found out about the murder three or four years after the event ('Devon's on a different planet, you know!'), when he had managed to get in touch with Dana, and was surprised to hear that George was out of prison already. He had imagined that the life sentence meant life. He had often intended to visit George in prison, but had never quite got round to it. It was 'just too complicated'.

When I asked him about his father and life at home, he could not contain his anger, spluttering insults and foul oaths, the bread from his sandwich splattering my jacket. I reached over to put a restraining hand on his arm – we were attracting attention from the Christmas revellers. He left me in no doubt as to his hatred for his father and Uncle Cameron, and seemed to have only contempt for his mother.

'Were you abused?' I asked quietly, leaning across the table to him.

'They tried it on wi' me. Them two got me upstairs in t' attic. I were just a kid, twelve I think. My dad held me down, while Cameron got me to . . . I can't say it. It were horrible. I didn't know owt about things like that. I bit him. My God I bit him! I nearly bit t' damn thing off. He never tried it on again. Gen me a good beating, though, when he'd stop screaming.'

'And your father? What did he do?'

'Oh, he joined in t' beating, all right. He loved gi'ing kids a good hiding. Got off on it, I think. *He* had a go at me once an' all. Crept into our bed in t' attic, mine and George's. When I realised what he were doing, I poked him in t' eye wi' my thumb, scratched him and bit a piece of his nose off. I'll gi' you one guess how he punished me for that.'

'Yes, I can imagine. You went through the mill, all right.'

'No. I got off easy. They weren't really interested in me. I were too difficult. Anyway, they had George. But it were t' lasses they really were after, as soon as they showed any signs of growing up. I can't imagine what they did to them poor little devils. I cleared out as soon as I could nick enough money from my mum's purse and *his* wallet when he were drunk, enough to get me to London and survive for a day or two. I were fifteen and stroppy and I'd had a bellyful.'

'I'm sorry. Sorry I brought it all back. All those bad memories. They scar you.'

He shook his head, emphatic, and stuck out his chin.

'Bad memories, but no scars. I'm fine, just fine.'

'Are you?'

Ryan downed the rest of his pint and planted his glass firmly on the table.

'If there were ever owt to get o'er, I got o'er it a long time ago.'

I tried to meet his eye, but he looked resolutely past me into the distance.

'That don't mean I'm not damnwell mad about it.'

I went to the bar to buy him another pint. When I returned, he was calmer.

'Did you ever tell anyone what your father and uncle had done, about the sexual assaults, I mean?'

'I'd have been too embarrassed. I'd have been ashamed to tell anybody my dad were like that. Anyway, nobody would have believed me.'

I left an awkward silence, in the hope that he would fill it, a tactic I had often used as a teacher. He did not oblige.

'And what about the beatings? Did you tell anyone about that?'

'Same thing, really. No point. It were done. If I'd told a teacher, what would they have done about it? Nowt. Probably have said we must have deserved it. Some o' t' teachers used to threaten you wi' telling your dad if you didn't behave, because they knew you'd be frightened o' gerrin a good hiding.'

'Did you ever think of telling *me*? I would have listened to you, I hope.'

140

'I were scared o' you. You were t' headmaster. I don't think you ever spoke to me once, all t' time I were at Harry Brearley. Perhaps once, when you asked me how George were gerrin on.'

I thought of Rabbie Burns' poem *To a louse* – 'to see oursels as ithers see us!' It was too late now, and too late to apologise, but I did.

This time I was the one who leapt in to fill the awkward silence that followed my apology.

'Do you remember Carly?'

He smiled. At least I had revived one happy memory.

'Aye, I do. She were only a little un, a toddler, when I left, a lovely kid, dark curly hair, all smiles. I felt bad about leaving her wi' them pigs. But what could I do? I often wonder what happened to her. God knows how she come out of it. You know what state Dana's in - and my big sister Nancy did away wi' hersen.'

He pushed his plate away. His appetite had deserted him. It was clear that he did not know where Carly had ended up, as I had been hoping he might. I asked him if he remembered his little sister, Tess. He had a vague recollection of her going away somewhere, around the time when they had 'tried it on' with him.

'She were always a sickly kid. Summat up wi' her.'

He brightened up considerably when I told him I could pass on her address.

'Is she okay?'

'As far as I know.'

I took out my notebook and copied her address for him onto a beermat. He picked it up, looked at it as though it were a work of art, and shoved it in his pocket.

'My little sister. Wow!'

I gave him enough time. This was his cue to ask for George's address or telephone number. He did not.

As we left, I handed him the A5 sheet with George's contact details. It was the right thing to do, after all. He folded it and put it in his inside jacket pocket, without reading it. I urged him not to mention to his brother that he had met me, as I wanted it to remain a secret at all costs. I invented the excuse that I did not want George to feel indebted to me, that it was in the way of a good turn for an old friend. It was an unnecessary precaution. I

141

knew that he would not try to get in touch with his brother.

Outside, on the pavement, I thanked him for seeing me and apologised for bringing back all those horrible memories. He shook my hand again and thanked *me* for listening, and for believing him. His voice cracked, and I believe I saw a hint of a tear, but in the gathering gloom and the rain I could not be sure. Either he was an excellent actor, or this was the first time he had told anyone his story. I waited for him to release my hand, but he had not quite finished.

'I wish I'd had t' guts to do what George did. I take my hat off to him. That pig deserved all he got.'

Ryan Campbell had confirmed all my suspicions about George's childhood and family life. But what was it that had caused this young man, by all accounts respectable, calm and reserved, to suddenly return home out of the blue and attack his father with such ferocity, after years of living a model, if silent existence away from the family home? Had the rage bubbled and brewed inside him until he could contain it no longer?

I feared that I was no nearer to the reason why George had finally snapped and delivered the death sentence for his father's sins. Why not Ryan? He seemed a far likelier candidate to exact revenge on his father. I sympathised with Ryan's verdict on George's crime, but I believe that what I truly wanted was to uncover something which would absolve my friend totally from the sin of patricide, would wipe the slate clean.

XIV

EN PRISE

(French: in a position to be captured. Describes a piece left undefended and thus exposed to capture, often by a less valuable piece.)

Proud of my achievement of finding Ryan and keen to take all the credit for myself, I picked up the phone to tell Les Bradshaw about my meeting.

'I know,' she said. 'Why didn't you tell me? I could have come with you.'

'How did you . . . ?'

'I checked up on a missed call and spoke to Natalie Campbell, who told me about her call to you and gave me her husband's mobile number. He told me he'd already spoken to you in a pub.'

'I should have told you, shouldn't I?' My answer must have been scarcely audible.

'So, are you going to put me in the picture? I'll tell you what – I'm free this afternoon, so why don't you come over and we can discuss it. Or I could come to you.'

I looked at Tuppence. He glared back at me. I couldn't possibly leave him alone again for the rest of the afternoon. I looked around the room. It was almost a week since Suzi's last visit and the house was correspondingly in a mess and not fit for admitting visitors.

'I'll be round in an hour and a half,' I said.

Tuppence looked away in disgust. I placed him, under protest, in his brand-new basket and carried him out onto the patio for his first taste of fresh air in over a week. I put on an extra pullover, a heavy coat, a hat and scarf and sat next to him to keep him company. His frustration at seeing the few remaining garden birds pecking at the nuts, seeds and scraps of fat that I had put out for them was palpable. It was as if the birds recognised his incapacity and were taunting him, mocking him, and avenging themselves for all the terror that he had wrought on them and their comrades. It was torture for the old tomcat. After half an hour I could bear it no longer and took him back indoors.

If I had expected Les to be cross with me for not keeping her in the loop, I was mistaken. She greeted me with a warm smile, congratulated me on my initiative and urged me to report back in full. I assured her that the credit was all hers; after all, it was her idea of distributing the leaflets which had borne fruit in the end.

I put her fully in the picture about Ryan.

'All this confirms what you thought about George's childhood. Is that enough for you, or do you need more? We have no mother and no Carly, and so those two avenues are blocked. What about this Uncle Cameron? He seems a key figure. Had you come across him before?'

I confessed that I had heard of Uncle Cameron during my time at Harry Brearley in the late seventies, but had forgotten about him.

'A pity. It might have been a good lead. We should go for him now, though. He may even still be in the area.'

Feeling a little like a naughty schoolboy who had not handed in his homework, I told her about the news item in *The Star* reporting the discovery of Cameron's body.

'And you didn't think to tell me about this before? David, you're expecting me to work with one hand tied behind my back! I need to know everything, however trivial

144

you think it is. Is there anything else you've not told me about your Mr Campbell and family?'

I considered owning up about George's recent disappearing act, but decided to treat her question as rhetorical. She sat grim-faced for a while. It was wise to remain silent. I was in enough hot water already.

'Well, that's another trail cut off,' she muttered finally.

Her sulk had made me feel angry, with her and with myself. Anger tends to bring out my little-used assertive side. On the drive over to Ranmoor, I had more or less decided to go to Spilsby to seek out Tess Campbell. I told her so. She nodded.

'It's a long shot, but our only chance is that she's kept in touch with her mother. You never know.'

She opened the file marked 'York', picked up her telephone and dialled a number. She was speaking to directory enquiries. She shook her head.

'No joy. The Tylers are ex-directory. I could find out the number, but it would mean calling in another favour, which I'm reluctant to do. In any case, a visit is always better than a phone call. It's easier for someone to fob you off on the telephone.'

'I agree. I had actually more or less made my mind up to go on Tuesday, just knock on her door and see what happens. As you said, you never know, and at least if I try I will have done my best.'

'Tuesday it is, then.'

'Do you mean you're coming too?'

'Of course. I wouldn't miss it for the world. We'll take my car this time. My big brother Jack has retired to a bungalow in Skeggy. He never invites me, and I've been wanting an excuse to go and see him for some time. We can stay the night. Anne will be thrilled.'

She pulled a face. Was I going to be embroiled in some family feud? Les spotted my reaction.

'Don't worry, David. They'll be pleased to have us. Jack's a grumpy old devil, and I enjoy teasing him. No fee, by the way. This is strictly *pro bono.* I'm curious. And I really would like to see my brother again.'

I clearly had no choice in the matter. Experience had taught me that it was dangerous to seek to thwart the plans of a strong-willed woman. In fact there was nothing I craved more than those two serendipitous days in the company of Lesley Bradshaw, private eye. I left Ranmoor excited at the prospect of this new adventure, but on the way home I remembered Tuppence! I would have to ask Suzi to come in for two days instead of one, so that she could look after him.

Les picked me up after lunch on the Tuesday for the drive to Skegness. Suzi lay in wait for her. Since Marilyn's departure for the care home, Suzi's role of gossip-monger and casual sprayer and wiper of kitchen and bathroom surfaces had metamorphosed into that of household matriarch, from whom no corner of the house held any further secret. Her new-found sense of ownership had, however, highly beneficial side-effects, in that every carpet in the house was now regularly vacuumed, every room ruthlessly tidied on a weekly basis, and no cobweb survived her feather duster. In recompense I had insisted on doubling her pay.

On seeing another woman step over the threshold, Suzi seized upon the opportunity to launch into a chapter-and-verse account of the disgracefully untidy state of each and every room in the house, followed us out onto the driveway and was still talking as we drove away, with Les almost in tears of laughter.

Jack and Anne seemed pleased to see us, and while Les was fending off questions about why they did not see more of her, why she had come in the winter instead of the lovely Skegness summer, and dodging an invitation to Christmas dinner, Jack shook hands with me and winked at me, nodding at Les.

'You'll have your hands full with that one!'

I put him straight. I had come with his sister on a purely business basis. She was conducting an investigation for me.

'Oh! She said a friend.'

There followed a minor embarrassment about how many rooms we required, which seemed to amuse Les no end. Anne blushed at her error and went off to make up another bed in the tiny third bedroom. I think I blushed in sympathy with her.

146

We spent a pleasant enough evening in their company. Conversation seemed to be mostly about family matters, but I chipped in whenever I could.

I slept badly, but was more than revived by the compulsory morning stroll in borrowed footwear along the enormous expanse of beach, where a glacial easterly whipped across the North Sea straight from the Urals. My cap was an early casualty, flying from my head at breakneck speed down the miles of sandy beach. Les pursued it for a hundred yards or so and then returned breathless, laughing and empty-handed.

'You need a chinstrap in Skegness in winter,' advised Jack, apparently in all seriousness.

After a communal pub lunch, we drove the short distance to Spilsby. I rang the Tylers' front doorbell. There was no answer. Les suggested we come back later, after the schools had turned out.

Tess Campbell opened the door to us when we returned at four o'clock. She looked at least ten years older than her actual age of 38. We explained that we were making enquiries on behalf of her brother, George.

'I don't think I can help you. I haven't seen him since I was five. Is it something to do with the murder?'

We persuaded her that it would be better to talk inside, and she invited us in. She led us along the hallway, walking with a pronounced limp. I noticed that her right arm was shorter than the left and slightly withered.

'My husband's not home yet. He has a meeting, and the boys have both got football.'

We questioned her about her family life in Khartoum Street, but unsurprisingly she remembered nothing. Yes, she had kept in touch with her mother for a number of years, although she had seen little of her since moving to live in Lincoln with her grandmother, Winnie Davies, who had died some years back.

'Are you looking for my mother?'

'We are. Can you help us? There's a great deal I think she could tell us.'

'I haven't heard from her since she joined the gypsies.'

'The gypsies?' I gasped.

This was a new development indeed.

147

'My mother's grandfather was a Romany, and I think my mother always had a bit of a fancy for the travelling life. She went off after my father died. Was killed, I should say. I haven't heard anything from her since. I don't think anybody has.'

'Anybody?' asked Les. 'Who do you mean, anybody? Are you in touch with another member of the family, a sister or brother, perhaps.'

I saw Tess colour up in response to Les's question.

'No,' she blurted rather too quickly. 'No one. No one at all. Why would I be?'

Methinks the lady doth protest too much, I thought to myself. Tess was blowing her nose, and Les exchanged a meaningful look with me.

'How was your trip to Australia, Mrs Tyler?'

'Who said I'd been to Australia?'

'No one. It's just that I noticed the boomerang mounted on the wall above the fireplace. And the poster in the hallway.'

Tess was becoming even more agitated, folding and unfolding her fingers.

'It's just the boys. They love that sort of thing.'

Les looked at me and gave a tiny nod in the direction of the telephone table. An address book lay next to the phone.

'Well, Mrs Tyler, if there's nothing you can tell us, then we'll leave you in peace. Would you mind awfully if I used your bathroom before we go. We have a long drive back to Sheffield.'

'It's upstairs on the landing and turn left.'

'You'd better show me. I'm hopeless in strange houses.'

I heard the two women climb the stairs. Les was following deliberately slowly. I snatched the address book and quickly scanned the names beginning with C, for Campbell, and for Carly. Nothing! I worked through the book looking for an Australian address or telephone number. Eureka! Thompson, PO Box ***, Mildura, 3500, NV, with a telephone number beginning 0061 – an Australian number! I scribbled down the address and phone number on the back of a £20 note. Idiot! I had nothing else to write on. Some detective!

148

Just as I was about to copy down the email address, I heard Tess hurrying back downstairs. I slipped the address book back onto the telephone table. I had had no time to look any further than T and crossed my fingers that Tess really had kept in touch with Carly, and that this was the address we needed.

Les came back downstairs and looked at me inquisitively. I nodded and couldn't resist a grin of triumph. In the car we exchanged a furtive 'low five', as Tess watched us drive away. I took the crumpled banknote from my trouser pocket and waved it in triumph.

'Do you think it's Carly?'

'I'm absolutely certain it is. They must have kept in touch all this time. Carly has obviously forbidden her to let on, because she's in Australia illegally.'

'Sometimes longshots come off, then, don't they?'

'Yes, David, you're a very clever boy. Take a house-point.'

She took her eyes from the road and turned to look at me.

'How do you feel about a part-time job as an assistant detective?'

I frowned. She had on a totally poker-faced expression.

'I'm not sure I'm entirely cut out for it, but I'll give it due consideration.'

'Lighten up, David. I wasn't being serious. A minimum requirement for my assistant would be the ability to keep his hat on in the wind.'

'I could always wear a chinstrap.'

We arrived back in Sheffield just after eight that evening. I said goodbye to Les, but was surprised to see her follow me into the house.

'You're not getting rid of me that easily,' she said, grinning. 'Put the kettle on. We'll leave it half an hour and then telephone Australia. They're eleven hours ahead of us. We can be fairly confident they'll be alive and kicking at 7.30 on a Thursday morning.'

I fumbled with the keyboard and set the telephone on speakerphone, then handed the receiver to Les, my hand trembling with anticipation. An older man answered, in rich Derbyshire tones.

149

'Thompsons. Hello. Bill speaking.'

'Could I speak to Carly, please?'

'That you, Tess? How are you doing?'

We heard him calling across the house: 'Carly! It's for you. Tess.' And then into the telephone: 'Hang on. She's on her way.'

'Hi, Tess. How's it going?' came a young voice in an unmistakably Sheffield accent.

'It's not Tess, Carly. May I call you Carly? My name is Lesley Bradshaw. I'm calling from the UK, in connection with your brother, George Campbell.'

'You've got the wrong number.'

The line went dead.

'Damn!' said Les, more exasperated than I had seen her. 'That is so frustrating.'

She handed me the phone.

'At least we know for sure that it's her,' I said, and then immediately became less certain. 'Don't we?'

Les gave me a reassuring nod.

'Oh yes. It's Carly, all right. The older guy threw her off balance when he assumed that I was Tess, who must be the only woman who calls Carly from the UK.'

'Shall *I* try?'

'No point. She'll be on her guard now. We should try again at a different time of day, see if we get different person answering, try and think of a new way of approaching this.'

I agreed to go round to Ranmoor at 10 o'clock the following morning, 9 pm in Victoria, when one of us would try again.

The second call was equally frustrating. I let Les do the talking once more. She was a professional, after all. A younger man answered, an Australian voice this time.

'Thompsons. Hello. Shane speaking.'

'May I speak to Carly, please?'

'Who is that?'

'This is Lesley, a friend of the family.'

'Oh yes? What do you want?'

'I'd like to speak to Carly, please. Carly Campbell, Tess's sister.'

'There's no one by that name here.'

150

'Carly Thompson, then. You have Carly Thompson, don't you? She answered the phone this morning.'

The line went dead.

'Sorry, George. I gave it my best shot.'

'It seems nobody wants to speak to us.'

'Short of going and knocking on their door, I don't know what else we can do. Except perhaps keep trying. Maybe *you* should try next time. Perhaps you can make someone listen. Seeing as you've spent most of your life doing just that.'

She smiled, but I could see she was not sanguine. She could not have felt more discouraged than I.

'You can bet your life somebody will be straight on the phone to Tess. We have definitely been rumbled. I don't fancy our chances of getting much further down the line with this.'

The following day at eight o'clock in the morning, 7 p.m. in Victoria, I dialled the number again, alone this time. An older woman, Australian, answered.

'Thompsons. Hello.'

'My name is David York. I am a very close friend of George Campbell, Carly's brother, and I'm anxious to speak to Carly. I'm trying to help George by finding out more about his childhood, and I am fairly certain that Carly can help. I don't wish her any harm.'

There was a seemingly interminable silence before the woman spoke again.

'Is this George Campbell in some kind of trouble?'

'I can explain better to Carly herself.'

The phone went silent. I could hear muttered conversation between the woman and a man, possibly the young Australian that Les had spoken to. The woman spoke again.

'Just a minute. Hold on.'

The young man, Shane, took the phone from her.

'Look, mate. I don't know who you are or what you want, but there's nothing for you here. We don't know any George Campbell. We don't want any more of these nuisance calls from you or your lady friend, so leave off, will you?'

Once again the line went dead. We seemed to have run through the whole family and alienated the lot of them. If only I had been slicker in my assistant detective role and copied down the email address! I am sure I could have written a letter of explanation persuasive enough to get Carly to talk to me! A letter! Of course! That's what I would do! Write to her. After all, writing was what I did best. I switched on my laptop and began to type.

It was after eleven when I finished the letter. I read it through carefully, editing out any repetition or lack of clarity. It was a heartfelt appeal to Carly's humanity, to the ties of flesh and blood that linked her to George, for any scrap of information about his childhood, his home, his relationship with his father, in short anything which might explain the fury that had seized him on the day of the murder, anything which might bring us a step closer to restoring George to full health. Surely no sister could refuse help to her brother in such circumstances! Pleased with my effort, I sealed the envelope and addressed it to Carly, no surname, as I was undecided whether to call her Thompson or Campbell.

I called Les to tell her about my phone call, my abortive conversation with Shane and my subsequent letter. She was philosophical about my failure to get through to Carly.

'It looks as though they've well and truly put up the shutters. The letter is a good idea, David. We can only hope that it works.'

'Do you want to read it?'

'E-mail it to me if you like, but I'm sure it's a brilliant letter. The snag is, no matter how brilliant it is, it won't work if nobody reads it. It may well go straight in the bin. Whatever happens, it may be some time before you get a reaction. It's a PO Box and it may not be picked up for a while. If I were you, I'd leave it till after Christmas before you try to contact her again.'

'Okay,' I said, discouraged. She had put a damper on my high spirits.

She was silent for a few seconds, an ominous silence. She was obviously giving up on the case and was wondering how to break it to me.

'I have some news for you as well,' she began, and paused.

152

'Oh?'

'Jan called me from West Bar. She's well aware of my interest in George Campbell, and she wanted to tip me off that her colleagues in CID had taken him in for questioning this morning over the death of his uncle, Cameron Campbell.'

'What! Questioning about what? The report said that there were no suspicious circumstances.'

'Look, I don't like talking about this on the telephone. Jan told me this in confidence, as a friend. She'll be in a lot of trouble if her boss finds out. I have to go into town today. Can we meet for lunch somewhere? I think we need to talk. And, take my advice, your friend George needs a solicitor right away. Do you know anyone?'

'No. I've never had cause to use a solicitor, except for buying a house or writing a will. Any suggestions?'

'There is one guy who gave me no end of trouble by the way he protected his client when I was investigating a crime. More than once! Roland Taylor-Smith is his name. You'll find him in the book. You should get him down there right away.'

XV

LUFT

(German: air. Creation of an escape route for the king to the safety of a flight square, in order to avert the danger of checkmate on the back rank.)

Taylor-Smith agreed to drop everything and 'dash to your friend George's assistance'. I took a taxi to his office, which was handily placed a mere hundred yards from the police station. He remained seated, as his secretary ushered me into the room, possibly out of poor social graces, but more likely because he would have had difficulty prising himself out of his seat, given his massively obese bulk. I shook his hand and received the full benefit of a garlic-laden belch as I did so. Taylor-Smith was not an attractive man. He presented a picture of total dissipation. Hogarth would have delighted in his flushed complexion, the hamster-pouches of his cheeks, the bulbous, pustuled, purple nose, the intricate network of broken capillaries that mapped his face, the goitre that rendered it impossible for him to fasten the top button of his shirt. I wondered where he bought his suits. I gave him a ten minute briefing on George's history, emphasising his mutism. He remembered the murder case, even though fourteen years had passed.

154

He muttered briefly to himself, twitched his nose to allow his spectacles to slide down an inch or so and peered at me over the gold frame.

'Mutism, eh? The strong, silent type is our George. Hm, the mutism could be our trump card. Any idea why they've arrested him?'

I pleaded ignorance, and we arranged to meet for a debrief in the *Kelham Island* pub, as soon as he had secured George's release, which he assured me he would have done within the hour. I watched Taylor-Smith drive off to West Bar in his Bentley, despite the very short distance.

'Always arrive everywhere in style. That's my motto.'

I suddenly realised that I had completely forgotten about Doris. She would almost certainly have no hint of George's detention, or she would have been on to me like a flash. Should I contact her at the school? I decided that there was nothing to be gained by worrying her unnecessarily early. I was doing enough worrying for the two of us, and furthermore, just at that moment, I did not feel up to coping with the hysteria that my phone call might provoke. Better to tell her face to face, when I knew more, I reasoned. I would leave it until we had George safely out of police hands. I called Les to arrange to meet her at the *Kelham Island* at two o'clock.

Les arrived on time, and five minutes later Taylor-Smith huffed and puffed his way into the bar, with George trailing in his wake. I almost upset the table in my hurry to get to George to hug him. He did not respond. I looked at him more closely. The blank stare of the old George gazed at me, or rather through me into infinity. God knows what trauma he had suffered during the police interview, what sleeping ghosts the experience had awakened. I remembered Paul Morgan's words the first time I approached him about George: 'Many patients, too many, cannot be cured. All we can do is manage their condition.'

Taylor-Smith stopped dead when his eyes alighted on Les; he pulled himself up to his full height of five feet six inches.

'DCI Bradshaw! What an absolute delight to encounter you again!'

155

Lesley did not rise to shake his offered hand. She nodded to him.

'Mr Taylor-Smith. I should be lying if I said I'm pleased to see you again.'

'Tell me, Chief Inspector, are you here in a professional capacity? I thought you had retired from pounding the beat.'

'I'm a friend of David's. David, shouldn't you introduce me to Mr Campbell?'

I apologised and made the introductions. George did not accept her offer of a handshake.

Clutching the large brandy that I had bought him, Taylor-Smith explained that 'some clever young bobby' had taken it upon himself to link the death of a certain Cameron Campbell with the strange behaviour and disappearance of another Mr Campbell whom he had encountered in the course of his duties several weeks previously, had added two and two and made five; that one of his superiors had subsequently looked into the matter, discovered the family relationship between George and Cameron, recalled George's conviction for murdering his father, and had requested a second, more thorough pathologist's report on Cameron Campbell's body. The first post mortem examination had returned a conclusion of accidental death from choking on his own vomit, after consuming a large amount of whisky; death had been hastened by the deceased's weakened lung capacity due to an advanced stage of lung cancer. This conclusion was overturned in the report of the second pathologist. A minimal amount of vomit was indeed found in Cameron Campbell's windpipe, but several fragments of goose down were discovered in his trachea, bronchi and lungs, goose down exactly matching that in the pillow found beside the deceased's head when his body was discovered, this evidence leading to a conclusion of death by asphyxiation caused by person or persons unknown. Subsequently, a forensic examination of the deceased's flat had been conducted and George's fingerprints found on an almost empty whisky bottle in the living room. The police had traced George's sister, Dana, and had interviewed her consultant; earlier that morning they had finally tracked down George's brother, Ryan, who had, presumably in the

156

best interests of his brother, given them chapter and verse on the physical, emotional and sexual abuse inflicted on George by his father and uncle. All this gave them a clear motive for George to suffocate Cameron Campbell. After all, he had been convicted of the murder of the father, and so he was a prime suspect for the murder of the uncle. He had offered no explanation for his disappearance from home for 48 hours, at a time which matched the pathologist's estimation of the time of death, and there was proof that he had been present at the scene of the crime. The police were now busy checking CCTV recordings from the area around the dead man's home.

Fortunately, George had been true to form and had not spoken a word during the police interview, much to the frustration of the CID officers, who had fired questions at him about how his fingerprints came to be on the whisky bottle and about his unwillingness to account for his movements on the 22nd and 23rd of October. Taylor-Smith had insisted that either they charge George with an offence, or they release him until such time as they had sufficient evidence to do so.

Taylor-Smith reassured us that the police did not have enough evidence, certainly not at this stage of their enquiries. A strong point in George's favour was that the lawyer was confident that it was now impossible to pinpoint the date of Cameron Campbell's death, even to within a week. His body would have been in an advanced state of decomposition, a process which would have been accelerated by the warm temperatures in the heated apartment. There was absolutely no possibility of establishing a precise link with George's visit, if indeed he had visited the flat – the fingerprints on the whisky bottle did not actually prove his presence in the room, only that he had handled the bottle. He had asked the question and discovered that a photograph, taken on his mobile phone by the enterprising constable who attended the call, revealed two glasses on the table with the whisky bottle. Significantly, the police had not claimed that either of these glasses showed George's fingerprints.

Taylor-Smith formed a twisted Churchillian pout, then grimaced, revealing a row of tiny yellow upper teeth.

'My fear, Mr Campbell,' – he turned to look George straight in the eye, his dangling jowls flapping from side to side as he jerked his head - 'my fear is that if indeed you did suffocate the unfortunate Uncle Cameron, your DNA will be plastered all over the pillow case and duvet cover of the said deceased. But please don't enlighten me – I know that's highly unlikely, anyway, given your, in the circs highly helpful medical condition. Keep us in suspense, dear boy, do. There's a good chap.'

He emptied his brandy glass.

'Chin-chin. Another round?'

I thanked him, but said we had better be going.

'What do we do now? Just wait? Will they want George back?'

'As sure as eggs is eggs, dear boy. As sure as eggs is eggs. And when they do, make sure that yours truly is there by his side. In the meantime, I shall cast an eye over the scene of the crime. But that can wait until the morrow, I think.'

I took a taxi to George's house, where I knew I must wait to explain the day's events to Doris and to face her fury at not being informed. To say that George was uncommunicative in the taxi is an understatement. He stared straight ahead and did not respond to any of my questions about his welfare, whether the police had given him a hard time, whether he approved of my sending him the solicitor.

We arrived at the house and George stood at the front door like a zombie. I had to ask him to produce the door key; otherwise I believe he would have just stood there immobile, inert. I made tea and handed him a mug. I'm not sure whether I was speaking to him or to myself when I asked the question.

'Was it you, George? Did you do it? Did you kill Cameron?'

He turned his head towards me, and I swear there was a look of sorrow in those ice-grey eyes. Perhaps it was my imagination. Perhaps not, perhaps it was because I had asked the question. After all, by asking the question I was revealing that I knew, or believed I knew that George had murdered his uncle. The logic of the police investigators

158

was sound. George had killed his father in a rage; his father and uncle had abused him; therefore, for the same reason, George had killed his uncle, but this time not in fury – there was no sign of a struggle or disturbance in Cameron's flat – but in a cold, premeditated act. Yes, I did believe that George was responsible for the murder, the asphyxiation of Cameron Campbell. His whispered words 'it's done' that night in Chapel–en–le–Frith now made complete sense. The job of exterminating the loathsome vermin, his father and uncle, was complete. Extermination was the correct word; this was not revenge. Like Ryan, his brother, I was still on George's side, although I was dismayed by the idea of this gentle man, whom I thought I knew so well, committing not one but two murders.

The phone rang. As George did not move, I answered the call. It was Doris. She was surprised to hear me, but pleased to know that I was keeping George company. She was going to be late and would not be back before six.

'You have to come home right away, Doris.'

'What's happened? Is something wrong? Is George okay?'

'I don't want to tell you on the phone. George is safe. He's here with me. But you have to come home. Now.'

Doris went very quiet.

'Okay. I'll be back in twenty minutes, half an hour.'

'Drive carefully,' I said, fearful that she might lose her head and have an accident.

She arrived white-faced and breathless, planting herself beside George on the sofa without removing her overcoat. She listened to my account of the day's events mostly in silence, from time to time closing her eyes in pain, or uttering an 'oh no!' or an 'oh my God! The thought of being angry with me for keeping her in the dark did not seem to occur to her, such was her distress. Her reaction was that of a mother with a sick child. She took George upstairs and put him to bed with hot water bottles.

When she came down, she flopped on the sofa and burst into tears.

'What are we going to do, David? What are we going to do now?'

It was clear to me that even in Doris's mind there was a strong suspicion that George had murdered his uncle.

159

That was the secret behind his two-day disappearance at the end of October. That was why he had sat traumatised in the car on Winnats Pass. I had frequently asked myself exactly where he had been heading in the car that night. On reflection, it was probably nowhere in particular; probably he had just driven and driven, away from the crime, until the fuel ran out and the car came to a halt. Then he had slumped, lifeless, until the police discovered him.

I made Doris eat a meal that I cobbled together from ingredients I found in the fridge, and then I left her around eight to go home. As I left, she tapped me on the shoulder.

'Thank you for looking after George, David. But why didn't you call me at work? You know you should have done, don't you? I had the right to know. I had the right to be worried, far more right than you, actually.'

We were eyeball to eyeball now. Her stare was unbearable; I felt my chin fall on to my chest.

'Don't ever do anything of the kind again, please. I'd like to know that I can trust you of all people.'

My answering machine was flashing. There was a message from Les, asking me to call her back. I sighed to myself, picked up the phone and selected her number.

'Well, David, now that I've met your friend, George, I can't say that I'm impressed. I've spoken to my contact, Jan, who tells me they are certain that George Campbell did kill his uncle, and that they are busy collecting every scrap of evidence from the dead man's flat.'

'It doesn't look good,' was all I could manage, my voice husky.

'You're still standing by him, though.'

'Yes, of course.'

'And if he is guilty?'

I swallowed hard, trying to move the lump in my throat.

'Then I'll stand by him. You don't know him like I know him, Les.'

'I think you're fooling yourself, David. I don't believe anyone knows George Campbell, really knows him.'

'He's a good man.'

'A good man who has almost certainly committed two murders.'

160

'To commit one murder may be regarded as a misfortune. To commit two looks like carelessness,' I muttered.

'What? What did you say?'

'Nothing.'

'Just so you know how I feel about this, I don't think I can help you any more with your friend George. I'm sorry.'

'Okay, Les.' My voice almost failed me. 'Just send me your account.'

'I will. At the end of the month. I hope you know what you're getting into here, David. Take care.'

She hung up. The house felt cold. I turned up the thermostat, kept on my outdoor clothing and sat down on the carpet in front of Tuppence.

'Just you and me now, Champ,' I said, feeling very sorry for myself.

That night I could not sleep and tossed and turned for hours until I finally gave up and resorted to listening to the radio. I remember hearing the start of episode two of *Tess of the d'Urbervilles*, but must have fallen asleep at that point and did not wake until after ten.

Tuppence was looking more like his old self and had already developed the knack of finding his way onto a window-sill, via a dining chair and the top of my writing desk. He was sitting there, his ears twitching at the sight of birds at the feeding table, when I arrived downstairs and called him for his breakfast of half a can of line-caught tuna fish. I thought it was fine to spoil him in his invalid state. I promised him an outing in the garden that afternoon.

After my breakfast-cum-lunch I called Taylor-Smith, or Mr Toad, as I now had begun to think of him. I asked him if he had been to the scene of crime.

'Of course, old boy. I said I would, didn't I? Couldn't get near, I'm afraid. They wouldn't allow me in. There was a uniformed lad acting as liftman, escorting all the tenants up and down. I had to show proof of bona fides before he'd even let me out at the right floor. The place was crawling with chaps in white overalls and slippers, with masks and magnifying glasses and tweezers and little plastic bags and the like.'

'I'd heard.'

'You'd heard? How come? No, don't tell me – your friend, the Chief Inspector, I presume. Well, if there is any evidence against our man George, then these chaps will find it, sure as eggs is eggs, old boy, sure as eggs is eggs. But don't worry, we'll have a trick or two up our sleeve.'

Taylor-Smith assured me he would keep me up to speed with developments, and we left it at that.

I kept my promise to Tuppence and gave him his hour in the garden, where he hopped around with admirable agility on his three sound legs, and did a good deal of sniffing and re-marking of his territory. Once back indoors, he spent the rest of the afternoon cleaning himself up.

I took note of the date: it was the 15th of December already and I had not written Christmas cards or bought presents. As I presumed I should not be seeing Michael and Claire this year, I resorted to Amazon to send presents to them, a couple of books on cricket that I thought he might like and novels for her. I spent the afternoon and early evening writing a mound of cards to people on the old Christmas list that Marilyn had compiled. I phoned Doris to ask how things were in the Campbell household. She told me she had taken compassionate leave until the end of term. The headteacher had been very understanding, after the initial shock of hearing that her husband was suspected of murder.

The following morning Doris called me early. I was still in bed.

'Have you seen the papers? They're absolutely full of it! Every front page headline! We are surrounded!'

I threw on some clothes and dashed to the newsagent's. It was true. Every newspaper, apart from the *Guardian* and the *Independent,* had front page block headlines and photos of George from the previous trial. It was hardly surprising. The news was sensational: a released murderer suspected of having killed again. I bought the *Guardian* and copies of three of the red-tops.

The broadsheet's editorial warned of the hazards of inadequate risk assessment of dangerous prisoners serving life sentences, before they were released into the community. Information leaked to *Guardian* journalists

162

from sources within Her Majesty's Inspectorate of Probation revealed fears that, 'in a substantial majority of cases', release plans for murderers, rapists and serial violent offenders were deficient. High risk offenders were too often unleashed upon the public, inadequately supervised, on a day-release basis. Three weeks previously, a prisoner released in this way simply had not returned to his Open Prison in Derbyshire and remained at large. In January of 2011, one murderer serving a life sentence at HMP Wakefield, a 'Category A' prison, had been released directly into the community, under the supervision of an amateur mentor, without even the key transitional trial period of day-release, and was now once again under arrest on suspicion of having re-offended. A shiver ran down my spine. The individuals were not named, but this clearly referred to George and myself. The editorial ended on a grave note, questioning whether lessons had been learned from the tragedy of the case of Anthony Bryant, serving a life sentence and released on licence in 2004, who went on to commit a violent murder only a few months later. On a further inside page the *Guardian* ran a large feature on the murder of Ian Stuart Campbell in 1998, including a profile of his son and murderer, George Campbell, as a mute, mild-mannered chess prodigy. The feature was accompanied by a press release from South Yorkshire police, saying that a Sheffield man had been taken in for questioning regarding the suspicious death of Cameron Campbell. The reader was left in no doubt as to who the Sheffield man was.

The three red-tops were less subtle in their approach, with headlines such as **SHOULD THIS MONSTER BE FREE?** and **DO KILLERS ROAM OUR STREETS?** above identical giant photographs of George. All three published *vox pop* interviews which unanimously derided the judgement of the Parole Board in authorising the early release of George Campbell.

I drove to the Campbell house. I could not get near to park the car. There was a throng of reporters and photographers outside the gate. Two were even at the front window trying to take flash shots of the interior of the house through a chink in the closed curtains. I pulled up the hood of my anorak and walked confidently down a driveway and round the back of a house three doors away. I climbed over three fences, damaging one of them quite badly, I'm afraid, and arrived at the end of my friends' back garden. Fortunately, Doris was in the kitchen and spotted me. She mimed 'no' and waved her arms. Reporters must have found a way round the back, possibly over the garage roof. I hid behind a bush for an eternity, until I saw her beckon to me that the coast was clear. I ran to the house and she let me in through the back door.

The phone calls had been incessant. Doris had now unplugged the landline and switched off her mobile; each time she switched the phone back on to attempt to make a call, it rang again immediately. I suggested she contact the phone company to arrange for a new landline number. In the meantime I lent her my mobile phone. We had a conference, in which George at least showed interest if he did not contribute, and decided that life like this would be intolerable. Our plan was for George and Doris to leave at the dead of night by the back garden – Doris knew a better route than I had taken, over the back wall and through the garden abutting theirs, attached to a house in the next street. From there they would take a taxi to my house, where they would stay for the duration of the siege.

Operation Back Garden Wall went smoothly. I had left the spare key under a plant-pot, to save them having to knock me up in the middle of the night, but I was awake anyway and came downstairs to welcome them and help with the suitcases and bags. It had been quite a feat to get their luggage over the back garden wall with the minimum of noise and without attracting the attention of the considerable numbers of press still lurking around the house, chatting, smoking, drinking from thermos flasks and hip-flasks and munching on inexhaustible supplies of sandwiches.

Late that afternoon Taylor-Smith phoned me to ask where the dickens George Campbell was. He had been calling him all day, but there had been no answer. The police wanted George in for questioning again. They had new evidence they wished to put to him. They had attempted to pick him up at his address, but had found the house empty. In answer to the police threat of launching a nationwide hue and cry, Taylor-Smith had maintained that Mr and Mrs Campbell had merely left the house to escape the attention of the press, and assured them that he would bring his client in to West Bar the following morning. I promised that George would meet him there without fail at 10 a.m.

The following morning's papers added a new dimension to the murder mystery. The police had seized Cameron Campbell's laptop, on which they had found thousands of images of child pornography, and had arrested seven men from the area in simultaneous dawn raids on their homes. All were charged with downloading and possessing indecent images of children, and newspapers were claiming that strong hints of the existence of a child-exploitation ring had been leaked to them by 'sources close to South Yorkshire Police'.

I ordered a taxi for George and Doris, and instructed the driver to take them to an address in the back streets near the police station. George wore an old trilby hat of mine and dark glasses, which I feared might be insufficient disguise. However, fortunately the taxi driver took no interest in him. I stayed at home to await developments, partly in the hope that Les might get back to me with some inside information, helpful advice or reassurance. Of course, she did not. I heard nothing further from her.

I waited on tenterhooks for the whole day. Eventually Taylor-Smith phoned me. There was more evidence against George. His presence in the flat had been confirmed by fingerprints found on the mouse and keyboard of Cameron's laptop and by traces of George's DNA, specifically hairs on the furniture. He had been captured clearly on CCTV, first parking the car several streets away from Cameron's block of flats, then entering the building in broad daylight at 4:10 on the afternoon of Monday, 22nd of October, and leaving in the early evening at 6:32 p.m.

George had not responded to any of the police questions, and Taylor-Smith had asserted his right to remain silent, especially as he was medically certified as suffering from mutism. The police quite rightly maintained that even a mute was capable of answering in the affirmative or the negative and that George was not incapable of writing an answer, or of making a statement.

165

They were therefore keeping him in custody overnight until questioning was resumed the following day. Taylor-Smith felt that we were very close to the moment when George would be charged with the murder. In fact, he could not understand why they had not already charged him. If George were to be charged, he would apply for bail, but, considering his client's criminal record, he was far from optimistic that it would be granted.

Doris returned home dejected, having forgotten in her distress to use subterfuge, as I had strongly advised her, when leaving the police station. Her taxi had been pursued by waiting reporters, and my house was now also under siege. I could scarcely blame her, but it was infuriating to have to endure that rabble at the gates.

'You may as well stay here now, Doris. You will have me for company, and there are more rooms to escape to, at least.'

Before the words were out of my mouth, the telephone rang. After half an hour of saying 'Who is this?' and cutting off call after call, I pulled out the plug on my landline. Doris handed me my mobile phone.

'You'd better have this back. I'm sorry. I'm an idiot.'

As Taylor-Smith had predicted, George was charged with murder the following day, Tuesday, 18th of December. On the Wednesday he made a short appearance in front of magistrates, where Taylor-Smith entered a plea of 'not guilty' on behalf of his client. The case was referred to the Crown Court; bail was refused and George remanded to HMP Doncaster. No date was yet set for the trial. Doris and I left the Castle Street magistrates' court in despair. We returned home to confront the onslaught of the jostling crowd of reporters, rubbernecks and sensation-seekers and their bewildering salvo of flashbulbs.

I confess that I felt totally impotent. I was out of my depth now; with no more Leslie Bradshaw, private eye, by my side to help and advise, and Mr Toad as my only comfort, I was of no further help to either George or Doris. I tried to imagine how he must be feeling, back once again in a prison cell, but only succeeded in making myself feel even gloomier, guiltier than ever about my role in George's wretched history.

XVI

KOTOV SYNDROME

(Named after Alexander Kotov, who described it: under time pressure, having thought long and hard long on a difficult position and having still not found a solution, a player makes a sudden and often very ill-advised move.)

I woke the following day after a surprisingly deep sleep, certain of what I had to do next. I made a call to Thomas Cook and enquired about immediate flights to Melbourne, Australia. The response was disappointing, to say the least. Flights were fully booked up until mid-January.

'It's the Christmas period, sir. The flights are always heavily booked. The last few seats went yesterday. You can phone Qantas direct, if you want to try for yourself.'

The travel agent gave me the number. I spoke to an airline representative, who promised to call me back if there was a cancellation, but warned me that there was quite a long queue on the standby list. I cursed myself for not having taken more decisive action before. I would just have to wait for a response to my letter. In the meantime I would be kicking my heels, seething with the frustration of inactivity. Why I thought that flying to the other side of the world would serve any purpose I am not quite sure, but this unattainable air ticket to Melbourne had become an obsession. I called Qantas from my study, out of earshot of Doris, every hour on the hour, until I was sure they were sick of hearing my voice. At 8 p.m. I called again; one last time and then I would call it a day, I told myself. The now familiar antipodean tones greeted me.

'Is that Mr York? I recognised your voice. And your number. I was just about to call you, Mr York. We do have a single seat which has fallen available, from Heathrow to Melbourne, but it's first-class and rather expensive, I'm afraid.'

'Never mind. Anything will do. When is the flight?'

'The flight leaves Heathrow on Sunday 23rd of December at 18:30 hours, arriving in Melbourne at 06:30 hours on Tuesday the 25th, changing at Singapore. Return flight Friday, 4th of January, leaving Melbourne at 10:30 a.m., arriving at Heathrow on Saturday, 5th of January at zero 30 hours. Again via Singapore.'

Christmas Day in Australia. I smiled at the irony. I had long dreamt of spending Christmas in Melbourne, of bringing Michael to the MCG for the Boxing Day Test. It was an odd way for a dream to be realised.

'I'll take it.'

I almost fell off my office chair when she told me the price and asked for my credit card details.

'Do you have a place to stay, Mr York, or would you like me to book your hotel accommodation in Melbourne?'

'Please do that. Thank you for your help.'

Why not? In for a penny, in for a pound.

I took a deep breath. Somehow I had to explain my Australian trip to Doris, who still knew nothing of my detective activities. Perhaps I would tell her I felt I simply had to get away. Whatever explanation I gave, I would seem to be a rat leaving the sinking ship. I was too exhausted for a confession that night.

I reflected on the strange paradox, or paradoxes that had governed, some might say blighted my professional and personal life. I loved order, symmetry and organisation, but lived and worked in the midst of a chaos of books, papers and personal belongings; I was one of the world's great procrastinators, and yet I loathed inactivity,

168

was maddened by the frustration of being powerless when confronted by a problem beyond my control.

As always, faced with a dilemma, I would procrastinate. I would confess my plans to Doris later. I thought of the irony of the words of Thomas de Quincey:

> *If once a man indulges himself in murder, very soon he comes to think little of robbing; and from robbing he comes next to drinking and Sabbath-breaking, and from that to incivility and procrastination.*

The world had been turned on its head, and the whimsy of de Quincey's words was strangely apt.

The following evening, my dilemma was resolved, when Doris announced that she was leaving the next morning for Oadby to stay with her mother, at least for the Christmas and New Year period, perhaps even longer. With luck, she might never find out.

I needed to speak to Ryan Campbell. I needed to know what exactly he had said to the police. I called his mobile. He told me he had been trying desperately to contact his brother, having seen the reports in the national newspapers.

'I meant to contact them before, but you know how it is, you're busy, you keep putting it off.'

I told him I knew exactly how it was.

'I needed to tell them, to warn them that the police had had me in and questioned me about when we were kids, in Sheffield.'

'When was that?'

'Tuesday. They knocked me up. Five o'clock in t' morning. Took me reight up to Taunton police station. They kept me for three hours.'

'Three hours? What did you tell them.'

'More or less what I told you. In that pub.'

'For three hours?'

'They kept on asking me more questions. Wanted more details.'

'And?'

'I couldn't tell them. Couldn't remember.'

I wondered if he was telling me the truth. He cleared his throat.

'I were supposed to be driving a wagon up to Immingham that morning.'

'Your boss understood, though?'

'He were all reight wi' me. Is George okay?'

I told him that George's wife was staying with me and asked if he wanted to speak to her. Doris gestured wildly at me. She did not want to speak to anyone.

'I'm sorry, Ryan. She's too upset to speak at the moment. I'll give her your number, and perhaps she'll ring back when she's up to it. George is in Doncaster prison, by the way, if you want to write to him.'

'Who was that?' asked Doris.

'George's brother. Ryan.'

'Brother? I had no idea he had a brother.'

As I plugged the telephone into its charger, it rang. It was Taylor-Smith, who, as I could tell from the familiar background noises, was calling from a pub. I wondered if this was how he usually conducted his business.

'I think I should warn you, old boy, that as soon as a trial date is set, we shall need to appoint a brief. All the top men are heavily booked up months in advance.'

'What about the top women?'

He was silent for a moment or two, but did not respond to my jibe.

'If you don't wish to go to the expense of appointing a brief, then of course Barkiss is willing. It is quite normal these days for a solicitor to appear in court. All the same, I would advise engaging a top brief. I think a top man can tear the prosecution case to shreds. Give it some thought. I'm just warning you in advance, old boy.'

He rang off. I thought of the extortionate fare to Australia. I had no concept of the cost of hiring an eminent barrister, but suspected it might well be astronomical, and though I did not share Mr Toad's faith in the infallibility of his 'top men', it appeared I might very well be obliged to hire one. I felt myself puff out my cheeks. Perhaps my son was right; perhaps the house would have to go.

This time I did not have the time to plug in the phone charger before it rang again. It was Paul Morgan. Until then I had thought of him as supremely calm and professional, but the exasperation positively crackled in his voice. His PA had been calling my number and the Campbells' all day.

'Finally she had the nous to dig out your mobile number. I do read the papers sometimes, David. What the devil's been going on?'

It was a long story. I realised how much I had not told him, about my conversation with Ryan, my abortive phone-calls to Australia, George's two-day disappearance, his questioning and subsequent arrest and murder charge, and now my plans to fly to Australia.

'I'm sorry, Paul. Things have been happening so quickly. I haven't had time to spit.'

My account seemed to have soothed his irritation.

'Yes, David, events do seem to have left me trailing behind. Where is George Campbell now?'

I told him.

'Perhaps I could take a drive up the A1 to see him, during the Christmas break. Remember, I have a lot invested in this too. Professionally.'

I gave him Taylor-Smith's contact numbers and suggested he get in touch with the lawyer beforehand.

'You will let me know how you get on down under, David, won't you?'

There was still just a hint of sarcasm in his voice.

It was an evening for difficult phone calls. I steeled myself for the call to Michael, to explain my plans for Christmas. Claire answered. I told her my news. The words flooded from her, sentences tumbling into each other; there was no question of my interrupting.

'First of all, we've read all the news and we're thinking of you. It must be awful. I keep on asking Michael to call you. I'm not surprised you want to get away from it all, but it's a monster of a flight to Australia. You're going on your own, you say? Are you sure you will be okay? We were thinking of asking you down here for a bit of peace and quiet – and Doris too if she wanted to come, but I suppose she has family. It must be hell, what with the press beating the door down and the daily headlines.'

Eventually she paused for breath, and then said she would pass me over to Michael.

'Australia, eh? You always said you wanted to spend Christmas in Australia.'

'I wanted *us* to spend Christmas in Australia.'

'Yeah, yeah. I don't know why you don't wait till next year though, for the Ashes.'

'Well, perhaps I can use this trip as a recce. Perhaps next year we could do that, together.'

'It's not going to happen, Dad. Like all those other things, it's not going to happen. Have a good time, and Merry Christmas. Here's Claire again.'

Claire wished me a safe journey and asked me to telephone to let them know I'd arrived safely. And that was that.

I looked at the pile of mail that I had not yet opened, from that day and the previous day. There was an envelope written in a hand I did not recognise. I opened it. It was from the daughter of my old friend and colleague, Bill Rodgers, informing me that her father had died on the 15th of December, peacefully in his sleep, aged 94. The cremation and service was to be held at Penmount Crematorium, Truro, on Thursday 27th of December, at 2 p.m.

Bill had been my indispensable second in command in my first headship. He had stayed on for a year to help my successor at Harry Brearley settle into the job, and then retired to a coastal village in Cornwall, where he and his wife could pursue their passion for sailing. We had kept in touch for over twenty years, and then our correspondence had dried up. His backing and moral support for me had never for one second been in doubt during my time at Harry Brearley, and his experience and gentle words of advice at critical moments had guided me through my early years of uncertainty in the post. I remained immensely grateful and indebted to him. And now I should be unable to attend his funeral. If this week's events were to have a last straw, then this surely was it.

•

172

The man has been banished from the maternity ward for two hours, so that the woman can rest before her ordeal. He is sitting amongst the few other spectators scattered around the boundary of a school cricket field in Canterbury. He has become totally absorbed in watching a tiny, blond, curly-headed boy, left-handed, who is using his bat like a cutlass to carve the bowling of far older, taller and stronger opponents to all parts of the park. The pavilion scoreboard shows that the home team has reached 204 runs for the loss of six wickets, and the small, curly-headed boy, batting at number 5, has accumulated 99 runs, when he flashes his cutlass one time too many at a wide ball and sends a straightforward catch to gulley. The man tosses his head back in sympathy and joins in the generous applause for the boy. Well played, young Gower, calls the cricket master from the pavilion steps.

The man consults his watch, jumps to his feet and runs to his car. He arrives at the maternity ward perspiring and out of breath. The woman is sitting up in the bed, propped up by several pillows. She is holding a tiny newborn baby to her breast. I missed it, says the man. I'm sorry. The woman nods her head in acknowledgement. Never mind, she says. Meet Michael. Michael, this is your father. Here, take him. I think we're done here.

The man takes the baby, awkwardly. He had no idea that babies could be so small. He studies the tiny, screwed up red face for hints of his own reflection. He wonders at the minuscule, perfect fingernails, at the power of the grip of the tiny hand around his thumb. He's strong, says the man, as the baby wriggles perilously in his arms. Hello, Michael, he says. I'm your dad. We're going to be big mates, you and me.

The woman's eyes have closed. Her breathing is slow and even. The man places the baby back in the crib, face down, the technique authorised in the baby book he has read. He leans over the woman and floats a tender, lingering kiss onto her cheek.

As he glides down the corridor, he punches the air and bursts into song: My boy Bill, he'll be tall and as tough as a tree! Nurses turn and giggle. The ward sister emerges from her office and shushes him.

173

XVII

SHARP

("Risky, double-edged, highly tactical. Sharp can be used to describe moves, maneuvers, positions, and styles of play."
Wikipedia.)

The longest distance I had previously flown was to and from the west coast of North America, a flight of 10 hours, which was already quite long enough for me. Experience told me that the flights from west to east were the ones which caused most problems with jetlag, and so I was expecting to suffer some effects on the outward flight to Melbourne. What I was not prepared for was the truly exhausting nature of a 25-hour flight, no matter how comfortable the surroundings. The fact that I slept for much of the journey in my comfortable reclining seat seemed to have surprisingly little beneficial effect. I arrived in Melbourne totally exhausted at 6.30 on the morning of a sparkling Christmas Day. For me it was still 7.30 in the evening on Christmas Eve, and my whole system was thrown into turmoil.

The Qantas agent had booked me in to the Melbourne Hilton and had had the foresight to pay the supplement that allowed me to check in early that morning. The shuttle from the airport would at that time of day normally have had to battle through rush hour traffic, but on Christmas Day the roads were blessedly empty. I fell into my bed and slept soundly and dreamlessly until late afternoon.

I slipped on shorts and a T-shirt and took a taxi for the five mile drive to St Kilda beach in Port Phillip Bay, where I knew there was a range of diners and restaurants. I planned to treat myself to a slap-up Christmas dinner. Christmas Day on the beach had long been a dream of mine, ever since a colleague had told me in glowing terms about his Australian Christmas experience. In the event the restaurants were all booked solid, and I had to content myself with strolling along the wide sandy beach and paddling up to the knees at the edge of the ocean.

It was approaching eight o'clock and I was ravenously hungry by now. The scores of families and groups of young people enjoying their evening barbecues only served to sharpen my appetite. A young man, early twenties, blond and bronzed, had clearly spotted me ogling their feast and called me over.

'You on your own, mate? Come on, grab a beer, join the mob and dig into the barbie! The more the merrier here, mate.'

I accepted gratefully and was soon deep in conversation with two pretty girls, Billie and Bev, who were curious first about what the heck I was doing here on my own on Christmas Day, secondly about my lilywhite skin, then thirdly my accent. Eventually, two of the young men came over:

'Typical pommy! Coming over here stealing our women! Here, grab another tinnie, mate. You look thirsty.'

I protested that I should be getting back to Melbourne, but they would have none of it.

'Hell with that, mate! Don't be a drongo! It's Christmas! She'll be apples!'

I had another beer. And another.

In my disoriented state, despite the alcohol, I did not sleep that night. Instead I watched a couple of films on pay-TV and read my book for a while. I must have dropped off around dawn.

175

It was Boxing Day, the first day of the Melbourne Test at the MCG. I asked at the hotel reception if it would be possible to buy tickets for the match. The young man behind the desk said he could do better than that – a guest at the hotel had a spare ticket and did not want it to go to waste. He had left it at reception, in case any other guest might like to take advantage of it. No charge. I tipped the young man ten dollars.

In fact, the MCG was only two thirds full, still a substantial crowd for a cricket match, as the stadium holds 100,000 spectators. I found myself sitting in the middle of a crowd of several hundred Sri Lankans, whose team were Australia's opponents. It was a miserable day's cricket for my new Sri Lankan friends, as they watched their team bowled out in little over 40 overs for 156, only Sangakkara offering resistance with a battling 58. By the end of the day the Australians had almost passed the tourists' score for the loss of only three wickets. The visiting supporters accepted the poor form of their batsmen with good grace and cheered uproariously when the first Australian wicket fell.

We were in full sun, and though the shade temperature was only in the mid-20s, the heat was merciless, and I drank a good deal of beer to slake my raging thirst. Whether from the alcohol or from the jetlag, I fell asleep in the late afternoon and was shaken awake by my neighbour, suffering from severe sunburn on my legs, arms and neck. I walked the short distance back to the hotel and slept the rest of the evening and most of the night.

It needed no genius to reason that I would be an unwelcome visitor to the Thompson household, and a visit close to Christmas would be even more irksome. I decided to wait a further two days, spent in the shade by the hotel pool, reading, relaxing and contemplating how I was going to approach the ticklish business of tackling Carly Campbell and her highly protective family. The first hurdle was that I did not know their home address. All I had was a PO Box number in Mildura, a town on the very edge of the outback. The fact that the family collected their mail

176

from the PO Box seemed to indicate that their farm or homestead lay some considerable distance from the town. I was not certain how easy it would be to find them, but my experience as assistant detective with Les Bradshaw had emboldened me to a degree.

I set out straight after breakfast on the Saturday morning. I had checked out the route to Mildura on the hotel's Internet service; the itinerary was uncomplicated and would present no navigational problems. I should cover the 350 mile stretch in under six hours, according to the route planner. I had only booked my car-hire on arrival and had been obliged to accept what the hire company had left to offer, a tiny mini manufactured in Asia and certainly not intended to be driven by a man as tall as I. A gangly youth, who had driven the car round from the compound, crawled out of the driving seat and handed me the keys rather apologetically.

'Going far?'

I told him Mildura.

'Good luck, mate. Rather you than me,' he grinned, then kicked the front tyre and added, reassuring, 'No worries. She'll be right.'

The temperature was already into the twenties as I left Melbourne behind me. I now regretted not having tried other car hire companies. This was going to be an uncomfortable drive. As I drove inland away from the conurbation, signs of habitation became fewer and further between and the temperature rose sharply. I switched on the car's air conditioning unit, which made a good deal of noise but had no effect. Approaching midday, the car's ambient temperature gauge registered 39°. I had opened the windows, but the external air seemed just as hot and brought with it the bonus of a cloud of dust whenever a vehicle passed in the opposite direction. By noon I had adopted the tactic of stopping at each petrol station I passed, to rest and replenish my water supplies.

'You all right, mate? You're looking a tad crook,' said Joe of Joe's Diner, where I stopped for lunch. 'Bushed, I'd say.'

I felt 'bushed', and there were still 200 miles to go. I rested up for an hour over a burger and fries and something that Joe called coffee, and then pressed on up

177

the highway northwards. I should have rested for longer, but had begun to think I had outstayed my welcome, as Joe returned repeatedly to refill my cup with his poisonous brew and ask if I had decided on dessert yet.

I have heard stories of how perilous it is to drive through Death Valley without excellent air conditioning, but I cannot believe that braving Death Valley could be any worse an experience than my drive northwards from Melbourne that day. I reached Mildura just after five in the afternoon, eight hours after leaving the hotel, and found the post office as it was closing. I handed over a slip of paper with the Thompsons' mailing address and enquired of the serious-looking man behind the counter if he knew them and could tell me their home address. He looked at me suspiciously.

'You're looking for Thompsons, and you don't know where their farm is?'

'I'm a friend of Carly's brother in the UK, and he asked me to look up Carly, Shane and Bill when I was in Victoria.'

He looked at his watch.

'You come far?' he said, looking me up and down.

I told him, and he frowned. He was obviously keen to shut up shop and, at another time, may have required more evidence of my bona fides. Either my desperate appearance or my name-dropping did the trick, however, and he gave me brief directions to the Thompson farm some 50 miles away, 'along the A20 Sturt Highway south-west out of Mildura, then take the road north to Merbein and then due west again from there'.

I soon found the turn-off for Merbein, reached the dusty little town in ten minutes, turned left at a crossroads and took the only road heading out towards the setting sun. An hour and a half out of Mildura on what had now become little more than a dirt track, I was beginning to lose faith in the post office official's directions, and I was grateful to finally spot a farm entrance, a high gateway in the fence running alongside the track, with a faded sign hanging from the crosspiece, reading simply 'THOMPSONS'.

I turned into the yard, drew the car to a halt beside a barn and opened the door. As I got out of the car and tried to straighten my cramped body and stretch my aching

178

neck, I was blinded by the sun's rays glinting from the roof of a large house entirely covered in solar panels. My head swam and my legs folded beneath me. I did what I had never done before. I fainted.

I have no idea how long I was unconscious. When I came round, my head was thumping and I was aware of two blurred female heads looking down at me. I had lost my spectacles. The older of the two was dabbing my forehead and lips with a piece of ice, while the younger one looked on, anxiously, I imagined. Behind them were two taller figures, men.

'He's coming round,' said the older woman.

The younger woman reached over and placed my spectacles carefully over my nose and ears.

'There we are,' she said. 'I bet that's better.'

The accent betrayed her Sheffield roots. It had to be Carly.

What followed was a tribute to Australian outback hospitality. I was offered a soothing bath, which went a long way towards restoring my energy, and a meal, at which we exchanged first names. We were joined at the table by a dark-haired teenage girl, Cathy, a younger version of Carly.

After the main course came the inquisition that I dreaded. What was I doing in the outback? Where was I staying? Why had I landed on their doorstep out of the blue? It had not been difficult for them to establish that I was no Aussie. My accent and my general demeanour revealed me as an Englishman.

I took a deep breath. This was the moment when they threw me out on my neck, exposed as the unwelcome snoop that I was. There was total silence, as I told them who I was and that I had come to talk to Carly about her brother, George. I asked Carly whether she had received my letter; she stood up and left the table, tears in her eyes.

'Come with me, Cathy. You don't want to hear this.'

Cathy protested, as Carly dragged her away from the table by her arm.

'What letter? Dad! What's going on?'

'Go with your mother, Cathy.'

Shane looked at me, fire in his eyes, pushed his chair back, fists bunched.

'Get the hell out of here!'

He had every right to be angry. I had abused their hospitality. I was sitting at their table under false pretences.

The older man, Bill, sitting next to him, placed a restraining hand on his shoulder.

'He's here now, Shane. He's come a long way for this. Let's hear what he's got to say. I'll give you this, mate, you're persistent. Tell us about this letter of yours. We've had no letter to my knowledge.'

I told them the long story of my quest to restore George to health, of Paul Morgan's theory that childhood trauma held the secret of his mutism. I thought it prudent to withhold the news of his recent arrest and the murder charge. There would be understandably less sympathy for a double murderer!

'That's a hell of a story,' said Bill, as I finished. 'But what exactly can we do for you? I don't see how we can help.'

'I want to understand what drove George, who I know is the gentlest of men, to go back to the family home and attack his father, and so violently, back in 1998. It's just possible that Carly has the answer, if she'll only talk to me, about her upbringing, her parents. She may even have been present around the time of the . . . the death of her father.'

'Carly wants to forget about those days. And you haven't any right to come here stirring things up from the past,' said Shane, fingers gripping the edge of the table.

The woman, Ellen, spoke at last.

'I think we need a family conference. Not now, in the morning. And you need to rest, David. You're not going anywhere tonight.'

Shane glared at her, but Bill nodded in agreement. I was shown to my bed, in the 'sleepout', a veranda converted into an outside bedroom, where I enjoyed a deep sleep, despite my apprehension about the outcome of the family conference.

Bill was cooking eggs and bacon in the kitchen when I emerged the following morning. I congratulated him on how good it smelled and asked if this was an everyday breakfast.

'No, David. Just the Sunday treat, to remind me of home.'

I drew up a chair, sat at the kitchen table, and remarked that it looked like another sunny day ahead.

'That's the problem in these parts this time of the year. Every day's a sunny day. Makes finding water tricky for the animals.'

I asked him what animals they had. He told me two flocks of sheep, about a thousand in all, on a thousand hectares.

'Poor land, though. That's why I picked it up cheap, when I came over from England.'

I asked him if he'd always been a sheep farmer. He said he had and told me he'd sold up in the early seventies when his parents died.

'The country was going to the dogs. Three-day week, power cuts, you name it. I took my chance down under, bought the land, some stock. The previous guy was bankrupt. A couple of jackaroos stayed on to give me a hand. I met Ellen and life was sweet. Hard work, but worth it.'

He spread his hands.

'As you see.'

'I couldn't help noticing that you have a wall full of books.'

I nodded towards the dining room.

'We're big believers in education in this family. No country yokels here. We sent Shane away to school in Melbourne, then Uni. Agriculture degree. He wouldn't have that for Cathy, though. Home schooling for her. We all pitched in. Didn't do a bad job, either. She's a reader. Like her mum.'

'Carly reads a lot?'

He nodded and planted a plate of two fried eggs and four rashers of bacon in front of me. I tucked in. The smell of frying bacon had made me ravenous, as it always does. I made short work of it. I piled the cutlery on the plate and sat back.

'I suppose you'll be wanting me out of the way this morning. You know, for the family conference.'

'It's done, mate. Shane couldn't wait. Made us sit at the table until we decided what to do. Said he wouldn't be able to sleep.'

I waited for him to tell me more. The tension was too much. I asked him.

'And what did you decide?'

'Shane is going to talk to you. He'll tell you what you need. But Carly stays out of this, you hear? And the lass. You seem a decent enough feller, David. Don't go letting us down.'

He looked beyond me to the far end of the kitchen. I turned to see Shane standing in the doorway.

'Do you ride, David?'

I told him I knew how to sit on a horse, as long as galloping was not required.

We cantered for ten to fifteen minutes in silence, Shane on a frisky chestnut gelding and I on a gentle old grey mare, along the course of a dried-up river. I was sweating a good deal and was grateful for the loan of Bill's wide-brimmed cowboy hat. The house was now well out of sight, despite the flat terrain. I still had not seen a single sheep. Shane reined in the horse, dismounted, and planted himself on a rock. I did likewise and felt the heat sear my buttocks through my thin jeans.

'I picked Carly up in London - no, that's the wrong word. I found Carly in London. June 1st 1998. In Soho, late at night. It was my twenty-first birthday, I was out with a mate, and I was in a good mood. Until we bumped into Carly. She was on a street corner, carrying a tiny child. Just a kid herself, but with a child. She looked a mess, and I'm pretty sure she was prostituting herself. Or trying to. Difficult to get customers with a child in tow. I took her home with me to the flat, and one of the girls in the house ran a bath and cleaned her and the kid up. She stayed with us, sleeping on the sofa for a while, until the landlord kicked up a fuss. We handed her over to social services and they found her a hostel.'

'What were you doing in London?'

'I was doing what all Aussies do, my year in Europe. Only in my case it was a year in London. I got some bar

182

work, and I loved the place. So different from what I knew. So much more exciting than Melbourne, even.'

'I can guess the rest. You and Carly fell in love.'

He looked away to the horizon, and there was just the merest hint of a smile.

'Something like that. Between us we sorted her out. She scrubbed up well. She's quite a girl, you know. And you couldn't help but love that little kid. Catherine, she called her then. She was a sweetie. In the end, Carly told me what had brought her to London. She was desperate to escape the country, I was young and stupid, and I bought them the flights to Melbourne, as soon as she was eighteen.'

'Did she ever intend to come back?'

'No. But we had to pretend that she did. For the immigration people.'

'So she's still here . . . illegally?'

He gave no answer.

'And Cathy too, I suppose.'

'This is confidential, Mr York. I'm putting a lot of trust in you, more than I'm comfortable with. I warn you, if you breathe a word, I'll . . .'

I raised a hand and shook my head, to prevent him from continuing.

'Not a word, Shane. Not a word to a soul.'

Yet another promise I would not keep.

Shane remounted, and I followed suit. We walked the horses on westwards and eventually I saw the flock of hundreds of sheep, in a slightly greener area of countryside, accompanied by a lone horseman and two black and white specks that must have been his dogs. Shane turned to me.

'You need to know about that night. The night that Carly ran away from home.'

'I was hoping you could tell me more about what happened the night George killed his father.'

'That's what I mean.'

I had been a sympathetic listener during the story of Shane rescuing Carly from her dire situation in London, but so far I had heard nothing surprising, nothing directly concerning the murder. Was Shane about to give me the information I needed? My interest was suddenly keener.

183

'I guess you know about the abuse. The stuff they did to Carly from being a little girl, from being about ten, and to the other girls - and to George, Carly told me. I don't know about you, Mr York, but I can't imagine the horror of living like that, year after year.'

'If they'd only told somebody!'

'I think they did, Mr York. That's the tragedy of it. Carly tried to tell one of her teachers, one she liked. She didn't believe her, or didn't find it convenient to believe her. She probably dismissed Carly as a hysterical, hormonal teenager.'

'God! I wish one of them had told *me!*'

'What would *you* have done, Mr York?'

'I would have acted, done something about it. I was the headteacher, when George and Nancy and Ryan were at Harry Brearley. It was my job to do something about it.'

There was a long silence before Shane spoke again.

'You don't think that maybe, just maybe Carly's brother George *was* perhaps telling you, Mr York – all that silence, all that strange behaviour?'

The words 'Mr York', again and again, accused me, stabbed at me. I knew deep down that this had been all along the source of my bad conscience, the reason for my determination to help to 'put things right', to atone for my sin of omission. The other two, Nancy and Ryan, I couldn't even remember from my Harry Brearley days.

'Maybe,' I mumbled.

He seemed satisfied with my answer.

'That night those two mongrels went too far. Shall we say they really excelled themselves in their vileness.'

It was a strange expression, but I knew what he meant.

'What happened? What did Carly say?'

'They took Catherine, Carly's baby – you've met my lovely daughter - not yet three years old, and they raped her. Took turns.'

He paused, and I watched his larynx jerk up and down, as he tried to swallow.

'Carly was beside herself. She rang George on the payphone at his house and told him what was happening. He lived only a few streets away and he ran straight over. He grabbed the kitchen knife, and the rest you know. The brother, Cameron, ran off. George gave Carly all his money and his father's wallet, told her to pack a few things and get out of there, go to London – he wrote the word 'London' on a bit of the evening paper. Carly still has that scrap of newspaper. It has her father's blood on it.'

'Where was her mother?'

'Out. Bingo, or something. I think she was the one who came in and found George with the knife and rang the police.'

'And what about the little one?'

'She was in a terrible state. Carly cleaned her up a bit before she ran. She was still only a baby. The damage was awful. When I found Carly in London, little Catherine was in a really bad way. Carly wouldn't go to a doctor, for fear of being sent back home – she was paranoid. We knew some medical students, and one of them stitched little Catherine up, looked after her - risked her own career doing that, bless her.'

I had been prepared for the worst, I thought, but nothing quite so horrific as this.

'Thanks for telling me. I think I can understand now why George did it.'

'Too right, mate. I'd have done the same myself. Totally. What about you?'

'I hope so.'

He stared into the distance. I waited, hoping for a continuation of the story, but afraid to intrude on his private thoughts, to break the confessional mood that he had drifted into. Eventually he spoke again.

'I went to see him once, in prison. Wanted to promise him I'd look after Carly for him. But he wouldn't see me.'

I remembered my conversation with the Wakefield Prison governor, about the visit of the mysterious young Australian. Shane winced and closed his eyes, as if trying to blot out an unwelcome sight.

'She still wakes every single night, screaming, around the same time, three o'clock, like she's got a little alarm clock somewhere inside her. We don't share a bedroom any more. It was killing me.'

He pulled on the reins; his horse tossed back its head and broke into a gallop, towards the flock of sheep. I did not follow. My interview was over. I patted my old lady on the neck and turned her for home. George's words, 'it's done', ran over and over through my head.

XVIII

QUIET MOVE

(A move that does not attack an opposing piece.)

Back at the house, Ellen greeted me with the choice of a long cold drink of fruit squash or a coffee. I chose the squash. Had I found out what I wanted? Good. She sat me down at the kitchen table and began to lecture me.

'Now look here, David. There's no way you are driving that little sardine can back to Melbourne.'

'I promise I'll take it easy.'

'Don't be a dill. We're going to put you on a flight from Mildura. Shane or one of the boys will drive the car back for you soon enough, when one of them goes into Melbourne.'

She picked up the telephone to call the airport. It seemed I had no choice. She was on the phone for a good ten minutes, before she announced the outcome of her negotiations.

'No flights until New Year's Day, and you're not flying back then – you'll be in no state to fly after our New Year's Eve party tomorrow night. So I booked you a flight on

January second, that's Wednesday. You'll be spending New Year at the back of beyond, in Sunraysia, David. Get used to it! Okay?'

'You are very kind, Ellen.'

'Reckon? You owe me a hundred and twenty dollars. Any time now will do.'

This was perfect for me. I did not fancy the hustle and bustle of the big city, and my flight back to the UK was not until the morning of the fourth of January. And a New Year's Eve party to look forward to into the bargain! I handed over the money with as wide a smile as I had managed for years.

Cathy breezed into the kitchen.

'I'm off, gran.'

'What are you up to?'

'Shooting foxes and dingoes, natch!'

I felt my eyebrows arch. I was curious.

'Is that allowed?'

'Oh, beg yours, David. Didn't see you there. Almost compulsory, I'd say. Anyway, I need the money.'

'Does your dad pay you, or grandpa?'

'Nope. The Government of Victoria! Ten dollars for a fox, fifty dollars for a dingo. Big money!'

She made a pretend scary face.

'They kill the jumbucks!'

'Well, good hunting! What are you going to do with all that money?'

'I'm saving up – for my trip to the mother country of course. Gonna come see Her Maj before she shuffles off this mortal coil.'

'Oh very literary!'

'Shakespeare's big in Sunraysia, didn't you know? Bye.'

Ellen shouted after her: 'I hope you're going to pay for the ammo! Not too far now – don't want you going back of Bourke!'

She turned to me, shaking her head.

'I don't know what we're going to do when she's eighteen, David. She's going to want to go off and see the world, like every young Aussie. The problem is, as far as the Australian government is concerned she doesn't exist. Just like her mum.'

'I see. So when she wants a passport, or a job maybe, that's when the problems will start.'

'Around here, she's Cathy Thompson to everybody, and her mum's Carly Thompson, Shane's wife.'

'I take it they're not married, then?'

'Cathy just thinks Shane's her dad. And he is, but there's nothing official. Fairly soon we're going to have to tell her, poor kid. You can see why Shane got a bit cranky when you came raking up the past.'

I did not envy them. It seemed an intractable problem. I knew there were ways of buying a false identity, but that was for gangsters, not people like me, and not for honest, hard-working country folk.

I resisted Ellen's attempts to feed me lunch and retreated to my veranda to mull over what Shane had told me about the night of the murder. I was with Ryan all the way. 'Bravo, George!' was my overriding emotion, although I knew that this was an uncivilised reaction. Although not a believer, I lived and breathed the Christian values of a country that had abolished capital punishment decades before, and yet I felt the same anger that afternoon that George must have felt ten times over, when he saw what that loathsome pair were doing to that mere baby.

I had the shameful waking nightmare of what I would have liked to do with those two monsters of depravity. I had a vision of them hanging by their feet from the rafters of a barn, naked, hands tied, while I sliced off their genitals and fed them to dogs. For my coup de grace I toyed firstly with the death of Edmund Ironside, son of Ethelred the Unready, who, at the behest of the famous Cnut, was impaled from beneath whilst answering the call of nature, and secondly with that of Edward II, who famously lost the Battle of Bannockburn, by means of a red-hot poker inserted where the sun does not shine! However, I settled upon the fate of King James I of Scotland. He hid in a cesspit to escape his would-be assassins, but was eventually discovered. He fought off the first two men sent to dispatch him, wrestling with them and holding their heads under the filth, but was run through by the sword of Sir Robert Graham who leapt in to the assistance of his two hired assassins. James died of a combination of his wounds and drowning in the ordure.

Yes, this would have been a perfect and fitting end for those two pieces of excrement!

Oddly enough, I felt much better for this explosion of anger. Perhaps it is just as well that I was not present that night in May 1998.

At five o'clock Ellen rescued me from my gruesome reverie and employed me peeling vegetables for the pot-roast supper. Cathy clattered in triumphantly, holding up two animal tails dripping with blood.

'Look at that, you guys! Sixty dollars there! How about driving me into Mildura tomorrow, David, to cash them in?'

I said I would be delighted. She could show me around the town while we were there.

'Good onya, Dave!' and a broad smile were my reward.

At the table that evening, the conversation became strained when Cathy began to ask me questions about England. Meaningful glances were exchanged between the adults, and halfway through the main course Carly made the excuse that she was feeling ill and went to her room, turning to throw me the dirtiest of looks as she left. Shane half stood to follow her, but thought better of it.

My trip to Mildura with Cathy was a rare treat. She was a mine of information about the area. I had no idea that the land around Mildura itself was so fertile and productive. The reason for that, she explained to me, was the Murray River, which ran through the town and fed the irrigation system for the surrounding land. Mildura, she assured me, was very highly rated for its oranges, lemons and limes, and almost all of Victoria's wine production came from local grapes. As we approached the outskirts of the town, she asked me if I had any fruit with me and made me throw a banana and an orange, my lunch, out of the window, as Mildura was a fruit-fly exclusion zone and no fruit could be brought in. I felt as if she was the teacher and I the pupil!

As first priority on arrival, she handed in one fox-tail and one dingo-tail and emerged triumphant waving her sixty dollars in the air, proclaiming 'easy money!' I reminded her we had to pick up the mail from the post office. The same man was behind the counter.

'You found them all right then, mate,' he chuckled at me. 'I wasn't confident.'

My letter to Cathy was amongst the clutch of envelopes. I offered to keep the mail safe in my backpack, and was able to smuggle my letter away and drop it in the garbage, while Cathy went 'to the dunny'.

Cathy was inordinately proud of the town, pointing out all its glories. As we passed the Working Men's Club, she told me it once had the longest bar in the world, according to Guinness. You could play any sport you liked in Mildura. She listed them, ticking them off on her fingers: Aussie rules, cricket – ('Dad loves Aussie rules and cricket! He goes off to Melbourne some weekends to see the matches'). Then there's basketball, baseball, horseracing, motorsport, drag racing, kart racing, motorcycle racing, speedway, watersports.

'Even soccer,' she grinned at me. 'For the Poms! Oh! I forgot golf. Golf for the oldies. I bet you play golf, Dave.'

I admitted that I had been known to, now and again.

She dragged me for hours through the shopping mall, which at the least had the blessing of being amazingly well air-conditioned.

'Give me Mildura over Melbourne for shopping, anytime,' chirped my young guide, as she browsed the umpteenth clothes shop. In the end she persuaded a young male assistant to sell her a dress at the price it would be in the sale, which did not start until the following day. One flicker of the eyelashes in my direction and I found myself handing over my credit card to pay for it. The shoe department was next, as a pair of heels to match the dress was suddenly a crucial object of desire. Funnily enough, I found myself paying for the shoes also. It seemed to be expected, not only by the shop assistant, but also by Cathy, who had found a sudden urgent need to inspect the display of tights.

I have only myself to blame for the fancy tights, skirt and top, as I could have called a halt right there at the shoe counter, but the shopping-machine was now at full throttle and I was somehow carried along.

Late lunch-cum-tea was coffee and cakes, which Cathy generously offered to pay for. I overruled her. Then she showed me the river. This seemed a refreshingly cheap option, but I had reckoned without the expensive two-hour paddle steamer trip. Finally, she sighed and declared that perhaps we ought to be going back home, but that first I must buy myself a boomerang. She would even show me how to use it, if there was time.

It is perhaps a blessing that I never had a daughter like Cathy, as that might well have been an express route to the debtors' prison; but expensive as it was on my pocket, I would have paid ten times over for the privilege of that blissful day in a small town on the edge of the Aussie outback. It was years since I had felt so light-hearted.

Cathy could hardly wait to show her mother her booty. She pulled each item out of the plastic bags, like a conjurer pulling rabbits from a hat, and flounced around the dining-room holding them up in front of her and posing for an imaginary camera.

'All that lot for sixty dollars?' said Carly, incredulous.

Cathy paused in her display, and turned towards me.

'Did David buy all this lot?'

'Well, he used his card.'

'That's still buying stuff, you dill!'

When Cathy had gone off to show Ellen her new acquisitions, I approached Carly.

'I hope you don't mind. I'm afraid it got a little bit out of hand.'

'No, I don't mind one bit. Anything that makes her that happy is okay by me.'

She turned on her heel and left me. It was the first time she had spoken to me since the evening I arrived.

Ellen had told me to expect lamb for supper followed by 'bush telly'. I was not disappointed. We were joined for the evening's festivities by two of Bill's jackaroos and their wives, who taught me a few words of 'Strine', Aussie patois. The meal was superb, and the 'bush telly' turned out to be a bonfire, around which we sat until midnight, drinking Ellen's delicious rum punch, playing charades, and then sang Auld Lang Syne – Bill's idea – hugged and kissed, shook hands and toasted the New Year. It knocked my 2012 New Year's Eve into a cocked hat.

New Year's Day was necessarily a quiet affair, considering the prevailing atmosphere of hangover. A late morning in bed was followed by an hour's instruction in the art of boomerang throwing, until Cathy gave up on me, frustrated by my incompetence.

'How far are you from London?' she asked.

'About two hundred and fifty kilometres, I'd say.'

'Well, if you're that near, perhaps you can show me around when I come to London.'

'No worries, cobber,' I said, with a little chuckle.

'What's so funny, Dave? You laughing at me?'

'Of course not. Why would I?'

The following day I said a sad goodbye to my new friends and flew back to Melbourne and the tedium of the Hilton Hotel. I had what I came for, the story of what happened the night of the patricide. I should have been content. Now I could only worry about what I could do with my information. I could tell George that I knew what had happened, and that I now understood what drove him to the crime. I could tell Paul Morgan, who would find my information helpful, perhaps even crucial. Taylor-Smith would of course want to know. I could tell Doris, to whom it might be some consolation. However, revealing the information to the authorities, who might consequently look more leniently on George's crime or crimes, would certainly endanger the wellbeing of Carly, Cathy and the whole Thompson family, and I would not be believed unless I betrayed my source. Wouldn't Doris insist that I did so? After all, she had every right to think first and foremost of her husband.

My dilemma tormented me on the flight back to Melbourne and for the rest of the day back in the state capital. I paced my room until mid-afternoon, and then drove down to St Kilda to watch the Victoria Women's XI play New South Wales. Even sitting in the shade behind the white palings of the picturesque Junction Oval, listening to the familiar, comforting sound of leather on willow, I found no peace.

The following day I felt easier in my mind. I had decided to tell all to Les Bradshaw, who would be guaranteed to provide the wise counsel that I needed. I also felt a burning compulsion to justify to her my faith in George as a good person.

I spent the morning shopping for souvenirs and gifts for Suzi, Alicia, Michael and Claire. And, of course, Tuppence. As the early afternoon heat built up, I ate a light lunch at a pavement café and then retired to my room for a siesta and to enjoy the television coverage of the second Test between Australia and Sri Lanka, in Sydney.

During the tea interval at the Test, I took off my spectacles and lay back on the bed. I must have nodded off, and I was woken by a knock at the hotel room door. I pulled myself together and fumbled for my spectacles. There was a second knock, louder. I called that I was coming, and stumbled to the door, still half asleep. It was probably cleaners, or room-service. Perhaps it was a message from home, from Suzi, or Taylor-Smith. Perhaps there had been developments!

It was not room service, not a message. Instead, it was the last person in the world I expected to see.

XIX

BREAKTHROUGH

(Breach of an apparently strong defence.)

'Carly! What are you . . . what brings you to Melbourne?'

'Can I come in?'

Perhaps it was my immersion in the Australian tones of my host city, but her accent sounded somehow even more Sheffield than ever. I showed her to the only armchair, offered her tea, which she refused, and sat on the bed waiting for her to speak. She remained silent.

'So, what does bring you to Melbourne, Carly? Shopping? The January sales?'

I winced at my sexist remark. I was forgetting my training.

'The sales? Of course, but mainly I came to drive your car back. I overruled Shane. Told him it was my turn for the big city lights.'

She opened her handbag.

'I've brought you the counterfoils from your hire documents.'

'Well, thank you. It was kind of you, driving that rattletrap all that way, just to save me the hassle. I appreciate it. How did you know I was here?'

'My daughter, the nosy one in the family, she knew where you would be.'

'Ah.'

I was still bemused by her arrival. This was the woman who had shunned me for the past four days.

She nodded towards the counterfoils lying beside me on the bed.

'That's not my only reason for coming to see you. Not the real reason.'

'Oh?'

'There's something I need to tell you. I've been wanting to tell somebody half my life. I couldn't tell Shane, or Ellen, and I can't tell Cathy. I . . . '

She stopped, put her head in her hands.

'What is it, Carly?'

I waited for what must have been a full minute.

'When I saw how you were with Cathy, and how she took to you, I . . . Do you have children, David?'

'One son, grown-up now, of course.'

'Then you might have an inkling, might begin to understand what it's like for a woman to hold a child who has grown inside her body, is her own flesh and blood. Literally. When you get home, ask your wife what she felt like.'

I hesitated, then nodded.

'I will.'

'You would do anything for that child, to keep her safe, to protect her from all the evils in the world, to keep her clean.'

'I understand that much. I've felt the same myself.'

'With respect, David, you can't possibly have experienced what I'm talking about. Not first hand, personally. You're a man! What I'm talking about is the mother instinct. You can't know what it feels to be so physically attached to a child. Men can't possibly feel that intensity! So don't tell me you've felt the same!'

Her tirade hurt me, but I bit my lip and held my peace.

She raised her hand in apology.

'Sorry, David.'

196

I forced myself to tell her it was okay.

'I was only a child myself when I had Catherine, but it was there in me, more powerful than you can ever imagine. I loved that baby, even in spite of the way she came to be in my body, and I would have done anything, given anything, made any sacrifice for her. I tried three times to run away from those scumbags, but they just came and found me, my parents so-called and that vile Uncle Cameron. They dragged me back home and made me pay. Big-time.'

Both her fists were screwed into a ball, and her knuckles were white with tension. I noticed a tear forming in her eye.

'It's okay, Carly. Take it easy, take your time.'

'Anyway, how would I have looked after her? I was just a useless kid myself. I needed their money, their food, their milk for the baby. I wasn't allowed anything for myself. Anything I got from the welfare, they took off me.

'I had Tess, though. They'd sent her away when my mother was expecting me. We'd only seen each other once, when I ran away to my grandma's in Lincoln with Catherine, but she used to write to me, send me photos and stories of going to the seaside and other exciting stuff. She liked the idea of having a little sister, I think.'

She paused. And smiled, no doubt remembering one of the few happy parts of her troubled childhood. Then she heaved a deep sigh and continued.

'And I had George. George always tried to look after me when I was little, before he left home. He was loads older than me, I always remember him as grown-up, but he kept in touch and used to come round to see me when he knew nobody would be in – when he had it, he gave me money to hide in a secret hiding place he'd made in the attic.'

'Shane's told me what happened, that night.'

She looked at me, then down at her feet.

'George didn't kill my father.'

I stood bolt upright.

'Shane told you what I told him, what he's always believed happened.'

'I don't understand. What are you telling me? George spent twelve years in prison for nothing?'

'Not exactly for nothing. For me. And for Cathy.'

197

The penny dropped. Suddenly everything was crystal clear.

'When I saw that they had taken Catherine out of her cot, I ran downstairs to find her. She was not there, either, and I suddenly had a horrible realisation of what they were doing with her. I grabbed the carving knife from the kitchen and ran upstairs to the attic. I don't have the words to tell you what they were doing to my baby, David, and it would break my heart if I tried. I flew into a rage and I stabbed and stabbed until I was exhausted. I think I only hit that foul scumbag Cameron the once, and he ran off, like the coward he is. When I'd finished, I was covered in my father's blood, from head to toe. I picked my baby up and we both cried.'

I waited, but was impatient to hear the rest.

'I suppose that was when you rang George.'

'Yes, I needed help. He raced straight round there. He helped me bathe little Catherine and looked after her while I changed my clothes and washed the blood off myself. He cried when he saw her wounds. It was the only time I saw him show any emotion of any kind. He gave me all the money he had with him and took our father's wallet and put it in my bag. He wrote the word 'London' on a scrap of newspaper, and I got the message.'

'My God! What did you do?'

'There was a bus to London from Pond Street. I knew I could afford the bus, so I got on.'

'And George stayed behind in the house?'

'Yes. I think my mother found him holding the knife, standing over the body.'

I could not help but wonder whether I would have had the courage to do what George did, or even the presence of mind to think of doing it.

'That was some sacrifice!' I murmured. 'How could you not say anything, Carly? You did nothing to help him. I mean, if you'd only told the police what those two men were doing to your child . . . '

'Don't imagine that I'm not ashamed of it. I think about it every day and every night of my life. For over fourteen years I've been trying to drive it from my mind, but it never goes away, never gets any better.'

I remembered the nightmares that Shane had told me about, and realised that it was not simply the horror of her experiences at Khartoum Street that disturbed her sleep, but also the guilt that she felt at leaving George to pay the price of her crime.

'And then Shane found you.'

'And we all lived happily ever after.'

She stood up and walked to the window, overlooking the wide street leading towards the MCG.

'I did it for Catherine. I kept quiet for her. She needed me. And all my instincts were telling me that I had to get out of the country, away from all that horror, start again, for her.'

'So you used Shane. Did you not love him?'

My words were harsh, but I was thinking of George and I was still angry with her.

'I love him to bits. Shane is my rock, my guardian angel, my hero, my other hero along with George. He's the best man in the world and a wonderful father to my girl. You've met her. We did well, didn't we?'

'You did.'

'So, what do you think? Was George's sacrifice worthwhile?'

I had no answer. I was not used to such difficult questions.

'What did you tell Bill and Ellen?'

'Shane came home, told them he'd found a girl in London and wanted to bring her home. They were happy for him at first. He hadn't shown much interest in girls before. Even when he told them about Catherine, they were understanding. They took the attitude that everyone makes mistakes. They welcomed me and my little girl into their family. It was only when they saw how young I was, that the alarm bells starting ringing.'

'What happened?'

'Shane had to tell them the whole story, well, part of it, about the sexual abuse. The rest, the murder, only came out when *you* started trying to contact me, before Christmas. We decided they had to know everything, well, everything Shane knew.'

'But back then, when you first came to Australia, they let you come to live here, as Shane's wife.'

199

'I'll never be any man's wife, David. No man is ever going to lay a finger on me ever again, while I live and breathe!'

I was confused.

'I've told you how I feel about Shane. He means the world to me. He saved my life, and Cathy's. God! he even educated me. I knew sod all about the world before I met him. You could write what I learned at school on the back of an envelope!'

She tossed her head back, a replica of those disillusioned teenage girls that have crossed my path so often.

'But we're not man and wife.'

I looked at her and shook my head, uncomprehending.

'Shane is not interested in us girls, David. Hard to spot, true, but if you know what you're looking for . . . '

'Shane is gay?'

She looked at me as though I were a halfwit. And nodded.

'It was a godsend to me that Shane took me on, but it was convenient for him as well, to take me home as his girl. Bill and Ellen didn't know he was gay. He'd kept it hidden away. It's not an acceptable lifestyle around here.'

'Do they know now?'

'I think they must. Nothing's ever been said, though. Cathy knows nothing, of course. She's always boasting about her handsome, sexy dad.'

I wondered where Shane took his comfort. He was an attractive, energetic man and would have the natural urges we all suffer or enjoy. Perhaps the occasional weekends he spent in Melbourne, ostensibly at sporting events, served more than one purpose.

'So, the separate rooms, then . . .'

'Oh, that's genuine enough. He has good reason not to want to sleep with me. I must be a nightmare. Sorry, poor choice of words there.'

I thought of that teenage girl, so desperate that she killed her own father, frightened half to death, with a tiny child to care for, alone in a strange city and with no knowledge of the world beyond Khartoum Street, no knowledge of real men, decent men. My anger softened. Her pain was real, and I did not have the first idea what to say to her, or how to comfort her, to show her I understood. I could not begin to grasp the extent of her suffering.

And so I made tea. It's what we do, we English. We make tea.

We drank it together in silence.

I could tell my good friend George that his sacrifice had not been for nothing. His sister had grown into a fine young woman, damaged, but feisty and courageous, and an excellent mother. His niece was a credit to her upbringing, and appeared blessedly unscathed by her early traumas. She had captivated me, for one, from the moment I met her and would certainly make her mark on the world.

I decided against telling Carly about the death of Cameron and George's arrest. It was the wrong moment. Her burden was already heavy, and she would know soon enough.

The shuttle bus dropped me at Tullamarine airport at 8.30 the following morning. I had over an hour to while away before boarding, and I sat in an upper-level café looking down on the travellers streaming into the check-in hall.

I am not sure if this is a common phenomenon, but all too frequently in my life, shortly after a friend or acquaintance has died, I have seen that person in a crowded place. The first time was when, as a little boy, I saw my Uncle Wilf, back in 1951, coming out of a football match with the throng of other spectators. I called after him, I was so sure it was him. Then I remembered he was dead; I had even been to his funeral. I felt very foolish and embarrassed, as if everyone knew and was laughing at me. The next time was at University, when I saw Ken Jones, my cricket chum, across the street near the student union building, wearing a university scarf and laughing and joking with a pal, as he always did. I ran across the road, through the busy traffic, but he had gone. It cannot have been him. He had drowned off the Aquitaine coast the previous summer. It happened to me three more times over the years. I suppose we all have our doppelganger somewhere in the world, our spitting image, perhaps several, or even many. Perhaps I had seen a look-alike. Or

201

perhaps the subconscious mind plays tricks on us. Perhaps on those occasions I was thinking of the people in question at a deep, subterranean level, and my brain played a trick on my eyes.

At all events, looking down on the crowds at Melbourne Tullamarine airport, I saw Bill Rodgers, trundling his wheeled suitcase along behind him, looking exactly as he did 35 years ago, the same neat grey hair with a centre parting, like the old-fashioned footballers I remember from cigarette cards, the same slow but purposeful walk. I stood to watch him pick his way dexterously, unhurriedly through the press to the far end of the hall, like a stately, slow-motion Stanley Mathews. Then I lost him.

I realised, sadly and more than a little ashamed, that I had not given a moment's thought to his funeral the previous week.

XX

PROPHYLAXIS

(A move or strategy that frustrates an opponent, provoking an error.)

The plane landed on time at Heathrow, and before two o'clock I was fast asleep in my room at the airport hotel where I had parked my car. I slept well and, after a leisurely breakfast, battled through the Saturday traffic around the M25 and up the M1 to Sheffield.

I had left Suzi in charge of Tuppence. She had been delighted to take the opportunity of living, as she described it, 'in luxury' in my house whilst I was away. She and Alicia were busy dismantling the bizarre Christmas trimmings she had introduced to enliven the house in her own unique style, while Tuppence looked on suspiciously from his throne.

He was as silent as ever, but he looked from me to Suzi, then to Alicia. I knew exactly what he was thinking:

'About time you were back! These two are a nightmare!'

I expected Suzi to greet me with a 'hello' at least, perhaps even a 'did you enjoy your holiday?' but this was not the case.

'This is very bad cat! He not do nothing that I tell him. And he try to scratch Alicia.'

'Well, I think he's very sensitive about his injuries, and he doesn't like stroking. Best to keep away from him, while he is in this mood.'

'Oh yes! We keep away from him. Tuppence is very bad cat. I would not have such a cat.'

I smoothed the situation over by paying her in crisp new £20 notes, and she left smiling to catch her bus home - she refused a lift, as always – the two creating such a charming tableau, as they crossed the street hand-in-hand, Suzi towing her gigantic suitcase, Alicia her tiny travel bag, that I was tempted to photograph them. I still have that image as the desktop background on my computer.

The following day, Sunday, I was tired, but having arrived back in the UK at a propitious time, I had avoided the worst excesses of jetlag. Uppermost in my mind was the fervent wish to pass on my knowledge that George had been innocent of the crime which sent him to prison for life, that my faith in him had been vindicated. Particularly to those people who did not believe in him! Most of all, I needed to tell Les Bradshaw, with whom I had parted on less than cordial terms because of that very issue. I phoned her.

'I need to see you. I have something to tell you, about George Campbell.'

'You know my position on George Campbell. But go on, if you must.'

'I'd rather come over.'

'Can't you tell me now, on the telephone?'

'This is something I need to tell you in person. It won't take long, I promise.'

I wanted to see the look on her face, when I told her I knew that George had been innocent all along.

It was a bitterly cold day, and as I left the house I was greeted by an icy blast of tiny hailstones that stung my face and drummed noisily against the car roof. By the time I arrived at Ranmoor, large, fat snowflakes filled the air, and my wipers were working full-time to clear the screen. Les ushered me quickly inside and hurriedly closed her front door against the freezing draught. The house was warm and smelt good – fresh coffee and cinnamon, I think. Even in my eagerness to spill my news, I noticed how well she looked. Her hair was cut a little shorter and differently styled. She offered me tea or coffee, which I refused. I was not going to stay long. We sat in her front room, in the same places as on my first visit.

'I have certain proof that George Campbell did not kill his father.'

I waited for my bombshell to take effect. Les frowned, examined her fingernails, looked down at the coffee table, then back at me.

'And do you know who did?'

'Yes.'

'And?'

'I'm afraid I can't tell you.'

'But you have proof, you say?'

'Straight from the horse's mouth. I have a confession.'

'But you can't tell me, or won't tell me, who did commit the murder?'

I signalled that this was the case.

'That's hardly going to hold up in court, is it?'

'I am willing to tell you, if you swear not to tell anyone else.'

'You know I can't do that. Once a copper, always a copper, David.'

'But a copper with a heart, I think. I hope. You have a daughter . . .'

She cut me off.

'We don't have hearts. We only have justice and the law. Please don't tell me any secrets. I shall have to act on whatever you tell me.'

She stood and walked to the door.

'Time you went, David, before you say something you'd regret.'

She opened the door and stood waiting for me.

'You see, I'm fairly sure I've already guessed. You look really well, David, and I don't think you got your tan from a sunbed. You haven't, by any chance, been to Australia, have you?'

I stayed in my seat and said nothing.

'I could find out easily enough.'

I stood and turned towards her.

'Okay, I have.'

'Nice time?'

'Excellent weather, Christmas Day on the beach with a barbie, caught a bit of Test cricket, that sort of thing. It was very rewarding.'

'You must show me your holiday snaps sometime. Goodbye, David. And a happy New Year to you.'

I left, chastened and demoralised, to drive home through the already snow-covered streets. I thought back to Ray Broomhead's description of Les, before we had met: 'Straight as a die, tough as old boots.' I had been guilty of a major misjudgement. Now, for Carly's sake, I could only hope that Detective Chief Inspector Lesley Bradshaw did have a heart.

After the underwhelming response to my discovery from Les Bradshaw, I was less enthusiastic about passing on my 'good news' to Michael and Claire. I phoned to let them know I was back safely, and we exchanged a few pleasantries about how we had spent our respective Christmases. Neither mentioned George, and so I decided to keep my news for a later date.

The next morning, I arranged an appointment with Taylor-Smith, for three o'clock that afternoon, to fill him in on my exploits down under. As the side streets had not yet been cleared of snow, I took the bus into town. I was a few minutes early, but Mr Toad's secretary showed me straight into his office. He was effusive in his greeting, although he did not rise from his seat, as though we had known each other for years, a trick I have often seen used by Members of Parliament and successful businessman.

After assuring me that he was 'the very soul of discretion' and that what I would tell him was entirely confidential and would remain within these four walls, he listened attentively, occasionally making notes on a pad, to my detailed explanation, first of Shane's account of the murder of George's father, then of the escape to Australia, and finally of Carly's revelation in the Hilton Hotel.

'Well, old boy, that's quite a story! One could almost write a book. But, you see, you've rather tied my hands by saying that we can't use this information. So, I'm not entirely certain why you've told me.'

'I suppose I thought it might make you do an even better job for George.'

In fact, I was not sure myself why I had needed to tell him. It was probably that I just wanted everyone to know what I knew, that George was innocent, had been unjustly convicted, and was still under a life sentence for a crime that he had not committed. I wanted everyone to know that he was a hero, a martyr maybe.

'It won't make a ha'p'orth of difference to the job I do for George Campbell. Stinking rich or skint, guilty or innocent, every client receives the full benefit of my expertise.'

I was clearly being reprimanded for uttering such a heresy.

'I'll give you this, it does turn on its head my opinion of our man George. Totally on its head. As to whether it helps us with the matter at hand, I'm not so sure.'

He told me that in effect nothing had changed since our last conversation. I asked him whether he had managed to see the scene of crime yet, and was disappointed to find that he had not. He promised me that, for what it was worth, he would arrange for the two of us to 'have a gander at the scene of the dirty deed'.

As I left, he called me back.

'I almost forgot. A psychiatrist chappie, Morgan was his name, said he'd been treating George, gave me your name, phoned to ask if he might go and see him in clink. I haven't heard any more from him.'

I called the Waltham Forest clinic when I got home and was put straight through to Paul Morgan. I warned him that I was relying on his professional discretion not to breathe a word of what I had to tell him about the murder of Stuart Campbell. He listened, without interruption, to my account of what I had found out in Australia. From time to time he let out a gasp of astonishment or horror. It all explained a great deal about the origin of George's psychological disorder, he told me. He had indeed driven up to see George, but it had been a waste of time. He felt that he had retreated even further into his shell, had responded to him in no way whatsoever, not even by looking him in the eye. He was now anxious for the opportunity to take George back into his care, but if his

207

patient's innocence was to remain secret, he would be unable to do so. Could I not persuade his sister to take responsibility for her crime? I was beginning to feel under increasing pressure to break my sworn promises to both Carly and to Shane.

This was my cue to visit my friend. Perhaps I could make a difference for George, cheer him up by telling him good news about his family. There is little or no restriction on visits to prisoners on remand, but I telephoned HMP Doncaster to announce my intention to visit George. Unexpectedly, he seemed pleased to see me. His eyes had shed their glazed, staring quality and had more sparkle. I shook his hand.

'I have some news, George. First of all, I need to tell you why I didn't visit over the Christmas and New Year period; I was in Australia.'

He turned his head slightly to one side, his recently acquired method of signalling curiosity.

'I found your sister, George. I found Carly.'

George sat up straighter, and I thought I detected some slight movement in his facial muscles.

'She's well, George. Little Catherine is seventeen now and she is lovely. She's a charming Aussie teenager, full of life and ambition. She's a real credit to her mother. And to you, George. Most of all to you.'

His hands were on the table now, fingers intertwined, and I saw his knuckles whiten. I lowered my voice to a murmur. I did not want to be overheard.

'She told me, George, about that night, about your father and uncle and her child. She told me the whole thing. I know you took the blame for everything, and I know that it wasn't you.'

He drew his right index finger up to his lips, the universal signal to keep quiet, not to tell.

'You've kept the secret for almost fifteen years, George. You've paid the price, made the sacrifice. It's done. I have no right to tell.'

He gave a short gasp, a gasp of relief.

'There is one thing I'd like to say, though, and I wish I could shout it to the whole world - what you did, I think it's the most noble and heroic thing that I have ever come across. Carly calls you her hero, and for what it's worth you're mine too. It's a privilege to know you.'

I took the hand from the table and the hand that was still held to his mouth, and I held them in mine.

The prison officer watching us turned away. The sight of two men, holding hands, with tears in their eyes, was too much for him.

On the Wednesday morning, Taylor-Smith and I went to see the flat at Callow Green. The caretaker, Mary Knowles, had been warned of our visit and was waiting for us outside the block with the keys. She was full of guilt and self-recrimination about not having discovered the body earlier, as she herself had noticed a 'funny smell' when cleaning the stairs the previous week.

'It were awful that t' poor man had been left there so long. God forbid it ever happens to me! We all thought he'd just died, and t' murder, that were just terrible. We've had some things, but we've never had a murder in t' flats. A lot o' t' old people are very worried and upset now. Some on 'em have asked to move.'

She prattled on, as the lift rattled slowly up to Cameron Campbell's floor. There were the obvious signs that the door to the flat had been damaged and then repaired and a new lock fitted. She unlocked the door, and I was relieved when she said she would wait outside.

The living room was surprisingly spick and span, everything tidy, with not a speck of dust to be seen, almost as though Suzi had passed through. I commented on it, and Mr Toad agreed that it was 'curiously shipshape'. The bedroom was equally immaculate, the bed made up with a crisp, ironed sheet and duvet cover. There were no pillows.

'This may not mean anything,' I commented to Taylor-Smith, 'but did you notice when you came last time, whether the door was mended?'

'No, I didn't. It was opened inwards and I probably didn't even see the damaged bit. Why do you ask?'

'Let's ask madame.'

He followed me out.

'Mrs Knowles,' I said. 'It's all very clean and tidy. Are you responsible for that? Or did the police do it?'

209

'Oh no, that were me. I thought I owed it to t' poor man. Anyway, folk were complaining, you know, about t' smell and that. So I went in and opened all t' windows, when they'd took him away, and cleaned up.'

'What did you do, exactly?'

I could feel Mr Toad breathing down my neck, very interested.

'I cleaned up. I hoovered, washed t' pots, dusted round and tidied up. T' place were in a mess. You know what men are like.'

'You hoovered everywhere, all through the flat.'

'Oh aye, I gi' it a good fettle.'

'Did you wash the bedding, Mrs Knowles?' came a quiet voice from behind me.

'I did. Straight away. It were horrible and it smelt. Like toilets.'

'Including the pillow-slips?'

'I washed all t' lot, sheet, duvet cover and pillow slips.'

'And the front door?' I said.

'I got t' council to mend t' door and put a new lock on straight away. They were very good about that. Said they didn't want looters coming in. You know what some folk are like, pinching stuff.'

Mr Toad planted a noisy, wet kiss on the caretaker's face.

'You are an absolute treasure, Mrs Knowles! There's a bouquet of roses and a box of Turkish Delight coming your way!'

As we waved goodbye to Mrs Knowles, I could see that Taylor-Smith was cock-a-hoop. He turned to me, triumphant:

'My joy is unconfined, old thing!'

I noticed the change from 'old boy' to 'old thing'. Was Mr Toad becoming affectionate?

'You know what this means, don't you?' he leered at me.

'I think I do,' I said, averting my gaze from the emetic vision of flapping jowls and fleshy red lips.

'It means, old thing, that we have them by the short and curlies! First of all, they have the problem of persuading the pathologist chappie to pin down the time of death to the day of our man George's visit, and no

210

professional worth his salt would risk his reputation with such a fib. Secondly, all they have is a few hairs on a sofa and a couple of sets of fingerprints – and why not? Our man merely paid a social visit to a long-lost, aged uncle, shared a glass of whisky with him for auld lang syne, looked up something for him on the Internet, bus times or train times, or the price of fish, and left him happy and healthy, then went off for a bit of a drive in the lady wife's jalopy and ran out of petrol, poor fellow. No trace of our man on the bedding, on the pillow - the presumed murder weapon - no trace of anyone, for that matter, thanks to the good offices of our friend Mrs Knowles.'

'Well done, Mr Taylor-Smith,' I acknowledged.

'Not a bit of it, old thing! Well done to you! I think the admirable professional skills of the fair DCI may well have rubbed off on you.'

'Can we get George out of prison?'

'We'll spring the blighter by the morning!'

We drove directly to West Bar police station, where Taylor-Smith demanded to see the investigating officer. All that was needed was George's continued silence, and we were home and dry. On the way, I left a voice-mail message for Doris, passing on the glad tidings.

Taylor-Smith gave the police and the Crown Prosecution Service enough time to come to their decision. It was, in the deplorable modern-day parlance, a 'no-brainer'. They had no choice, so flimsy was the evidence they could present against George. Convinced of his guilt, they had clearly been hoping to force a confession by misrepresenting the strength of their case. It was sharp practice, and belonged to the grey area between legal and illegal. They had been rumbled.

XXI

ABSOLUTE PIN

(A pin against the king, where the pinned piece cannot move because it would expose the king to check.)

We returned together to the West Bar station the following afternoon, expecting to hear that the charges against George had been dropped. To our surprise, Taylor-Smith was ushered into the office of the superintendent of CID. He emerged half an hour later, even redder in the face than usual and looking furious. He marched straight past me at a rate of knots that I had not dreamt was within his capability. I ran after him and caught up with him in the car park.

He told me the worst. The good news was that the charge against George for the murder of Cameron Campbell had been dropped, as we had expected. The bad news was that George was still to be held in custody, pending a hearing before a judge the following Monday in Leeds, to face charges on five counts of breach of parole licence.

'What!'

Taylor-Smith pulled out a note-book from his jacket pocket.

'Item 1: absence from his agreed place of residence without prior agreement over two days around New Year 2011–2012.

'Item 2: absence from his agreed place of residence, without prior agreement, for two days and nights, October 22nd and 23rd, 2012.

'Item 3: unsupervised train journey from London to Sheffield, without prior agreement, on Saturday 8th of September, 2012, at a time when he was, by prior agreement, still under the supervision of a psychiatric clinic.

'Item 4: failure to attend an arranged appointment with the Offender Manager, on March 27th, 2012.'

'Unbelievable! They must know that was the day of Marilyn's funeral.'

'Item 5: failure to complete unpaid work requirement of 300 hours, within the deadline of 18 months from the day of his release, a deadline already extended from 12 months because of mitigating circumstances, viz the offender's frail state of health upon release and the two months he spent in a clinic under psychiatric treatment. He was three hours short, by the way.'

'Unbelievable!'

I was almost speechless with rage, and clearly the range and quality of my vocabulary had shrunk.

'Apparently, these matters have only just come to the notice of the Offender Manager.'

'It's a shabby trick. You'll appear for him on Monday?'

'Certainly. I shall cancel my other appointments.'

He shook his head slowly and his chin fell onto his chest.

'I shall do my best, but I am not sanguine. They wouldn't have trumped up these charges if they didn't mean business.'

The jaunty, hail-fellow-well-met self-assurance had evaporated. The ebullient Mr Toad had slipped into sombre mood.

I called Doris, who told me she already knew about the charges and was about to drive up the M1 from Leicester. The solicitor and I set off directly for Doncaster to inform George of the day's developments. Taylor-Smith drove the Bentley – I was far too angry and in no fit state to be at the

213

wheel. Even the normally phlegmatic Mr Toad was grim-faced; he gripped the steering wheel fiercely, never leaving the outside lane and flashing his lights aggressively at any driver who dared to block his way.

The governor intercepted us to tell us that George had already been informed of the charges brought against him by the Offender Manager. Taylor-Smith asked how he had received the news. The governor shook his head.

'I told him myself. He didn't blink an eyelid. I thought he might be furious.'

I personally was still boiling with anger.

'George doesn't get angry. He's the calmest, most gentle man I have ever met.'

The governor raised his eyebrows, like a cartoon character.

'He's a better man than I, then. I understand they have dropped the murder charge. I haven't told him. I'll leave that to you.'

George did not seem surprised to see us. I gave him brief details of our visit to the scene of the crime and our elation at discovering the weakness of the case against him. He shook his head slightly at the news that the charges against him had been dropped.

As we were leaving the prison, Doris arrived. Her joy on hearing the news of our scene-of-the-crime triumph had, like mine, turned to despair and anger. I hugged her long and hard. Taylor-Smith shook her hand and assured her he would do his damnedest in court.

On the way back to Sheffield, both Taylor-Smith and I had recovered our composure. Taylor-Smith asked me what I thought had really happened in Cameron Campbell's flat, a question to which I had already given a good deal of thought.

'There are several possibilities. The obvious one is that George tracked down his uncle, went to see him, got him drunk and into bed, then smothered him, look at it how you will, as a punishment, or revenge, or just as you might put down a mad dog.'

'I'm with you there, old boy. That's the obvious conclusion, and that's what our friends in the CPS think. They're convinced he did it, especially as he's served time for murdering his father. Same motivation. They can't get him back sewing mailbags quickly enough.'

'It's just possible, just possible that George tracked him down, went to see him, shared a whisky with him, and left him alive and well.'

'Can't say I buy that one, old boy.'

'Me neither. I'll tell you what *is* a possibility, though.'

Taylor-Smith turned his head ninety degrees and looked interested. Anxious for him to keep his eyes on the road, I went on.

'George went to see him, intending to do him in, but found someone else had done the job for him. There must be plenty of candidates, anybody who found out what he was up to, perhaps even with their own children.'

'Hmm. I'm not convinced. How would our man have entered the apartment with the unfortunate uncle dead as a doornail? Your murderer would hardly have left the door conveniently unlocked.'

'Ah, yes. A snag. I hadn't thought that through.'

'But I will tell you what *is* a realistic scenario – our man George tracks down the evil uncle, curious to discover if he's a reformed character, no intention of terminating the aged relative, sits down innocently at the computer to check his lottery numbers, discovers a bucket-load of filth, draws his own conclusions and decides that society is better off without this child-molesting scoundrel. And quite right too.'

'We mustn't rule out one other possible scenario.'

'Oh? Enlighten me, do, old boy.'

'The possibility that this was an act of charity, of altruism.'

Taylor-Smith, alarmingly, once again took his eyes from the road ahead, this time for a full ten seconds.

'Cameron Campbell had terminal lung cancer and was probably living in constant misery. Perhaps this was a mercy killing, even requested by Cameron himself. The heavy consumption of whisky fits in with that scenario.'

'So, who dunnit?'

'Possibly George, possibly another, unknown person, a friend or relative of Cameron. The fact is that we don't know. And we never shall, unless George tells us.'

'It's a neat theory, I'll grant you that. In any case, old boy, we don't have to worry our pretty heads about that any more, unless George blabs to the bobbies, which I'm sure you'll agree is unlikely, given his predilection for silence. Our immediate problem is to fend off these trumped-up charges on Monday morning.'

I visited George on each of the intervening days between then and his appearance in court. I bought him a high-octane-level chess software package and a top-specification laptop computer, to occupy his time and keep his chess skills honed. He seemed pleased. It was the very least I could do.

The following Monday, the judge upheld all five charges of breach of licence, despite the stout defence offered by Taylor-Smith. George Campbell was dispatched to 'A' Wing of HMP Leeds, the ghastly fortress of Armley Gaol, to sit out the rest of his life sentence. He was refused the right to appeal.

That morning in the Leeds Crown Court, I watched George's face, as the judge pronounced his decision. It was the old George, pale, still, with no sign of emotion on his face; the dull stare was back in his eyes. He did not turn his head to the body of the court, to the solicitors' bench, to Doris, nor to me. The court officer led him down from the dock and out of sight.

I sat alone in the row of seats behind Doris, who was flanked by her mother and brother. I watched as Taylor-Smith hauled himself to his feet, and, white with anger, reacted to the judge's words.

'Your honour, today I am ashamed to be part of our system of justice. I protest that this is a decision which rests on technicalities, no more. In no way has my client breached the spirit of his parole licence.'

The judge warned him that he was exposing himself to the danger of a charge of contempt of court, and Taylor-Smith collapsed back onto the bench, an abject figure, head down, cramming his papers into a battered attaché case.

Doris turned to leave the court. She was in tears, but she stood erect. I walked closer to hug her, but she took me by the shoulders.

216

'I'm so sorry, Doris.'

'It's not over, David. We're not finished yet.'

She squeezed my shoulders and left the court, followed by her grim-faced mother and brother, to meet the gathering horde of reporters, photographers and television cameras. I walked down to shake Taylor-Smith's hand and thank him for his efforts.

'Sometimes,' he said, his lips taut and opening a mere slit as he spoke, 'sometimes the law is an ass, old boy.'

This was not the flippant, cynical, self-indulgent, pretentious, pompous, mercenary clever-dick that I had taken him for. I had discovered a new respect for Mr Toad. And a grudging affection.

I went out of the building with him and stood beside him on the steps of the courthouse, as he and Doris acted out the conventional post-trial scene, Taylor-Smith expressing his disappointment at the court's 'ill-advised and erroneous decision', Doris avowing her determination to fight on.

Over the following days, controversy raged in the British media as to whether, in this case, the law was indeed an ass. The red-tops were unanimous that justice had been done; a dangerous man was back safe within prison walls. **GOTCHA** was the headline on the *Sun*, its front-page article pointing out that if the law has 'got it in for you' they'll find a way, evidence or not, of 'sending you down', a somewhat ambiguous vote of confidence in the justice system. The broadsheets made much the same point, in rather more literate mode, but in their case to point up flaws in the system. Taylor-Smith's angry comment to the judge had been picked up and developed in more than one editorial. The following Sunday's *Observer* ran a four-page feature expressing discontent at the state of our justice system, with George's case at its heart. It was clearly widely understood that George had been thrown back into prison on a technicality, failing sufficient evidence for a conviction in the Callow Green case. The *Mail on Sunday*, in contrast, was muted in its criticism, pointing out that removing a dangerous criminal from our streets was perhaps an example of the end justifying its rather dubious means.

Doris appeared on Radio 4's breakfast-time news programme, where it was pointed out early in the interview that her husband was indeed a convicted murderer. She was asked whether in her view George had committed the recent second murder of which he had been accused. She became flustered and was reduced to repeating several times that a man is innocent until he is proven guilty. It was not the impression that any of us would have wished to create. I felt that she had been what the police and criminal fraternity call 'stitched up'. Doris was in tears when I spoke to her about it. It was a poor start to her campaign to turn George into a *cause célèbre*. When we parted, she wore the same troubled look I remembered from when I first knew her, as a young probationary teacher.

I saw little of her for the next two weeks. At the end of January, she called to tell me that she had resigned from her post at Harry Brearley and intended to devote herself full-time to the campaign to free her husband. I congratulated her, wished her luck, and offered my support in any possible way. I added that I was very proud to know her and to be her friend. We agreed to meet the following day, to sketch out a plan of campaign.

I had suggested that we engage a high-profile publicist to promote our campaign, but Doris, who considered publicism, marketing and public relations all to be 'meretricious professions', vetoed the idea impatiently and without compunction. We were thus left to our own amateur devices. Doris, assuring me she had learnt from her first unfortunate radio experience, took on the task of communicating with the media. I would use contacts built up over the years to lobby for George's release.

From mistakes that I had made during my first headship, I had learnt the benefit of developing a reputation for Robespierrian 'sea-green incorruptibility', not out of any superior moral rectitude, but because I had realised the value of the moral high ground. Although it is at times inconvenient to be obliged to eschew the easy and practical solution of the amoral pragmatist, in the long term a reputation for being the even-handed paragon of honesty, scrupulousness, consistency, steadfastness and dependability can take a man a long way, gain him a level of respect he otherwise does not warrant. In short, paradoxically, I had found that the truly pragmatic course in professional life was to become known as an idealist, an altruist, for idealism and altruism are all too frequently mistaken for wisdom. I make no apology for this. What harm could I have done?

Of course, to confess to or be discovered in this duplicity would have been tantamount to professional suicide, and I contrived to carry off the egregious deceit for the final two decades of my career and beyond, without arousing more than the faintest occasional suspicion from a close collaborator, or from friends and colleagues who had known me in earlier less righteous days. Only Marilyn, if I am not mistaken, was fully aware of my feet of clay. This is not to say that I have been a bad man. On the contrary I have made it my business to be publicly good, saint-like almost in my moral rectitude, if admittedly not what my old friend Bill Rodgers would have called 'twenty-four carat'.

In any case, I convinced myself that there is a strong argument to be made that true altruism cannot exist, that no one ever performs a good action for no reward. To claim that an act is truly altruistic is to discount the inevitable personal gratification that comes from performing that act. Who amongst us does not feel better for doing a good deed for a friend or a stranger? Does not everyone feel a sense of satisfaction from making a gift to charity? Furthermore, it is often difficult to distinguish altruism from the feelings of duty, moral obligation and guilt inculcated into our superego from childbirth. Many acts of altruism can be accounted for by fear of God and hellfire, or a misguided ambition to attain the afterlife. Even the saintly, self-effacing Mahatma Gandhi has been accused of 'pathological altruism', mental illness rather than sainthood!

At all events it was time to call in favours from my contacts in high places. Because of my hard-earned reputation – being upright, honest and forthright is not easy – in the first two weeks of the campaign, I was able to rally behind George's cause a cabinet minister, a bishop, a European Commissioner, a member of the Shadow

Cabinet, an MEP, a former prison governor and a high-ranking BBC executive. After inspecting the cards of condolence received when my wife died, I was also able to enlist the help of her good friends at *Amnesty*. I knew from my wife's experience of volunteer work for *Amnesty* that this would almost certainly be a long war of attrition, but at least I had made a good start.

I also approached my contacts in the chess world, where George had by now established a glowing reputation as an outstanding player who had risen rapidly through the national rankings, despite being a good deal older than most entrants to the field. One of my contacts was James Harcourt, chairman of the English Chess Federation, and a former national champion. I had done battle with him several times as a student, when he played number one board for Oxford University, and had on one occasion beaten him. He was delighted to hear from me, had already read the feature in the *Observer* and, recognising George as the new rising star of British chess, had followed the newspaper reports on his arrest, detention and return to prison. This was a piece of luck! He was easily convinced that a man of George's talent was a cause worth fighting for.

'Leave it with me, David. I have an idea.'

He was not willing to go into detail, in case he was later forced to disappoint me, but left me with the strong impression that he intended to concoct some publicity stunt. I had no inkling of how rapidly and dramatically this doyen of the chess establishment would set the events in motion that would lead to a national soap opera centred around a man imprisoned not only within four stone walls, but also in his own silence.

XXII

BRILLIANCY

*("A spectacular and beautiful game of chess, generally
featuring sacrificial attacks and unexpected moves."
Wikipedia.)*

Young Cathy had insisted that I leave my contact details
with her, when I left the Thompson farm, and I received
three e-mail messages from her during January and
February. Along with what little news there was from
Sunraysia, she peppered me with questions about life in
England, how easy it was for a young Australian to find
work and accommodation, especially in London, and
finally asking if she could stay with me initially when she
came over. She certainly had the bit between her teeth,
and already seemed to be plotting her 'escape from
Sunraysia' with two or three girlfriends, as soon as they all
reached their eighteenth birthdays. I wondered if her
parents knew that she was writing to me in this vein.

I managed only one visit to George during this time. He
was restricted to three one-hour visits per month, and
quite naturally Doris wanted to keep these to herself. I saw
him towards the end of February, when Doris was

221

recovering from a bout of influenza, and was willing to let me go in her place. He was paler than ever and the creases around his eyes had deepened. I believe he was pleased to see me, but he was certainly unable or unwilling to attempt his recently acquired half-smile. It was hardly surprising; he had little to smile about. I tried raising his spirits by explaining my efforts to drum up support for his release, by telling him about his niece Cathy's e-mails and her ambitions to see the world. I took him a couple of chess magazines and he gave me a tiny nod of acknowledgement.

At the end of February I received a phone call from Harcourt. He was in ebullient mood. He had persuaded four of the leading British professional chess players, three men and one woman, to play two boards each against George, live online, courtesy of a leading Internet service provider, who would reward both them and George with a sizeable fee. He had already negotiated with the prison governor at HMP Leeds, a woman and a well-known liberal, for these matches to be permitted to go ahead. The only conditions were that George's fee would be paid into a trust to be accessed only on his release, and that he would not be seen on screen. His moves would be electronically represented, but on the other hand, his opponent would be shown pondering his or her every move. The matches were to be played against the clock, each player allocated one hour per board. All he needed now was George's signature on a contract that he would e-mail to me. He had assumed that I would act as George's manager and agent, and had already advised the prison governor, Laura Jameson, that I would be approaching her. For me the suggestion that I be George's agent was a stroke of genius. It meant that I would have the excuse to wangle extra visits. I discussed the offer with Doris, who was very enthusiastic – she felt it would be excellent for George's morale and, in any case, recognised the value of anything that would keep him in the limelight.

Ms Jameson had already warned George about the events that Harcourt wished to arrange, and he was not surprised when I turned up with his contract. As he signed, with as much enthusiasm as a man of George's temperament ever shows, I realised just how much progress he had made since the day of his release from Wakefield Prison two years previously. I could never have dreamt of George putting pen to paper, or responding by look or gesture to any question or suggestion, or most importantly developing his friendship with me and, crucially, his relationship and marriage with Doris.

I saw him now as a man who, despite his innate reticence and his disabling mental illness, relished competition, and the stiffer the better. It was a bizarre paradox.

In the short run-up to George's series of matches against the leading professionals, the nation was bombarded with e-mails advertising the contest; advertisements sprang from webpages, not all of them in good taste, flashing onto the screen George's photograph and those of his opponents, interspersed with a chessboard shown as a gory battlefield on which knights, bishops and kings were slaughtered by a sword-wielding queen flanked by castles dripping with blood.

The matches, played over four consecutive days, were a dazzling success, the website receiving many millions of 'hits'. I wondered by how much the ISP's advertising revenue had multiplied during the course of the week. I was allowed to attend the matches, sitting in the room with George and a prison warder, as technical experts transmitted his moves to the control room. There were no cameras. George performed brilliantly; against two of his opponents he won both boards, whilst against the other two he won with the white pieces and played comfortable draws with the black pieces. I was in awe of the level of concentration that he maintained over the four intensive days of competition, each time against a fresh opponent and a different style of play.

The event was reported each evening on the national news and closely followed by the broadsheet chess experts, who wrote daily bulletins and transcribed the games in their column. A few days later, the Internet service provider which had arranged the event offered George a lucrative sponsorship contract, which was to run for five years. It was a bold move and, financially, a risky one, which only a hugely wealthy organisation such as this could have contemplated. George was not an obvious candidate for sponsorship. In the first place, he was, for the moment at least, unable to travel, and travel is an essential part of the life of the chess professional. Secondly, it is also unusual for an older chess player to remain competitive, and George was already well into his forties. Above all, at the top level, chess is the supreme psychological battle, and all champions have a fiercely ruthless streak. I was not sure how strong George would prove in psychological warfare against the great minds of the game.

Nevertheless, sponsorship was a godsend for George Campbell, as it is to any chess player who has an ambition to gain international success and recognition. There are very few young professionals who are not also financially secure before they embark on their career. Even so, most have to rely on teaching and writing for the bulk of their income, fields which were not open to George. His one trump card was his notoriety, and the sponsors had clearly recognised the value of having on their books a notorious murderer who was at the centre of a controversial legal dispute.

I suggested to George that he 'snatch their hand off', which he did, much to the delight of Doris. The one snag was that the prison authorities insisted that only a small percentage of the money would be paid to George, the rest into a trust fund until such time as his eventual release.

More was to follow. In the first week of April, Harcourt also organised matches, on a similar basis, with first the Dutch champion, Johan van Gaal, and then the Swedish champion, Sven-Inge Johansson, both of whom George defeated with dazzling performances. His reputation was growing rapidly, and not only among the chess fraternity. He was now a household name, compared without any real justification to such as Fischer and Karpov. Furthermore, as Harcourt told me proudly, 'chess was back on the map'.

The week after the match against Johansson, Harcourt announced to me triumphantly that he finally had his man. When I asked him to explain what he meant, he told me that the matches against the six previous opponents had been arranged to lure the British champion, Lawrence Keefe, into a contest with George. Now the national champion could not possibly refuse, for fear of seeming to be 'running scared'. It would be fantastic publicity for the game of chess and a great advertisement for the national championships coming up in the summer. Again, George's opponent would receive an attractive fee from the ISP, his sponsors and the organisers of the event. The masterstroke was that this time the match would be shown live on Sky Sports 4, in afternoon sessions, with highlights nightly at 10 p.m. on Channel 5.

The six-board match was to be played during the early part of May, running from Sunday to Sunday, with two days of matches followed by a rest day, then a further two days of matches, and so on, cumulating in a two-day climax over the second weekend. This time George was to be seen on camera, as the match would be played at HMP Leeds, with the two players face to face across the table.

As the date for the opening day of the match approached, the nation was already gripped in a chess fever similar to that at the time of the great Reykjavik showdown between Bobby Fischer and Boris Spassky, four decades before. The BBC re-ran a documentary on the life of Bobby Fischer. ITV showed the documentary film *Game over: Kasparov and the machine*, detailing the battle between the man regarded as the greatest chess player the world had ever seen and the IBM supercomputer, Deep Blue, back in the nineties. Film 4 even joined in the festival, screening the moderately successful chess-based feature film, *The Luzhin Defence,* starring John Turturro and Emily Watson. Channel 4 ran a 45-minute profile of George Campbell, as the troubled, silent, withdrawn chess genius with the hidden potential to be world champion. The title of this documentary was *Madman or Genius?* and before the final credits, the director showed on the screen the rhyming couplet from John Dryden's *Absalom and Achitophel:*

> *Great wits are sure to madness near alli'd;*
> *And thin partitions do their bounds divide*

Membership of chess clubs burgeoned. The broadsheets featured articles by famous players; their resident experts had their work cut out producing enough copy to satisfy editors keen to surf the wave of enthusiasm for the game.

As the big day approached, George appeared increasingly distracted and withdrawn. The old distant look had returned to his eyes, and I frequently had a strong feeling that he was not listening to me when I spoke to him. Doris and I became more worried each time we were permitted to see him in the weeks before the event, which was in any case seldom.

In the first game of the series, playing with the black pieces, George was savagely mauled by the British champion. Even to the layman, the extent of his opponent's superiority must have been evident, without the commentary of the expert pundits. It was a highly disappointing anti-climax, not only for his supporters, but also for the organisers and expectant followers of the event. I was allowed, as George's manager and coach, to meet him to discuss and analyse the game. I told George that there was no point in our attempting to conduct a post mortem on the defeat, as his performance had been a travesty of his skills. He had shown no glimpse of the form that had allowed him to dominate his six previous opponents.

'It's okay if you don't want to carry on, George. Everyone will understand. The pressure on you must be enormous. No one will think the worse of you for it.'

I put my arm around him and felt him stiffen and move away from me. Then he held up one hand, signalling 'stop', took a deep breath, stood erect and made a 'calm down' motion with both hands. He was telling me that everything was okay, under control.

'Okay,' I said. 'I believe you. It's all under control.'

I told him I would be there to lend moral support, but that there was no technical advice that I could offer to him; his skills were vastly superior to mine, as he had demonstrated so often in the past. I said goodbye and wished him a sound night's sleep.

On the second day of the match, the Monday, George played more solidly with the white pieces, but without the inspired level of ideas and stratagems that had brought him his previous victories. After several hours of play, exhausted, he had to settle for the draw offered by Keefe,

226

from what had earlier seemed a winning position. At least he was still only one point down, and there was a rest day to follow.

In his post-match interview, held in the bare prison room which served as the venue for the match, Keefe came across as happy and relaxed. His rimless spectacles glinting in the television lights, and looking even younger than his 35 years, he was every bit the supremely confident, urbane Ivy League professor, an image he was reputed to cultivate. When asked about the prospects for the rest of the match, he turned to look at the tiny chess table, with its remaining scattered pieces, and grinned:

'Well, let's say that everything has gone according to plan so far. So, as long as I bring my A game, or even my B game, I see no problem. Perhaps Mr Campbell will have learnt how to shake hands by the end of the match.'

It had been noticeable that George had not shaken the champion's hand either before or after the two games, an accepted convention in the chess arena, as in most other forms of competition. Either this comment was a case of the patrician taking a cheap shot at his plebeian opponent, or perhaps George had got under Keefe's skin a little after all.

George, who had remained in the room for the interview, showed no reaction to the barbed comment. There seemed little to be gained from a discussion of the game that evening, as George appeared far too weary. I arranged with the prison governor that I should return the following afternoon to discuss playing strategy with my man.

I telephoned Harcourt that evening. He was as disappointed as I was with the way that the match was turning out. This was in no way the blockbuster performance that he had been hoping for, the uplifting battle to heighten public interest in the game. I asked him what he thought of George's play, and he immediately confirmed my own impression. In the second game George had been solid, but no more. There had been none of the surprises, the unexpected moves and gambits so typical of the matches that I had watched him play over the previous two years.

'You're the coach, David, but I know what I'd be telling him. He's played far too many standard moves, obvious moves, and he's making it far too easy for Keefe. He's got to make him think, make him raise his eyebrows, scratch his head, put his thinking cap on. That's what I want to see!'

It was already in my mind to adopt the very same approach with George when I saw him the following day, but I was relieved to have the distinguished man's confirmation of my planned advice.

George was resting on the bunk in his cell, as I had requested he be allowed. He seemed relaxed enough, but with George it was so difficult to read his mood. He reacted well to my summary of the match so far, and listened attentively, while I pointed out without mercy how flat and lifeless his performance had been.

'Do you know George, I think I could have beaten you myself in those two games, you were so ordinary. Is that what you want?'

He sat up and looked me in the eye. I did not let up in my attack.

'What I should like to see more of is the real George Campbell, the one who smashed Johansson and van Gaal, the one who plays the off-the-wall moves, the astonishing changes of direction, the shock tactics.'

He nodded almost imperceptibly. I hoped he had received the message loud and clear.

The next day, as I accompanied George to the match-room, I leaned towards him and whispered:

'Whatever you do, George, don't shake hands.'

He stopped, turned and looked at me. I should like to say quizzically, but there was no more expression than usual on his face. We continued on into the tiny arena for the third game of the series of six. Two minutes later, Keefe strode in, accompanied by his two seconds, stopped to smile for the cameras and took his place opposite his opponent. He offered his hand to George, who ignored it.

Keefe, playing white, built up a stronghold in the centre of the board, and, after 30 moves, he was a knight and a bishop up and had developed what appeared to be a winning position. He smiled expansively to the cameras and to his seconds. George sat impassive, leaning so far over the board that his head and Keefe's almost touched at times across the tiny table.

At move 32, George, his king threatened by the white queen and two knights, played hurriedly, without reflection, an apparently random move with his remaining bishop, leaving it easy prey for one of the white rooks. Keefe swept the bishop from the board, almost contemptuously, and then, from the look of horror on his face, immediately realised his error. I thought back to my board against George so many years before in the Staff v Pupils match at Harry Brearley, and how that thirteen-year-old had tricked me into complacency. This time George was not to win the game, but had turned a certain defeat into a draw, by forcing a position from which he could threaten perpetual check on the white king.

Keefe, clearly angry and frustrated, offered the draw and reached his hand across the board. George nodded, stood and moved away from the table. I clapped him on the back.

'Well done, George! That was more like it! They'll be calling you Houdini if you carry on like that!'

Keefe was cross and unsmiling at the post-match interview, which he cut short when the interviewer asked him how he had allowed Campbell to escape from such an impossible position.

I left HMP Leeds that night in a much more optimistic frame of mind. I felt there was more to come from my silent genius. Gentle George was at last up for the fight! And the next day he would be making the first move of the game.

Doris, who, I knew, had followed every second of the match, analysing each development as though it were a matter of life and death, more than shared my optimism. She was convinced that her man had turned a corner, was at last 'into his stride', as she put it. I tried to persuade her not to set herself up for a huge disappointment. Chess and chess-players at this level could be unpredictably volatile.

George did not let us down. He played the popular Queen's Gambit opening, brushed aside Keefe's Queen's Gambit Refused response, emulating the famous dismantling of Yusupov by world champion Anatoly

Karpov. It was clear that Keefe knew exactly what George was doing at each stage of the game, but was powerless to respond. There were none of the surprises I had come to expect from my friend, but the relaxed pose and the clear gaze of concentration that had so impressed me in our first games across my dining-room table were back. He had decided on the simplest and most secure way of winning the fourth game with the white pieces and had stuck to his plan ruthlessly. As the game reached move 40, I noticed Keefe's knee and thigh begin to tremble, and his head begin to twitch. After some twenty minutes of uncomfortable shuffling, he stood, reached his hand across the table to offer resignation. George did not meet his handshake, and the champion was obliged to topple his black king, before storming out of the match-room. The match was all-square after four games.

The fifth game, on the Saturday afternoon, showed us George at his very best. Playing black, he made his moves rapidly and confidently, while Keefe pondered long and hard before each move, struggling to work out exactly what traps his opponent was setting for him. George sacrificed minor pieces extravagantly, but forced Keefe into an endgame where the white king became trapped on the back rank, alongside his dark-square bishop, and eventually fell to a combination attack by George's queen and rook.

At a subsequent press conference called by Keefe's team, with the British champion pale and silent, his manager complained about the conditions of play, the fact that his man was severely disadvantaged by having to perform in the claustrophobic prison environment so alien to him, that he was being adversely affected by the unsporting psychological tactics of his opponent, who did not even possess 'the basic decency to look his opponent in the eye, let alone shake his hand when he had won a game'.

It was clear to me that the match was won already. Keefe was a beaten man. George had only to play a solid game with the white pieces and force a draw, in order to be victorious.

In the event, the match ended in anti-climax. The following lunchtime, Keefe's camp gave the excuse that he was suffering an acute attack of gastro-enteritis and would not be able to play the final game of the series. George had won! He had beaten the British champion!

Doris and I toasted George's victory and his glowing future in the chess world in champagne that night. I received calls from several old friends that I had not seen for years, as well as from Harcourt, who congratulated us on George's famous victory and apologised for his champion's disappointing capitulation. Claire rang to say that the whole family was very proud of me. I pointed out that it was George who had won, but I confess I was delighted to bask in the reflected glory. Taylor-Smith rang my doorbell, flushed with excitement and flourishing two bottles of Bollinger.

'Reinforcements, old boy! Thank goodness the confounded spectacle is over! I have never watched so much television! Sorry to barge in like this! Not my style at all.'

He had followed every move.

As to George, I am not sure if or how he celebrated, as because of the abandonment of the match, I had not been allowed to see him. When I arrived at the prison on the final Sunday afternoon of the match, ready to meet my player, I was given the news of Keefe's withdrawal, sent away and advised to return the following morning at 11 a.m.

When I did, Laura Jameson took me into her office, her face grim. She had received a phone-call the previous morning from a Home Office official, instructing her that 'this absurd circus' had to stop, and that she was to be relieved of her duties with immediate effect and would be well advised to accept the early retirement package that would be offered to her.

'And there was I, believing that what I was doing was beneficial to prisoner morale, was improving the image of the prison service,' she said to me, with a dejected, wry smile.

I commiserated with her and assured her that I was not alone in my admiration for her good work and her approach to prisoner welfare. We chatted over coffee for the best part of an hour, during which she revealed that she had believed all along that George's re-imprisonment

231

was unjust, and that this had been a major factor in her decision to stage the chess matches.

Once again, the dead hand of the establishment had suffocated the future of my friend George, at the first sign of hope. I was allowed, at least, ten minutes to congratulate him on his anti-climactic victory. I thought it best not to tell him, on that day of all days, the discouraging news of the governor's dismissal. If anything, he looked disappointed that Keefe had pulled out, although that could have been my imagination working overtime. Was he secretly relieved, as I was, that it was over, or would he have liked the opportunity to finish the job of defeating his opponent? I am ashamed to admit that I was not fully confident of the mental stamina of my timid, gentle friend.

The callous *double entendre* of the headlines in the expanding chess pages of the Sunday broadsheets, prior to the aborted final game, had no such doubts. **CAMPBELL REVEALS KILLER INSTINCT IN SHOWDOWN** headed the *Sunday Times* report, whilst **KILLER INSTINCT OF SILENT GENIUS** led the *Observer* column. I winced at the *Sunday Times'* deliberately tactless description of George's play in the fifth game as 'relentless suffocation of the white king'. The *Sunday Telegraph* chess correspondent described him as the 'steely-eyed assassin with ice in his veins', whilst the *Observer*, more poetically, hailed 'the new uncrowned champion with the face of a mild-mannered, middle-aged bank-clerk that conceals a razor-sharp mind and a heart of pure Sheffield steel'.

We were fated never to learn whether George Campbell had the necessary 'ice in his veins', the ruthless streak of the great champion that he promised to be.

.

XXIII

PERPETUAL CHECK

(When one player places the opposing king in a theoretically never-ending series of checks, thus forcing a draw.)

In the week following George's demolition of Keefe, the media campaign for his release intensified. The matter was aired on BBC television's current affairs discussion programme, *Question Time,* and on Radio 4's *Any Questions?* broadcast the following evening; a heated debate ensued amongst the panel and the audience on both programmes. *The Times* published a full-page open letter to the Home Secretary, demanding George's release, signed by one hundred International Grandmasters. Over 3,000 chess players from around the United Kingdom signed a petition supporting their new hero.

Seizing the moment, I pressed my other contacts to intensify their lobby, whilst Doris gave impassioned interviews on local and national radio. The issue was revived both in the broadsheets and in the red-tops, who took up a predictably kaleidoscopic range of stances; at one end of the spectrum stood those pleading for George's human rights, at the other those making a case for justice and retribution and the protection of the public against a convicted murderer who was suspected of having re-offended.

Finally, on May 20th, the Home Secretary was obliged to make a statement. Under no circumstances would the decision of the court be overturned. George Campbell would continue to serve his life sentence for the murder of his father, Stuart Ian Campbell, until such time as the Parole Board decided that it was safe to release him. He had wilfully broken licence agreements on five separate counts and had with every justification been returned to prison.

As far as the Home Office was concerned, the matter was closed.

The statement had been leaked to the press in advance and was reported in every national newspaper. Doris was distraught, and I felt at a lower ebb than at any point in the campaign. I was not sure how George would react to this latest blow. After a brief council of war in the *Kelham Island*, Doris, Taylor-Smith and I resolved that we would fight on through the European Court of Justice. Somehow or other, we would raise the money to carry on the campaign. But I could see from the lawyer's demeanour that he was not sanguine about our chances of success, certainly not in the immediate future. When our meeting broke up, he held me back on the pavement outside the pub, as Doris drove away, and spoke quietly in my ear.

'This business of our man George's sister, the confession – I suppose you are sworn to secrecy, old boy?'

I nodded.

'I promised I would say nothing, to Carly *and* to George.'

'There is no question of you snitching to the bobbies, then?'

I shook my head emphatically.

'It would help our man if something happened to slip out. After all, he is as white as the driven snow in this matter, as innocent as the proverbial lamb.'

I agreed that it was the most frustrating part of the whole story of George's nightmare life, and yet the most uplifting.

'No one else knows, not Doris, not the sister's husband? Nobody apart from George and his sister?'

'I only told you and his doctor.'

I remembered my visit to Les Bradshaw and my hand went involuntarily up to my mouth. Taylor-Smith detected my moment of doubt.

'Are you sure? Who knows about your expedition down under? Come along now, old boy, spill the beans to Uncle Roland.'

I confessed that I had almost told Les Bradshaw, and how she had jumped to her own conclusions.

'As you and I are sworn to secrecy on our honour, then we shall have to hope the Chief Inspector does her duty to God and the Queen, shan't we, old thing?'

I shuddered. If the truth were to come out through my error of judgement, George would have his freedom, but, each for their own reasons, neither he nor Doris would ever forgive me.

That night I dreamed of Marilyn, for the first time since she had died. She was young, as I presume I was too, and wore a cotton print dress belted at the waist, which emphasised her elfin form. She was happy and gay, cooking a meal, whilst I sat at the kitchen table reading a newspaper and commenting on the articles that I read.

It was unmistakably the first home we had shared, a two up two down stone-built terraced house in Oxford, but the situation was entirely different. The house now sat on the edge of a precipice, with nothing but the wide front step between the house and a sheer drop into infinity. Bill Rodgers came to see us; we had apparently invited him to dinner, and he had brought us a housewarming present, a set of carved ivory chessmen, with the kings and queens as Chinese emperors and empresses, the bishops as mandarins. He was older, the same age as when I had known him at Harry Brearley. He advised us that we needed to fix a safety net under the front door-step, and I assured him that this would be done, although I knew I had no intention of acting on his advice. It was an odd dream, and I have no idea of its significance, if indeed it had any, but its effect was that I woke refreshed and in a good mood.

I took my morning coffee into the garden and joined Tuppence on the sunlit patio. He was now as fully recovered as he would ever be, but could only sit watching the birds, swishing his tail, frustrated at the loss of agility, brought on by age and injury, that had ruined his sport.

I surveyed the jungle of my enormous garden. It was time. Michael was right to ask what on earth I was doing, living alone in a house of this size, with a garden I could not hope to maintain, or even enjoy. I knew that it was a reaction to the disappointment and frustration of the Home Office decision, and that it was probably not a wise moment to make a life-changing decision, but my mind was made up. I would bring in a team of gardeners to put the wilderness back in order, and then I would sell the house.

I turned to Tuppence.

'You're not going to like this, Champ, but I hope you'll come with me.'

He stretched, yawned and limped off down the garden, disappearing into the long grass. In disgust, I presumed.

The estate agent was happy to employ a firm of gardeners, who would do 'just enough to get things shipshape'. In the meantime she would take interior shots and prepare the brochure. The house would go on the market in two weeks' time, the second weekend in June.

'Quite a lot of older people decide to downsize, as they find the house and garden getting too much for them, or when they want to liquidate their capital. From what you are saying, I may have just the thing for you, not quite in such an up-market area of the city, but pleasantly quiet, and ready for immediate occupation, as soon as we succeed in selling your house, which should be no problem at the price you are asking.'

I arranged to meet her at the house which would be 'just the thing' the following afternoon.

And I did a crazy thing.

Some people might say that the fact that I had taken to holding one-sided conversations with my cat, since I had begun to live alone, was already bordering on madness, but the man who takes his pet as a consultant on the possible purchase of a new house must be, by any standards, in danger of a visit from the men in white coats. That is, however, exactly what I did.

236

Sheffield is often, and with justification, called 'the largest village in England', probably because of its geographical isolation, surrounded as it is by a ring of seven hills, but also because of the tendency for its inhabitants to stay from cradle to grave, and for those who come to live there to put down roots. The house lay in a modest suburb on the outskirts, but was still only twenty minutes by bus from what marketing experts now call 'The Heart of the City', although I confess I have never managed to locate the exact geographical location of this mythical quarter.

The house itself was equally modest, a stone-built, two up two down end of terrace building situated at the bottom of a cul-de-sac. Because of its end position, the back garden was level and wider than those of the others in the row, and backed on to a beech wood. I liberated Tuppence from his basket, and he set off immediately to investigate, apparently unabashed by the foreign territory. I followed him down the garden, which lay in full sunlight. There was an apple tree and a pear tree, both with a promising load of fruit. Further down I found an equally laden plum tree, and at the bottom of the garden a small, neglected greenhouse and a shed.

The house itself had that musty, 'old people' smell, but the estate agent assured me that this would disappear when the previous owner's furniture had been removed, the windows opened and the whole place properly aired. The rooms were sadly in need of decoration, but the two downstairs rooms and the bedrooms, all of a similar size and shape, were adequate for a man living alone, and I was delighted to find that there was not only an attic but also a cellar, both sound and dry, if a little dusty. My imagination was already at work. I would remove the wall between the two downstairs rooms, install a large patio window at the rear, and then the house would indeed be 'just the thing'.

The estate agent was a clever young woman; although I said nothing, she sensed that I was favourably impressed and offered to leave me there 'to get the feel of the place' on my own. I could drop the keys off through the office letterbox.

I looked out through the kitchen window. I realised that I had been so delighted by the tranquillity and simplicity of the back garden that I had already resolved to buy the house even before I had walked through the door. I ambled through the rooms several times, imagining the delight of putting my own stamp on the place where I lived, for the first time ever. I fetched Tuppence indoors and showed him round. He appeared less impressed, but I already felt at home and resolved to offer the asking price.

The sale of my family house was equally simple. On the first weekend it was advertised, there was one viewing only, by a Chinese couple in their forties, accompanied by their three children. Mr Wu declared the house to be 'a palace', whilst the three children and Mrs Wu, who revealed herself to be a horticultural therapist, rhapsodised endlessly about the garden. None of them displayed the faintest trace of the inscrutability so often misguidedly attributed to the stereotype of their race!

It was immediately obvious that they intended to buy the house. The family were moving to the city from London, had already sold their previous house and were presently living in the spare room and caravan of relatives in Rotherham. They told me they would offer the asking price and would like to move in immediately. We were clearly made for each other! I insisted on only one condition: that they retain Suzi as their cleaner. I gave her a glowing reference, and they were only too pleased to accept. Mrs Wu told me she had been about to ask me if there was anyone I could recommend, as both she and Mr Wu were busy professionals.

The sale of the two houses was concluded in a few days. Contracts were exchanged, deposits paid, and a moving date set for July 25th, some six weeks later. The difference between the selling prices of the two houses was substantial; for the new house I would pay little over a quarter of the price of the old. Even after renovation of the more modest property, a considerable amount of capital would remain. It would form the basis of the George Campbell fighting fund.

At least, that was my intention, although at the time I told no one, not even Doris. But 'the best-laid plans o' mice and men gang aft agley'; events, and one event in particular, were to overtake me.

XXIV

RESIGNATION

(Conceding the loss of a game, traditionally by tipping over one's king.)

Four weeks after the Home Office had effectively condemned him to spend the rest of his days behind bars, during the night of June 16-17th, George Campbell took his own life.

I received the news by telephone from the temporary acting governor of HMP Leeds, Jim Welch, formerly Laura Jameson's deputy. He had been unable to track down Doris Campbell, but knew of my close connection with George because of the series of chess matches.

Shocked, I asked Welch to explain the circumstances of the death. It seemed that George had used the money that he was receiving from his sponsor to buy narcotics on the prison black market. He must have acquired and stashed a large enough supply over the previous weeks to create a fatal dose, which he had injected that night.

'How can you be sure that it was suicide?'

'There was a note.'

'What did it say?'

I think I was hoping for some revelation, some inkling of the depth of the torment that George had undergone, perhaps even a personal message to me.

'It just said "NO MORE", in block capitals. Nothing else.'
No more. It was as simple as that. George could not face the prospect of spending another day in that awful place. The news wrenched me from the mood of self-gratulatory euphoria induced by the prospect of my altruistic plan. For that afternoon at least, I shared some tiny corner of the despair which my friend must have suffered.

Passing on the news to Doris, as I had agreed to do, was the most distressing and painful task I have ever undertaken. At first, she simply refused to believe me. It was impossible. George would never take his own life. He would never give way, after all he had endured. There followed an equally heartrending conversation with her mother. I am only grateful that I was not present in the same room as the two women. To put down the telephone was cruel enough, but to turn my back on them, to leave them alone with their agony, would have been intolerable.

The following day, a slim package was delivered to me. The envelope bore a postmark indicating it had been sent from HMP Leeds, but the address was written in an uneven scrawl, with upper and lower case letters randomly employed. A thin paperback book fell from the envelope. There was no accompanying letter. The book was an account of the famous world championship match between Bobby Fischer and Boris Spassky, in Iceland, in 1972, entitled *Fischer v Spassky: the match of the century* and written by a famous Yugoslavian grandmaster. I felt an eerie sense of *déjà vu*, as my eyes fell on the cover, but could not place where I had seen the book before. Perhaps it had been in some bookshop, or on a library shelf. I had certainly neither owned nor read it. The book was brand new, although I saw that its publication date was November 1972. There were three lines of writing on the flysheet, in the same clumsy hand as on the envelope.

To My Friend David
Thank you
From George.

I was touched beyond words by this simple, final gesture of friendship.

George's death was, of course, national news. I found the presence of the press and broadcasting companies at his funeral both unwelcome and oppressive, as I am certain did Doris. We would have preferred to say our goodbyes in private, but George was now a famous figure, in many eyes notorious.

The funeral ceremony was of a non-religious nature, and George was buried in a woodland setting, without a headstone, next to a cherry tree, planted by Doris and bearing a stainless steel plaque with the simple inscription:

GEORGE CAMPBELL
1966 – 2013

Doris had asked me to give the eulogy, which I did, more nervous than I had ever been, before the large congregation, which spilled out of the wide-open doors of the hall onto the courtyard. I spoke, with as much warmth and humour as I could muster, of my first encounters with him as a boy, of how he had toyed with me across the chessboard, how fate had thrown us back together again, how he had supported me when I had needed a friend. I spoke of his genius, the depth of which we had surely not yet fully plumbed, of our hopes for his future in the chess world, to which he had still so much to give.

I searched amongst the mourners for friendly, encouraging faces to hearten me, as I stumbled through my prepared speech. I spotted a sombre Roland Taylor-Smith, resplendent in a brand-new black suit and tie, and sporting a white carnation in his button-hole. Behind Doris and her mother was a grim-faced Ryan Campbell, hunched between his sister Tess and another woman, his wife, I presumed. Suzi sat in the front row beside Doris's brother, constantly dabbing her eyes with a pocket handkerchief. On the opposite side of the hall, in the middle, I could see Harcourt and, next to him, to my surprise, Lawrence Keefe. There were dozens of other faces that I recognised from the chess world, along with many who were unknown to me and who, out of solidarity, wore a tie showing the crest of the English Chess Federation.

And there was Laura Jameson, bless her!

Finally, standing silhouetted in the doorway, the sun behind her head, I spotted Les Bradshaw. I wanted so badly to go over to her, shake her by the shoulders and scream in her face: 'Is this your justice? Is this your law?'

At the end of the ceremony, we emerged from the hall into bright sunlight. It was one of the many dazzling days that we were privileged to enjoy during that magnificent July, the best summer month that I can remember. It was a day for picnics under the trees, for lazing in outdoor pools, a day for children to splash each other in back gardens, for watching a village cricket match, for sipping a cooling glass of beer in a pub garden. With a friend.

It was no day for a funeral.

As we walked towards the car-park and then joined the procession of vehicles leaving for the burial ground, I shaded my eyes to try to catch a glimpse of Les.

She was gone.

A blessing.

•

I had a surprise phone call from Carly at five o'clock one afternoon during the week following the funeral. I looked at my watch and made a quick calculation. I worked out that it was three o'clock in the morning in Victoria.

'Hello, Carly. Is anything the matter?'

'No, it's just that I couldn't sleep.'

'The nightmares, I suppose.'

'No, they're gone for good now. I shall not be having any more nightmares. I was wondering how George's wife was doing. And you, how are you?'

'It's been a bad time, Carly. Doris was heartbroken, but I think she'll pull through. She's a brave woman.'

'We've been celebrating Cathy's eighteenth birthday today, I mean yesterday.'

She paused, but I said nothing. I sensed that she was struggling to express herself.

'There's something I need to do, David. I always promised myself I would, as soon as Cathy was grown up.

243

I hope you're not going to be angry with me. I know you'll think it's too little too late.'

I knew what she was going to say.

'Please, Carly, no, not now, not after all this time.'

'I have to do it, David. I have to hand myself in.'

'George has paid already, paid more than enough.'

'You don't need to remind me of that. I remember it every day, every time I see my little girl.' Her voice cracked. 'That's why I have to do it. For George. I knew, as soon as I heard that he had . . . that he had died. It made my decision easy.'

'And what about Cathy? What will happen to her?'

'Ask yourself what will happen to her if I don't do it. Remember, she doesn't exist, she's a non-person.'

I tried for half an hour or more to talk her out of confessing, insisting that there must be another way, that there were ways of buying false passports and identities on the black market, and that it was just a question of finding the right contacts – I talked a great deal of nonsense, I am afraid - but her mind was made up.

I realised that I had been standing for the whole duration of this long phone-call, my hand gripping the telephone so hard that I could hardly replace it in its cradle. I collapsed into my armchair. I thought of the futility of George's twelve miserable years in Wakefield Prison, with only the likes of murderers and rapists for company; of his squandered talent; of his tragic, needless death. And now all his sacrifices had been for nothing!

I calmed down a little and thought again. It had not all been for nothing. He had saved a tiny, innocent child from a life of misery and ensured that she grow into a fine young woman; he had probably saved the sanity of his seventeen-year-old sister. And he had done it willingly, out of love. Now, that sister wanted to pay back the favour, to give him back his good name, and to clear her own conscience, to banish her own nightmares once and for all.

The following day Carly Thompson drove to Mildura Police Station and declared herself responsible for the death of her father, Stuart Campbell, in 1998. She was escorted back to South Yorkshire by the British police four days later.

Just before 11 o'clock, on the morning after the news of Carly's arrest and extradition hit the headlines, my doorbell rang. It was Les Bradshaw. She stood silent on my doorstep.

'This is a surprise.'

'Can I come in? There's something I need to say to you. Preferably in person, not over the phone. Knowing you, I thought that was what you would want.'

I invited her in, and she found a seat in the living room. I still felt angry with her, and to give myself breathing space to make up my mind how to react to whatever it was she had to say to me, I went off to the kitchen and made coffee. Let her stew for a while, I muttered to myself, but I knew the real reason for my reluctance to look her in the eye. I had admired her, professionally and as a person, and thought of her as a good friend, a new friend, but a good friend. I felt that, even taking into account her life's work as a police officer, she had let me down not once, but twice. I went back into the living room and poured the coffee.

'I read about George Campbell's sister, about handing herself in.'

I nodded.

'I always did respect what you were doing for your friend, David – the time, the effort, the money. After all, *I* don't come cheap for a start.'

I laughed, bitterly I am afraid.

'I would pay ten times the amount to have him back.'

'And I thought you were naive to have such faith in him. So now I owe you a huge apology. You were right all along.'

I have always been a pushover for the softly spoken apology.

'Okay. Apology accepted, then.'

'Truce?'

'Truce.'

'I'm really sorry about your friend George.'

'I saw you at the funeral. A good job I didn't find you after. I might have said something I regretted.'

'I saw the look in your eye. That's why I made myself scarce.'

She looked around the room and seemed to notice for the first time the piles of packing cases and boxes.

'It looks like you're moving.'

'Spot on, Detective Chief Inspector.'

'Not out of the city, I hope?'

I shook my head: 'I think I'd shrivel up and blow away, if I moved from Sheffield.'

I gave her a card with my new address.

'You're looking very well,' I told her.

She was. She had a healthy glow about her.

'Thank you. Everyone says so.'

'Oh?'

She lowered her eyes, like a bashful teenager. A new look for her.

'I have a new man.'

'That's good news,' I said, forcing myself to say the right thing.

I expected her to tell me more, but she remained coy, fidgeting with her skirt, smoothing it out across her knees.

'Who is he? Someone special?'

'It's an old colleague of my ex, a guy from the tennis club. He asked me to be his doubles partner for the club knockout. I was flattered – he's one of the best players, with a backhand like Roger Federer!'

She laughed, no doubt imagining some winning crosscourt backhand drive.

'And then I realised he was hitting on me - and I was even more flattered.'

She dropped her head down onto her right shoulder, as if stretching out a stiff neck.

'He's a bit younger than me, but we can cope with that.'

She smiled, gave an involuntary, nervous shrug of the shoulders and gazed into the distance beyond me. I assured her that the age difference would not matter. My compliment was sincere.

'I'm very pleased for you. Good luck. I hope you're very happy.'

She left shortly afterwards. I was relieved that we had parted on good terms once again, and if I had been twenty years younger, I would have given that young whippersnapper and his backhand a run for their money.

Doris took the news of Carly's confession and arrest very badly indeed, which was hardly surprising in the circumstances. As far as she was concerned, this young woman had taken advantage of George's kind nature and caused him immeasurable harm. Because of her he had spent over twelve years in a high security prison, had suffered tremendous mental and emotional trauma and become even further entrenched in his disabling mutism. She had effectively sacrificed his life to her own interests, to avoid what would probably have been a minimal prison sentence. Doris's reaction was one of the deepest resentment. I had not thought her capable of the pure, unmitigated hatred that she displayed towards her sister-in-law. Any attempt to reason with her would have resulted only in her venting her spleen on me. The last thing I dared venture was to tell her that I had known about Carly's guilt long before George's suicide. I was complicit in his untimely death, and I was far too much the coward to admit it to Doris.

Taylor-Smith had offered his services to Carly, and we went together to HMP Foston Hall, near Derby, where she was detained prior to the trial. She was upset at Doris's reaction, although unsurprised.

'I would have felt exactly the same way as her,' she said, her eyes filling with tears. 'She has every right to hate me. I hate myself. I should have spoken out earlier. I could have saved George.'

She was right. She should have spoken out earlier. Perhaps I too should have spoken out, ignored George's wishes, broken my word to Carly and saved his life. Perhaps Les Bradshaw was right to believe in the sovereignty of justice and the law. It certainly made life simpler. I did not have the excuse of Taylor-Smith and Morgan, bound by the rule of professional confidentiality. Perhaps there are times when we have to act against the express wishes of those close to us, in their own interest, for their own good, for their own protection. Hiding under the umbrella of my own promise, I had been too cowardly even to do this. I certainly had no right to criticise Carly's action. She did what she did for the sake of her child's life and well-being, justifiable conduct by any lights.

Back in Sheffield, Taylor-Smith and I sat in miserable companionship in the *Kelham Island,* he with his large brandy, I with my pint of ale. I was surprised when he confessed to me pangs of conscience at his own complicity in George's death.

'What we should have done, old boy, is work on Carly Campbell to own up to the bobbies, instead of relying on this farcical farrago of the European Court, which would have taken years, anyway.'

We both needed to take some action to salve our conscience, perhaps more practically to ease the pain Doris was suffering. I mentioned to him that the money I had set aside from the sale of the house, earmarked for the campaign to free George, now lay depressingly idle. Perhaps Claire and Michael would be able to do something useful with it. I was feeling far too sorry for myself to have any constructive ideas, and it was Taylor Smith who came up with the suggestion.

I jumped at it.

XXV

BUILDING A BRIDGE

(Creating a safe pathway for the king by providing protection against check by queen, bishop or rook.)

Doris was still staying in Oadby with her family. I arranged a day's outing with her in Leicestershire, on the pretext of getting both of us out into the fresh air, which her mother agreed would do her good, as she was spending her time doing little else but mope, bemoan her ill fortune and express her total disillusionment and hatred of the world in general and Carly Campbell in particular.

I picked her up around half past eleven in the centre of Leicester, where she had been shopping, and we took a circuitous route through country lanes to Ashby de la Zouch. There we ate a pub lunch in the *Bull's Head* in the high street. Afterwards we wandered among the castle ruins. It was here, sitting on an ancient stone, that I outlined our plans for the *George Campbell Trust*, a charitable fund for the support and education of children who had suffered abuse.

I do not recall ever witnessing such an outburst of emotion as I saw from Doris at that moment. It was as though floodgates had opened and released all the pent-up feelings of the past weeks - the love, the loss, the sadness, the frustration, the anger, the resentment and the hatred. She wept in my arms, and I was at a loss to know what to do to comfort her.

I explained to her that I had considered offering myself as director of the Trust, but had decided that it was the work of a younger person, and in any case we wanted her to be the director. I would help initially to raise funds for the project. Taylor-Smith had agreed to be both a trustee and our legal adviser. The other trustees would be myself, Claire and Michael, the two of whom had volunteered their advice and guidance in the setting up of the charitable trust, a field in which they were expert. I had thought it best that all these arrangements were ready to be put in place upon Doris's agreement. She was delighted beyond words and declared that she would be honoured to be the director. She stood straight and tall, and the energy that flowed back into her body was almost tangible, as she accepted the responsibility for running the trust.

That evening, back at her mother's home, the three of us held a long conversation about Carly Campbell and her actions. I confessed about my visit to Australia and told the Shane Thompson version of his meeting Carly and taking her and her child to safety in Australia. I thought it wise to withhold from Doris Carly's confession to me in the Melbourne Hilton. I needed her as a friend, not an enemy. I have since vowed to myself that, as long as I live, I shall not reveal to her what I knew before George took his own life. Others will have their view on my decision, may decry it as cowardice or moral turpitude. I cannot hurt Doris any more than she has been hurt. It would be too cruel. I shall have to live with my own conscience.

Mrs Day and I managed to talk Doris round to accepting that what Carly had done had been motivated by her fears for her young child, that George had taken the blame for killing their father upon himself willingly, for the sake of his tiny niece, to save her from the kind of life that he and his sisters had suffered. I witnessed the weight of resentment falling from Doris's shoulders before my very eyes, as her mother told Doris that she would have done exactly the same for her, if she had been in the same situation. What George had done had been admirable. He

250

had acted out of love and human kindness. We should all be very proud and privileged to have known such a man.

The following week Doris moved back to Sheffield, into the house she had shared with George, and we began work on setting up the *George Campbell Trust*. Shortly afterwards, Cathy and Shane arrived on my doorstep, as we had arranged by telephone. I had expected Shane to be resentful, to blame me for the fact that Carly would now have to serve time in prison. There were no such recriminations, although he remained grim and unsmiling throughout his stay. Cathy had had no problem obtaining a British passport, she told me, but declared that she was really still 'an Aussie girl' and was very optimistic of being granted Australian citizenship in the long run. In the short term, she would be allowed back into Australia on her UK passport. I feared that her mother would not enjoy such a privilege ever again, but decided to keep that to myself. The youngster already had enough to contend with.

I drove Cathy and her step-father to Foston Hall for an emotional reunion with her mother. Taylor-Smith is confident that Carly's sentence, for manslaughter, mitigated by temporary insanity, diminished responsibility and provocation, will not be too severe. I am less optimistic, as I fear that her long silence and the fact that she knowingly allowed her brother to take responsibility for her crime will weigh heavily against her in the eyes of the judge. Common sense and natural justice say that George has already paid for her crime, but we are not dealing with common sense, we are dealing with the law and British justice. Only time will tell.

The following week I played my trump card. Shane had flown back to Australia, where he was needed for farm business. I invited Doris and Taylor-Smith to my house one evening for supper and a charitable trust meeting. Cathy did the cooking, a lamb casserole, grandma Ellen's recipe, she told us. I introduced her to the guests. I suspect that she put on a specially exaggerated Australian accent for the occasion.

'Hello, Auntie Doris. I am so delighted to meet you. I've heard such a lot about you and about Uncle George.'

Doris appeared overwhelmed, firstly to meet unexpectedly, in the flesh, the object of George's altruistic sacrifice, and secondly to be called 'Auntie Doris'. When Cathy flung her arms around her neck and hugged her, it was all too much for her, and she fell back speechless into an armchair. Cathy, in all innocence, took me to one side and whispered in my ear: 'Did I do something wrong? Have I upset her?' I explained that English ladies were perhaps not used to such effusive behaviour from someone they had not met before, even if it were a relative. Cathy clearly had not given a second's thought to the possibility that her aunt might resent her part, albeit innocent, in her husband's suffering.

In the event, all was well. Doris recovered from her initial shock at meeting her niece and, like everyone else who met Cathy, was totally won over by her naive charm. The key moment was probably when the teenager spoke about George.

'My Uncle George must have been a wonderful man. I wish I could have met him. And Mum says he was amazing at chess, probably would have been world champion. I would have been so proud to know him!'

The long and short of the matter is that, before two more weeks had past, Doris declared that it was not proper for a young lady to be living alone in the same house as a man not related to her. What would the neighbours say? She offered to take Cathy in to stay with her. The reconciliation appeared to be complete. As Cathy's presence in my house over the past weeks had not always been relaxing, I was happy to agree, although I confess I was just a little hurt at the alacrity with which the teenager took up her aunt's invitation!

Yesterday morning, the two women came to my house and planted one hundred spring flowering bulbs in my garden. Doris also brought me a housewarming present. It was a large box and quite heavy. Cathy, still a child at heart, helped me open the parcel. It was a carved, soapstone chess set, with Chinese emperors and empresses as kings and queens, mandarins as bishops, prancing horses as knights and replicas of the terracotta warriors as pawns.

Doris and I share a love of the game of chess, and her choice of present was logical. But I thought of my dream of

Marilyn and of Bill Rodgers' gift, and I could not help thinking that this was more than just a coincidence.

After lunch, Cathy surprised us by asking if we would take her to see her uncle's grave. It seemed an odd request, but she was insistent and said 'please' several times. She also was adamant that all three of us should go together. When we reached the burial ground and approached George's grave, she stopped and held us back.

'I hope you don't mind, Auntie Doris, but I've had a little change made to Uncle George's plaque.'

Doris frowned, her face like thunder. She was not best pleased. The girl had gone too far, had overstepped the bounds of hospitality this time! I felt most uncomfortable. Cathy noticed the change in her aunt's demeanour and began to look very nervous.

'It's just one word,' she said, quietly, and pointed with a shaky index finger to the plaque on George's cherry tree.

Doris and I leaned over in unison to read the inscription:

GEORGE CAMPBELL
1966 – 2013
HERO

Doris bit her lip and shook her head slowly.

'You know you shouldn't have done that without asking first, Cathy, don't you?'

The girl's chin dropped onto her chest.

'You promise that you will never do anything like that again?'

'I promise,' said Cathy, a tear leaking from the corner of her eye and trickling down her cheek. 'I'll have the old one put back.'

'No you won't, my darling. It's a beautiful thing that you did, Cathy. Thank you. It was a very kind thought.'

'Yes, a beautiful thing,' I agreed. 'And very fitting.'

I was relieved to see Doris hug her niece.

Epilogue

Last night in bed I was woken by a rustling sound and gentle pressure against my leg. I had fallen asleep while reading, and so the bedside light was still on and I was still wearing my spectacles; I saw everything clearly, as if by daylight. Marilyn was sitting on the bed. She was elderly, but beautifully groomed, as she used to look before she succumbed to dementia. She wore an elegant, sleeveless, black sequinned ball-gown that I had not seen before, set off by the single string of pearls that I remembered buying her for our pearl wedding anniversary.

'Hello, Marilyn,' I said out loud, surprising myself. 'You're back.'

I dared not sit up or move towards her in any way, for fear she would disappear, and so I must have been aware in my dream that it was a dream. She smiled, rather condescendingly I felt, and then leaned over and whispered in my ear.

'It's done.'

I turned my head to kiss her cheek, but she drew back, tutted and wagged an admonishing finger. She stood and walked towards the door, then turned back and handed me a book. The title, printed in gold leaf on the cover was *Die Traumdeutung*. It was Sigmund Freud's book on the interpretation of dreams, in the original German, and was covered in dust and cobwebs. I opened it, blew on the pages, revealing a surreal print of a naked woman, and made myself sneeze with the dust. I sat bolt upright and woke with a start. I was indeed holding a book, but it was the novel I had been reading when I fell asleep.

Freud's book is now on my Christmas present list.

Today is the last glorious day of the Indian summer of 2013, if we are to believe the meteorologists. I am content to sit alone in the suntrap of my new back garden blessed by the surprising warmth of this first October Sunday.

The few garden birds that have remained to winter here are undisturbed by predators, for the time being at least. I last saw Tuppence on the day I moved house, ten weeks ago. He watched the removal van arrive, turned on his heel and limped to the end of the street. At the corner, he stopped, turned and looked at me. A long hard stare. If cats can say goodbye, then he was saying goodbye. I have requested that the Wu family leave the cat-flap free for a while, in case he returns. They have promised to detain him and inform me immediately, if he does.

One day, about three weeks ago, tired from an unpleasant motorway drive, I returned absent-mindedly to our old house, not realising my mistake until I arrived outside. On the driveway stood a young cat, entirely black except for the milk-white tip of its tail. It was the very image of Tuppence, but without the battle-scars. It was almost certainly an ancestor, a son or grandson of the Champ. I got out of the car to take a closer look, but the youngster darted off into a neighbouring garden.

I still hold out a faint hope that one day Tuppence will turn up on my doorstep, to take up his place of honour as though nothing has happened. Cats are resourceful, and he is the most resourceful of cats. If he does want to come back to me, I am confident that he will find a way.

Progress on setting up the *George Campbell Trust* has been promising. The experience and wise counsel of Claire and Michael has proved indispensable. Claire's parents have matched my own contribution, in a spirit of charity, I hasten to add, rather than of competition. Roland Taylor-Smith has donated his fee for defending George and has contributed £10,000 of his own money. The local chess club that George and I attended together has organised a 'chessathon' over a weekend in November and has so far raised several thousand pounds in sponsorship for the Trust. Their idea has been taken up by over a dozen clubs nationally. Lesley Bradshaw has also donated her fee for the detective work she carried out for me last year. Generous personal contributions flood in daily.

I have spent the afternoon leafing through my journal one last time, trying once again to make sense of the strange story of my relationship with George Campbell. It is the story of a schoolmaster and his pupil, a story of a guilty conscience and a quest for expiation. It is George Campbell's story, a story of wasted talent, of sacrifice, of courage, of 'grace under pressure', as Hemingway put it so well.

But it is also my story, because it is a story of friendship. Less than two years ago, I felt alone and without a friend in the world. The journal entries from those dark days did not make for amusing reading.

January 31, 2012 - It is the human condition to be alone, at birth, at death, and in between. The greatest gift we can bestow on another human being is to make him or her believe that this is not so, however temporarily.

It is true that we can never fully know another. I hold with the iceberg theory, that we rarely know more than the one tenth of the true nature of our friends and lovers that appears above the surface. I am certain that I, for one, have never revealed my true self to others; sometimes I doubt whether even I know who or what I really am. Did I really ever know Marilyn, for instance? Her secret thoughts, her true essence have probably always remained out of reach to me, her husband and life partner. George Campbell, admittedly, is a special case. No one knew him better than I, but for me to say I knew him truly would be an egregious exaggeration. And yet I have attempted to write his story and to draw my conclusions. We spend our whole life writing other people's stories and drawing our conclusions.

Entries made at the time of Marilyn's death are equally chilling.

March 30th, 2012 - As far as I can see, life is nothing more than a series of leave-takings and lost loves.
March 31st, 2012 - There are many common experiences, but there is no such thing as common experience.

I must forgive myself for the pessimism. I was emotionally at a low ebb, and after all there is a grain of truth in both these latter entries. Nevertheless, despite their underlying truth about the human condition, these entries do not constitute a philosophy to live by, and I am determined to consign them to oblivion with the rest of the contents of the journal, on this evening's garden bonfire.

I am alone now, but I have known true friendship. I have felt closer to the hero of my story at certain moments of silent communion than I ever thought possible. Our friendship has armed me with a new optimism in these my last years; it has taught me much about the limitless resources of courage, of strength of character in adversity, that we humans possess. Collections of quotations are replete with statements, wise, witty or cynical, about the essence of friendship. Aristotle maintained that 'he has no friend who has many'; the American historian, Henry Adams, declared that 'one friend in a lifetime is much; two are many; three are hardly possible'. I am inclined to agree, as I do with the assertion of seventeenth-century worthy, Thomas Fuller, that 'if you have one true friend, you have more than your share'.

I have had more than my share.

Martin Luther King, somewhat hard on the rest of us mere mortals, proclaimed that if a man does not discover something he is prepared to die for, then he is not fit to live. George Campbell certainly found something worth dying for. My accomplishment is slighter: I have found something worth living for; and today I am resolved to live for ever.

•

The man sits back comfortably in his office armchair, his feet on the coffee-table, tie loosened. He is more relaxed than at any time he can remember since his student days. Normally at this time of the day, he would be patrolling the building, making his presence felt, beaming that all-encompassing smile of goodwill, whilst simultaneously exuding control and power. Today he simply cannot be bothered. He has just received telephone confirmation of the important promotion he has set his heart on, a new challenge, a clean slate, in a rural paradise, with all those messy, intractable problems left behind for his successor to solve.

In the sunlit staff car-park stands a scruffy youth, wearing a torn pair of faded jeans and a blue tracksuit top, staring towards his office, half hiding behind a car, the man's car. He has been there for several minutes. The man decides that it is not his problem, so long as the youth does not damage his car, but stands up and moves to the window to take a closer look. From the man's experience of studying hundreds of teenage faces, he discerns that the youth is seventeen or eighteen, although he is shorter and slighter than average. He has a distinctly undernourished, uncared for appearance. The man sees that both his basketball shoes have holes in them, and that he is, surprisingly, carrying a small book. The book looks brand-new. There is something nigglingly familiar about the youth, as if the man has met him before, but cannot place him.

The man opens the window. Away from the cars please, he calls. The youth, startled, ducks down behind the car. A woman in her fifties hears the man call out and marches purposefully towards the youth. The youth evades the woman easily and runs across the car park towards the exit. As the woman does not pursue him, the youth stops, turns, looks towards the man's window once more and opens his mouth, as if to speak. What is it? says the man sternly. What do you want? The youth says nothing, carries on walking towards the exit, head down.

The next morning, the youth appears again on the car park and stares at the man's window. He is wearing the same clothes as the day before, but the book now juts from the zip pocket of his tracksuit top. The man looks up, sees the youth, shakes his head and continues with his work.

The man leaves his office earlier than usual today. It is Friday and he intends to celebrate his promotion with his family. There are puddles in the car-park from the afternoon's heavy thunderstorm, and he has to tread carefully. On the bonnet of his car, tucked up against the windscreen, is a slim paperback book, about eight inches by five and no more than a quarter of an inch thick. It is sodden; the pages are stuck together and have almost turned to pulp. The cover, thicker and shinier, still shows the title of the book clearly enough: Fischer v Spassky The chess match of the century. The name of the author, Svetozar Gligoric, whom the man knows to be a Yugoslavian chess grandmaster, is still just legible.

The man carefully peels back the cover to check for an owner's name. There are three uneven lines of writing on the flysheet, but the ink has smudged, obliterating all but the first four letters of the top line, written in a cramped, childish hand:

> *to MR....*

and the end of the third line, which he reads as the number 11.

He shrugs, walks to the nearby waste bin and drops the book in with the day's litter. What a shame, he says out loud. What a shame.

•

also by JOHN FOSTER

NINE TIMES IN TEN:

stories short and long

"**Nine times in ten** the heart governs understanding."

Lord Chesterfield. Letters, 15 May 1749

MATADOR PRESS (2012)
paperback, 309pp
ISBN 9781780882666

... a kaleidoscope of stories laced with humour, pathos,
love, murder, drama and suspense,
all with a common theme:
the human condition.

John Foster's books are available on line at

www.johnfosterstories.com

from Amazon

through your local bookshop

and as e-books